Revenge of the Crafty Corpse

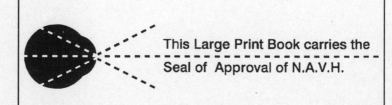

This Large Print Book carries the
Seal of Approval of N.A.V.H.

AN ANASTASIA POLLACK
CRAFTING MYSTERY

REVENGE OF THE
CRAFTY CORPSE

LOIS WINSTON

THORNDIKE PRESS
A part of Gale, Cengage Learning

GALE
CENGAGE Learning®

Detroit • New York • San Francisco • New Haven, Conn • Waterville, Maine • London

GALE
CENGAGE Learning

LIBRARY OF CONGRESS CATALOGING-IN-PUBLICATION DATA

Winston, Lois.
    Revenge of the crafty corpse : an Anastasia Pollack crafting mystery / by Lois Winston.
        pages ; cm. — (Thorndike Press large print mystery)
    ISBN 978-1-4104-5754-7 (hardcover) — ISBN 1-4104-5754-0 (hardcover) 1. Single mothers—Fiction. 2. Mothers-in-law—Fiction. 3. Handicraft—Fiction. 4. Large type books. I. Title.
PS3623.I666R48 2013b
813'.6—dc23   2012051210

Published in 2013 by arrangement with Midnight Ink, an imprint of Llewellyn Publications, Woodbury, MN 55125-2989 USA

Printed in the United States of America
1 2 3 4 5 6 7 17 16 15 14 13

For Jack, Zoe, and Chase, who have left permanent handprints on my heart

ACKNOWLEDGMENTS

To the usual suspects:

Terri Bischoff, Midnight Ink acquisitions editor, and the other members of the Midnight Ink team who all work so hard to make Anastasia look her best and give her such incredible support once she leaves the nest, including Connie Hill, Steven Pomije, Courtney Colton, Donna Burch, Lisa Novak, and any other staff member who has worked on the series.

To Carolyn and Ashley Grayson for not only having my back but for their continuing friendship.

To Denise Dumars for introducing Anastasia to Midnight Ink.

To my family: Rob, Chris, Scott, Jen, Megan, and the very special trio mentioned in the dedication.

To my fellow founding members of Liberty States Fiction Writers: Gail Freeman, Melinda Leigh, Caridad Pineiro, Kathye

Quick, Michele Richter, Rayna Vause, and Anne Walradt for their amazing friendship, their constant support, and their ability to keep me sane.

In addition, for offering their expertise during the research phase of *Revenge of the Crafty Corpse,* special thanks to John-Michael (J. M.) Jones of the Gray Funeral Home in Westfield, NJ and Officer Tomasso Campisi of the Union County Police Department.

ONE

"If that damn woman doesn't shut up, I'm going to strangle her!"

My mother-in-law had been settled into the Sunnyside of Westfield Assisted Living and Rehabilitation Center for all of ten minutes before she began carping about the accommodations. Uppermost on her list of complaints was her roommate, a woman we'd so far only heard, due to the mauve and burgundy floral print curtain separating their beds and a one-sided phone conversation detailing the latest episode of some cable soap opera — in a syrupy sweet Southern accent quite at odds with her blunt vocabulary. At least, I hoped she was summarizing a soap opera. I'd hate to think, given the X-rated play-by-play, that she was gossiping about actual people.

"Shh. Lower your voice, Lucille. They can hear you in Hoboken."

"Don't you shush me! And I don't care if

that prattling twit or anyone else hears me. This is unacceptable. I want a private room." She tightened her hand into a fist and pounded it against the arm of her wheelchair, but given her weakened state, the punctuating gesture left negligible impact.

"Medicare won't cover a private room," I told her, forcing my voice to remain calm as I unpacked her suitcase.

Three weeks ago Lucille had suffered a minor stroke. Subsequent tests revealed a brain tumor, which may or may not have accounted for some of her more bizarre behavior over the last few months. With my mother-in-law, it was hard to tell.

Lucille had weathered the stroke and surgery remarkably well for an eighty year old. The tumor proved benign. After a brief hospital stay, she was now ready for some minor rehab to help her regain her strength and coordination. Hence, today's resettlement.

"If my son were alive, he'd never let you dump me in this hell hole."

She should only know that her son had tried to kill her to get his hands on her life's savings — which he then proceeded to gamble away, leaving me to clean up the mess after he conveniently dropped dead at a roulette table in Las Vegas. Trusting wife that I was at the time, I thought Karl was at a sales meeting in Harrisburg, Pennsylvania.

Given his knack for pulling off such a duplicitous life, Karl should have been a CIA operative instead of an auto parts salesman. At least then our sons and I would be receiving a fat government pension. As it was, Dead Louse of a Spouse left me in stratospheric debt and at the mercy of both an army of bill collectors and Ricardo the loan shark. Not to mention his mother and Manifesto, her French bulldog, AKA Mephisto the Demon Dog to the rest of the family.

Ricardo now resides in a federal facility. However, barring some philanthropic leprechaun gifting me with his pot of gold, I'm stuck with the bill collectors, Lucille, and Mephisto. The bill collectors treat me better. And yet I continue to refuse to divulge to Lucille the truth about her precious Karl, no matter how much she goads me.

My name is Anastasia Pollack, and I'm a glutton for punishment. Welcome to my dysfunctional world. I hope the universe is taking note because as far as I'm concerned, I definitely qualify for sainthood at this point.

"Hell hole?" I glanced around Lucille's

half of the generous, well-appointed room, equipped with abundant creature comforts, including her own flat screen TV, a leather recliner with heat and massage, and Wi-Fi. "Hardly."

"You're not the one stuck here. If you possessed an ounce of consideration, you'd allow me to remain at home and drive me to rehab every day," she said. "But I know the truth. This is all part of your grand scheme to get rid of me permanently."

I wish. Sunnyside was more an exclusive country club than a hell hole, right down to its exclusive country club–like fees. I placed the last of her circa nineteen seventies polyester pantsuits in the dresser, slammed the drawer shut, and spun around to confront her.

"How exactly am I supposed to shuttle you back and forth to rehab *and* go to work? Are you suggesting I quit my job? Alex, Nick, you, and I can live out of my eight-year-old Hyundai and Dumpster dive for our meals just so Lucille Pollack, the diehard communist, doesn't have to share a room with a talkative stranger for a month? Very politically correct of you, Comrade Lucille."

"How dare you mock me!"

I needed to get out of there and back to

work before I did some strangling of my own. And it wouldn't be the faceless voice currently detailing her skepticism over the supposed sexploits of one Mabel Shapiro, who, according to Lucille's roommate, couldn't satisfy a man twenty years ago, let alone now.

"I told you, Lucille, between Medicare and your supplemental insurance, you're only covered for a month's stay. After that, whether you're ready to come home or not, you're back living under my roof."

"This is all your fault!" she continued.

"My fault? Just what about your situation is my fault? Did *I* force you to jaywalk across Queens Boulevard? Did *I* drive the SUV that mowed you down? Did *I* make you keep your life's savings in shoeboxes under your bed instead of in a bank? Did *I* torch your apartment building, leaving you homeless and penniless? How is any of that *my* fault, Lucille? I'm the one who opened my home to you when you had nowhere else to go."

"Charging me exorbitant rent! You're no better than a slumlord."

"You're paying exactly what you paid each month on your apartment in Queens. Not a penny more. And for that you're receiving a place to live *and* all you and your dog can

13

eat. Besides, I only asked you for room and board *after* your son left me broke and up to my eyeballs in debt, but I suppose that's my fault, too?"

She glared straight ahead, refusing to make eye contact with me, her lips pinched into a straight line, her post-surgery shaved head making her look even more like Mephisto than usual.

Of course, she blamed me. She's been blaming me for everything since the day Karl introduced us. Hell, she probably even blamed me for her stroke and the brain tumor. So much for hoping the removal of that tumor would improve her personality. "If you don't like the arrangements, you're free to make your own at any time."

Which, unfortunately, she wouldn't because Lucille had it far better at *Casa Pollack* than anywhere else she could afford. And she knew it.

"What are you gawking at?" she demanded.

I glanced over my shoulder and followed her laser glare to the middle of the room where I found myself staring at Laura Ashley. Or what Laura Ashley might have looked like had she lived into her nineties, complete with pink-tinged white pin curls, poorly applied makeup caked into the crevices of deep wrinkles, and looking like she'd been transplanted from Wales, UK to Westfield, NJ.

I hadn't seen so many ruffles and such an over-abundance of Cluny lace since my cousin Susannah Sudberry's English garden–themed wedding back in 1992. The most god-awful lace-edged, pouf-sleeved floral print bridesmaid's dress ever created still resides in my attic. However, I might have to hand over that designation to Lucille's roommate's outfit. At least my bridesmaid's gown didn't have the addition of a coordinating yo-yo trimmed cardigan sweater.

At some point the soap opera play-by-play had ended. How long Lucille's roomie had been eavesdropping on us was anyone's guess, but before Lucille could hurl another barb, I crossed the room and held my hand out to the woman. "Mrs. Wegner? I'm Anastasia Pollack." I knew her name from the nameplate tacked to the wall outside the room. Lucille's name had already been added beneath that of Lyndella Wegner.

She took my hand in a surprisingly firm grip for such a petite and elderly woman. "Pleased to meet you, sugar. And call me Lyndella. Mrs. Wegner was my mother-in-law, bless her hard-hearted soul."

Looks like I'd found another loser in the mother-in-law lottery. I nodded in Lucille's direction, "And this is my mother-in-law Lucille Pollack, your roommate for the next month."

Lyndella nodded toward Lucille. "Not too happy to be here, are you, sugar?"

A part of me (the nasty part I kept tamped down as much as possible) wanted to tell her that *happy* wasn't in the commie curmudgeon's lexicon, but she'd learn that for herself soon enough. Instead, I said, "I'm afraid Lucille has been through quite a bit the last several months."

She directed another question to Lucille. "So what's your story, sugar?"

I stifled a giggle. Lyndella Wegner's strong accent seemed right at home juxtaposed against her Laura Ashley-meets-Blanche Dubois demeanor, but totally at odds with twenty-first century Westfield.

"Mind your own business," muttered Lucille. "And I'm not your *sugar.*"

Lyndella ignored the rudeness. Or maybe she hadn't heard Lucille. Modern hearing aids are so tiny, I couldn't tell if Lyndella wore any underneath her pink pin curls. She glanced at her watch and said, "I'm afraid we'll have to postpone our get-to-know-each-other chat until later, girls. It's time

16

for my needlework class, and I can't be late. Those other women, bless their Yankee hearts, would be lost without my expert guidance." Then she ducked behind the curtain divider.

Lyndella reappeared a moment later. In one hand she held a ball of pink crochet cotton. She cradled a length of finely crocheted extra wide pink lace and a crochet hook in her other hand.

"That's exquisite work," I said.

"Of course, it is, sugar."

I held out my hand. "May I?" She placed the delicate lace across my fingers. I examined the stitching closer. "Did you also crochet the lace on your dress?"

She executed a flat-footed pirouette to show off her workmanship. "I make all my own clothes. Always have. And they're of a far better quality than anything you'll find in any department store."

And how modest of her to say so. I had to admit, though, the dress fit her like couture, and her attention to detail rivaled anything strutting down New York's Fashion Week catwalks.

Lyndella flipped up the hem of her skirt and held it out for me to inspect. "See here, sugar. French seams. I dare say, you won't find any of those hanging on a rack at Macy's or Lord & Taylor."

"Probably not," I agreed, although I failed to see the need to French seam poplin when pinking shears worked just as well and took much less time and effort. However, I kept that judgment to myself.

"I'll tell you a little secret, sugar. Handwork keeps both the mind and body sharp." She tapped her temple with an index finger. "Mark my words, you young people will regret your store-bought ways when you get older, but it will be too late. You'll wind up doddering old fools, sipping Ensure and drooling into your mashed bananas."

I certainly hoped not, but I had no desire to engage in a debate over my generation's future with this woman.

"Believe it or not," she continued, "I'm ninety-eight years young."

"What's not to believe?" asked Lucille.

Lyndella heard that comment loud and clear. She shot Lucille a glare of contempt. "For your information, I still have all my teeth *and* all my faculties. People tell me I don't look or act a day over seventy. I credit that to my creative talents. Among other things."

I couldn't resist. "What other things?"

"Sex and whiskey, sugar. As much of both as I can get."

18

I should have exercised better restraint.

How often did Lyndella hit the whiskey, and when had she last looked in the mirror? The roadmap of deep wrinkles lining her face made her look every one of her ninety-eight years, if not more.

As for the sex, were ninety-eight year olds even capable of having sex? Wouldn't everything have shriveled up and dried out decades ago?

But what did I know? My own mother still claimed to have an active sex life at sixty-five, with no signs of stopping anytime soon. As for me, let's just say it had been a while. A long while.

However, whether Lyndella Wegner was actually getting any action or merely thought she was getting some, who cared? Every woman should be that alive at her age. It certainly beat the alternative.

As I studied the delicate lacework, an article for a future magazine issue began to germinate in my brain. "Mrs. Wegner, I'm the crafts editor at *American Woman* magazine. I'd love to do a profile on you and perhaps some of the other women in your needlework class."

"Well, bless your heart, sugar! You mean I'd have my name and picture in a magazine?"

"Yes."

"I'd be famous?"

"In a manner of speaking. Our circulation is upward of three hundred thousand."

"Three hundred thousand?" She placed her hand on my arm. "Trust me, sugar, you don't need anyone else. My work is far superior to that of anyone else around here and far more creative."

"I thought I'd showcase a variety of crafts."

"When it comes to handcrafts, you name it, and I've done it. Tell me, sugar, how many people do you know who can create museum-quality paintings using dryer lint?"

Dryer lint? "Not a single one."

"Well, now you do. My re-creation of Michelangelo's *David* in lint will blow away your little Yankee mind." She winked, then added, "In more ways than one."

I'll bet it would. "May I see it?"

"Later, sugar. I have my class now." Her face took on an almost wicked grin. "Wait till Mabel Shapiro hears this. Bless her frigid Yankee heart, that woman will positively shit in her Depends!"

Soap opera Mabel "can't please a man" Shapiro?

From behind me I heard a loud *harrumph.*

"Must go," said Lyndella, removing her

20

crocheted lace from my hands. "We'll talk later."

"Insufferable!" said Lucille after the door closed behind Lyndella. "How do you expect me to live with that woman for a day, let alone a month?"

"You'll just have to make the best of it. You've had plenty of practice living with someone you don't like."

"Thanks to you."

An old argument. When Lucille first came to live with us, Nick was forced to double-up with Alex in order to give Lucille a room. Whenever my mother arrived for a visit, she and Lucille became reluctant roomies. Lucille and Mama got along as well as Mephisto and Mama's corpulent Persian kitty Catherine the Great got along. In other words, they fought like cats and dogs.

I suppose that's to be expected when a blazing Bolshevik is forced to shack up with a self-proclaimed descendant of Russian royalty. Given that Mama makes a habit of extended stays whenever she's between husbands, Lord only knows how they've kept from murdering each other to this point, not to mention how I've managed to maintain my sanity.

"Would it kill you to be civil?" I asked Lucille.

"These places are nothing but dumping grounds run by mercy killers."

"Give it a rest, Lucille. Sunnyside has an excellent reputation. No one is going to murder you in your sleep."

"And if you're wrong? It will be no skin off your teeth, but I'll be dead. I demand you take me home at once!"

"That's not going to happen. Not until you're permanently out of that wheelchair and capable of managing entirely on your own. You can barely brush your teeth right now, let alone dress yourself. You're just going to have to tough it out."

"I'll sign myself out."

"And go where?"

"To one of my sisters."

The *sisters* in question — no blood relations — were the dozen other members of the Daughters of the October Revolution, all like-minded, octogenarian communists who followed my mother-in-law, their Fearless Leader, like lemmings. However, had any of them wanted Lucille on a permanent basis, I would have gladly provided a means of transportation to deliver her. Lucille's *sisters* might love their Fearless Leader, but much to my dismay, none had come forward to offer Lucille a home after she lost hers. So much for the communal spirit of communism.

"I'll stay only if you bring Manifesto here," said Lucille.

Who but my mother-in-law would name a pet after a communist treatise? As previously mentioned, the rest of us had dubbed him Mephisto the Devil Dog. Lucille cared more about that dog than she did her own grandsons, whom she never referred to by name. They were always *those boys.*

And no, I didn't name them after dead Russian czars out of spite. The boys were named for my grandfathers — Alexander Periwinkle and Nicholas Sudberry. "Sunnyside won't allow you to have Mephisto here," I said.

And yes, I said *that* intentionally. So sue me. I'm not perfect. And I'd reached my limit.

"Manifesto! His name is Manifesto!" She pounded the arm of the wheelchair, again not producing the impact she intended. "And you're lying. I hear dogs barking."

"Their owners are permanent residents, capable of caring for their pets. You're here for rehab and not even capable of caring for yourself at this point, let alone a dog."

"I'll manage."

"I'll ask if I can bring him for a visit, but he won't be allowed to stay."

Lucille folded her arms over her sagging boobs and jutted out her chin. "We'll see about that."

Yes, we would. I didn't bother to respond, though. Why bother? Besides, we were interrupted by a knock, followed by the door opening.

"Mrs. Pollack?" Shirley Hallstead, Sunnyside's director, stepped into the room and nodded hello to me. I'd met her previously when I scoped out the facility for Lucille and made arrangements for her month-long stay. "All settled in?" she asked Lucille.

"I'm not staying."

Shirley turned to me. "What's going on?"

"She's staying," I said.

"I see." She turned back to Lucille. "Your reaction is normal, but we here at Sunnyside will do everything within our means to make you as comfortable as possible and facilitate a speedy recovery."

She sounded as though she were parroting from the *Assisted Living Director's Manual, Chapter One: Dealing With Problematic New Arrivals.* However, even though her words conveyed kindness, Shirley Hallstead's body language suggested otherwise. From her not-a-hair-out-of-place jet black waves to her double-breasted cherry-red power suit, down to her four-inch designer

24

stilettos, the fifty-something Shirley Hall-stead reminded me more of a cutthroat executive than a benevolent assisted living center director.

I do believe Lucille may have met her match.

"Let's get some light in here," said Shirley. She stepped around Lucille's bed and yanked the curtain divider back to the wall.

"Lovely," said Lucille, her tone thick with sarcasm. Not from the sunshine now spilling across to her side of the room but from what the drawn-back curtain revealed.

Holy crafts overload!

No denying Lyndella Wegner's love of the handmade. Every square inch of vertical space held crafts, some framed, some taped or pinned to the walls — needlework, string art, quilling, scherenschnitte, stenciling, calligraphy, quilted and appliquéd wall hangings. An enormous ivy plant hung from a macraméd plant holder in the far corner of the room. Stained glass sun-catchers dangled in front of the windows. Fabric yo-yo dresser scarves covered a bureau and nightstand. On them stood an assortment of painted ceramic and polymer clay figurines, mosaic and decoupage covered boxes, and a variety of soft-sculptured dolls in various sizes. An intricately patterned appliquéd quilt was draped over Lyndella's bed, a crocheted afghan folded at the foot. A latch-hook rug covered part of the floor.

However, the *pièces de résistance* were the lint reproductions hanging on the wall above her headboard. "She wasn't kidding about doing it all." I stepped closer to inspect a three-foot-tall, two-dimensional rendition of *David.* Sure enough, Lyndella had recreated Michelangelo's masterpiece, down to every anatomical detail, completely in dryer lint and minus any censoring of a certain body part. "I don't know whether I'm impressed or horrified."

Thank goodness Lucille couldn't see these from the vantage point of her wheelchair. I'd never hear the end of it.

"Picasso had his Blue Period," said Shirley. "And Lyndella has her *Blue* Period." She indicated the polymer figurines. I took a closer look. Many were reproductions of ancient fertility gods, complete with over-sized members.

"I think she creates these just to drive me crazy," said Shirley. "And this lint kick of hers? Heaven knows where she came up with that, but she insisted the laundry save every scrap of dryer lint for her. She spent weeks sorting and bagging colors, then months working on those —" She paused for a moment to clear her throat. "Pictures. Thankfully, she became bored with lint after awhile and moved on to *smaller* pursuits."

I examined the rest of the lint paintings, half a dozen in all and each replicas of some of the most graphically anatomical and erotic art of the ancient world, including a series of paintings from the bath houses of Pompeii.

"As you can see, Lyndella doesn't do anything in moderation," continued Shirley. "She's our very own X-rated Martha Stewart."

"With a personality to match," muttered Lucille.

My mother-in-law knew who Martha Stewart was? Lucille considered television too low-brow a form of entertainment for someone of her intellect. Did she secretly indulge a daytime TV addiction when no one else was home? Maybe I should ask Zack to set up a granny cam to catch the hypocrite in action, considering how she mocked what I did for a living.

Shelving that idea to explore later, I pulled out my camera and started capturing Lyndella's handiwork.

Shirley stepped between the camera lens and a quilted wall hanging I'd focused on. "What are you doing?"

I quickly explained my idea of a feature article for *American Woman.*

"Absolutely not," she said.

"Don't worry. I won't use any of the racier pieces."

"You won't use any of them. Period. I don't want my facility looking like Kitsch Central. You'll irreparably harm my reputation."

Her facility? *Her* reputation? If Lyndella and some of the other residents agreed to an interview, I didn't see where Shirley Hallstead had any veto power. I was about to tell her so when the door swung open.

An extremely thin girl in her late teens shuffled into the room. She kept her head down, watching her feet as she methodically placed one in front of the other, as if making a concerted effort to keep from tripping herself. Her Minnie Mouse print scrubs hung over a nearly skeletal frame that screamed anorexia.

"About time you got here," said Shirley.

The girl mumbled a nearly inaudible apology, something to do with a Mrs. Grafton and a missing shoe, but she stopped mid-excuse when Shirley grabbed her by one thin arm and spun her around to face Lucille.

"This is Reggie Koltzner. She's one of our

28

aides and will be taking you on a tour of the facility."

"I don't need a tour," said Lucille. "I told you I'm not staying."

"Your doctors say otherwise." Shirley again addressed Reggie, ignoring Lucille's very loud harrumph of protest. "When you're done with the tour, take her to physical therapy. She's got a ten o'clock appointment with Alvarez. Don't be late."

"Yes, ma'am." Reggie pulled on the wheelchair handles, but Lucille didn't budge.

Shirley shook her head and sighed loudly. "The brake, Reggie?"

Reggie bent and fumbled with the brake release, then wheeled a very pissed Lucille from the room.

"Damn vo-techs," said Shirley. "Can you believe this is what they're turning out? Our tax dollars at work."

If she expected a nod of agreement from me, she wasn't getting one. I'd suffered my share of bullies over the years, first as a child and later in the workplace. Reggie Koltzner had my sympathies. "Maybe she needs a mentor," I suggested.

"A mentor? The last thing I need is tying up one of my nurses to hand-hold an incompetent aide. That girl's already on probation after the stunt she pulled last week. One

29

more strike and she's out of here."

"Stunt?"

Shirley waved my question away. "Sorry. Patient confidentiality. But nothing you need to worry about as far as your mother-in-law is concerned."

Her assurance aside, I wondered about the wisdom of leaving Lucille in Reggie's obviously less-than-competent hands but reasoned Shirley wouldn't risk Lucille's well-being. She'd be crazy to set herself up for a lawsuit. Whatever the *stunt,* I doubted it had anything to do with patient safety.

I took my leave of Shirley Hallstead with the excuse of having to get to work. We walked out of Lucille's room together; Shirley turned left toward her office, and I headed right for the exit. As I passed the front desk, though, I stopped. "Which way to the needlecraft class?" I asked the receptionist.

"Down that hall, through the double doors," she said, indicating the direction with a wave of her pen. "It's the second room on your left."

"Thanks." Shirley's objections aside, if I checked out the class for an article, I was on Trimedia's dime. All in the name of research. I wouldn't have to give up half a day's pay for picking up Lucille at the

30

hospital and transporting her to Sunnyside this morning. I'd used up my few personal and sick days for the calendar year way back in February when my not-so-dearly departed husband left Las Vegas in a pine box.

The door was propped open, so I stood in the hall and surveyed the room, a space at least three times the size of a normal classroom and divided up for different purposes. One corner was dedicated to drawing and painting, another to sculpture and pottery. Four large worktables with chairs filled the center of the room.

At the opposite end of the room two dozen elderly women, ranging in age between early retirement all the way up to ancient, congregated around four more tables and worked on a variety of needlework projects. Three women hunched over whirring sewing machines positioned along the far wall.

I spied Lyndella Wegner holding court amid a group of three other women. Both her mouth and her hands worked at warp speed. I don't think I could crochet that fast if my life depended on it, and I was more than half her age.

"May I help you?" A very pregnant woman with a riot of strawberry blonde curls and a face full of freckles waddled toward me from

31

the side of the room. When she stood about three feet away, she stopped and stared. Her jaw dropped; her eyes grew wide. "Anastasia Periwinkle?"

I stared back, wondering how this woman knew me.

"You don't recognize me, do you?"

I shook my head. "Afraid not."

She spread her arms wide. "It's me. Kara Kennedy."

Kara Kennedy? I knew that name. Then it hit me. Kara Kennedy. Oh. My. God.

FABRIC YO-YOS

Did you have visions of a colorful rounded plastic spool, a piece of twisted string, and tricks like *Around the World* and *Walk the Dog* when Anastasia mentioned Lyndella's yo-yo cardigan sweater? Rest assured, Lyndella wasn't wearing dozens of toys hot glued to her sweater. Instead, her cardigan was embellished with fabric yo-yos.

These yo-yos are circles of fabric gathered into rosettes. They're an ideal way to use up scraps of fabric left over from other projects. The fabric yo-yo is incredibly versatile and can be used as either a decorative embellishment or sewn together to create both wearables and home décor accents. Anastasia will share a variety of yo-yo projects

32

throughout the pages of this book. For now, here's how to make a basic yo-yo.

BASIC YO-YO

Materials

5″ × 5″ piece of cardboard
compass with pencil attached
scissors
fabric marker
quilting thread
sewing needle
5″ × 5″ piece of lightweight cotton or
   cotton-blend fabric
button (optional), invisible thread (optional)

Directions

Using the compass, draw a 4″ circle on the cardboard. Cut out the circle. Use the circle as a template to trace a circle onto the wrong side of the fabric. Cut out the fabric circle.

Hold the fabric circle with the wrong side facing you. Fold 1/4″ of the raw edge toward the wrong side of the fabric and using the quilting thread, hem with a running stitch. When you reach your starting point, and the circle is completely hemmed, pull the thread tight to gather the fabric. Smooth and flatten the yo-yo so the hole is in the center. This is the right side of your yo-yo.

Knot the thread and snip excess.

Depending on the end use, you may want to sew a button over the center hole of some or all of the yo-yos. Use the invisible thread for projects where the yo-yos are whip stitched together.

Yo-yo Stitching Tips

Always use quilting thread. Regular sewing thread is not strong enough and will break when gathering the yo-yo.

Begin the first gathering stitch underneath the fold of the hem to hide the knot.

Use a minimal amount of stitches when sewing yo-yos together to keep the yo-yos from being pulled out of shape.

Always hand wash yo-yo projects.

Make smaller or larger yo-yos by increasing or decreasing the size of the circle template. A 4″ circle template will make a 1 3/4″ yo-yo, a 5″ circle template will make a 2 1/4″ yo-yo, and a 6″ circle template will make a 2 3/4″ yo-yo.

TWO

Kara Kennedy and I were roommates first semester freshman year. She fell head-over-heels for some senior football jock whose name I'd long ago forgotten. When he was drafted by the Forty Niners, Kara transferred to a school in San Francisco and moved with him. We soon lost touch. I hadn't thought about Kara Kennedy in nearly twenty-five years.

"You haven't changed a bit," she said. "You look exactly the way you did freshman year."

Thanks to the *Freshman Fifteen*. Which I still hadn't lost and probably never would. Those pounds enjoy hanging out too much with the additional ten I'd gained after the birth of each of my sons. Speaking of which, I ogled Kara's baby bump. "And you look —"

"Pregnant?" Kara patted her tummy. "My little mid-life crisis. I woke up one day and

35

realized I wasn't quite ready for empty nest syndrome."

Better her than me. I couldn't imagine being pregnant at forty-two. "So when did you move to New Jersey?"

"Five years ago. Chad accepted a coaching position with the Giants."

Chad. Now I remembered. Chad Kulakowski. NC-double-A All-American. Don't ask me which position. Although I'd grown up rooting for the Mets, the lure of football escaped me. I didn't know a tight end from a punter, and that's after years of living with sports-obsessed teenagers and a husband who'd apparently bet on a lot more than his company's annual Super Bowl pool. "You're the art therapist here?" I asked.

Kara nodded. "And you're my replacement?"

"Replacement? No. My mother-in-law is in rehab here. You're leaving?"

"I'm on maternity leave as of the end of the day today. Sunnyside hired someone part-time, but they're still looking for an additional person. The arts and crafts classes are an important part of the program here. Interested?"

"I have a full-time job."

"Doing?"

"I'm the crafts editor at *American Woman*

36

magazine."

"Hey, I sometimes pick that up at the supermarket!" Kara cocked her head and wrinkled her brow. "I don't ever remember seeing your name mentioned."

"I took my husband's last name when we married. I'm Anastasia Pollack now."

Kara pulled a frown. "You should've kept Periwinkle. I always loved your name. Anastasia Periwinkle always sounded so whimsical. Anastasia Pollack?" She dismissed my name with a wrinkle of her freckle-spattered nose and a flick of her wrist. "Pedestrian."

I didn't remember much about Kara, but I did remember she never minced words. Apparently, she still lacked a diplomacy gene. I shrugged. "Seemed like the sensible thing to do at the time. I thought about hyphenating. For all of about ten seconds."

"Anastasia Periwinkle-Pollack?" Kara chuckled. "I see what you mean. Quite a mouthful!" She grabbed both of my hands in hers and squeezed. "Well, you'll always be Anastasia Periwinkle to me, and I'm so glad to see you after all these years."

Given the blow I'd received from Karl, maybe I should have remained Anastasia Periwinkle. In more ways than one. Who knows what my life would be like had I not fallen for the drop-dead gorgeous hunk who morphed into Dead Louse of a Spouse? On the downside, I wouldn't have Alex and Nick, but on the upside? I wouldn't be doggie-paddling fast and furiously to keep from drowning in a sea of red ink. And I definitely wouldn't have Lucille, the communist albatross, weighing me down.

Alex and Nick were worth all the other grief, though. I couldn't imagine a life without them.

"Sunnyside needs someone an additional eight to twelve hours on the weekends," Kara continued. "Think about it."

"I don't know. I play catch-up on weekends. Laundry. Shopping. Bill paying." When I have money to pay bills.

"The pay's damn good," she said, continuing to sell me on the idea. "And who can't use a few extra shop-till-you-drop bucks?"

Bull's eye. She'd found my Achilles' heel with her first arrow. Only my shopping till I dropped centered around the supermarket sales circular these days. "Define good."

"Thirty-five dollars an hour."

I strained my math-challenged brain to multiply thirty-five times eight. Two hundred eighty dollars. Then thirty-five times twelve. Four hundred twenty dollars. "How long will you be out on maternity leave?"

"My insurance gives me twelve weeks, but I may decide to take a few additional weeks without pay."

More straining of left-sided brain cells. I'd make somewhere between thirty-three hundred sixty dollars and five thousand forty dollars. Even after taxes, that was serious change that would make a serious dent in at least one of my maxed-out credit cards.

She had me at thirty-five dollars an hour, but I didn't want to admit my financial desperation. Not to a woman who considered over seventy grand a year plus benefits *shop-till-you-drop bucks.* "I might be able to help out for twelve weeks or so."

Kara beamed. "You always were the best, Anastasia! I'll talk to Shirley. I'm sure she'll love to have you, and the residents will be thrilled. They weren't happy over the prospect of losing some of their class time. Hell, some of them won't even be alive when I return."

"Kara!" At least she spoke in a low enough voice that none of the women in the room heard her. They all continued with their handwork and their own chatter, oblivious to us.

"We're talking nursing home here, sweetie. It's a revolving door. On any given week, two or three leave by ambulance and never

39

return. Others arrive to take their beds. Circle of life."

"You sound so callous."

"You have to develop calluses — no pun intended — in the geriatrics business. The key to survival is not getting too attached to any of the residents. If you do, it's like losing a member of your own family. Who needs that grief on a weekly basis?"

"I suppose that makes sense."

"Trust me, if you do take the job, don't get attached to anyone. I speak from years of experience."

"Lyndella Wegner, you're full of shit!"

We both turned to the back of the room. A woman with a tight gray perm and thick, rhinestone-studded, black-framed glasses glared across the table at Lucille's new roommate.

Kara glanced up at the wall-mounted clock. "Ten minutes without a fight breaking out between those two. I think that's a new record."

"Well, bless that ugly disbelieving Yankee heart of yours, Mabel! Why in heaven would I lie about such a thing?" Lyndella stood up and pointed toward me. "Ask her yourself, why don't you? She's standing right over there."

"Wait. I'm confused," said Kara. "Lyndella's your mother-in-law?"

"My mother-in-law's roommate."

"Of course. That makes more sense. Lyndella goes through roommates the way I go through pantyhose."

"What? She crafts them to death?"

Kara laughed. "Lyndella is one of our more *challenging* residents. She's an extremely bossy, in-your-face know-it-all, disliked by all the other women, not to mention the entire staff."

"I'll admit, she has a very high opinion of herself, judging from our brief conversation."

"Yes, no one does anything as well as Lyndella. According to Lyndella."

"From what I saw, though, her bragging rights are justified."

"True. Especially for a woman of her age, but her personality, not to mention her less-than-mainstream tastes, leave much to be desired. Shirley found it best to bunk the temp rehabs with her."

"She sounds just like my mother-in-law. Minus the X-rated art."

Kara laughed. "If that's the case, they might wind up talking each other to death."

The woman Lyndella had shouted at hoisted herself out of her chair, grabbed hold of a walker, and shuffled her way toward me. As she drew closer, I noticed both the legs and the wheels of her walker were decorated with pink rhinestones. A small wire basket, with satin ribbons and silk flowers woven through the mesh, hung from the front of the walker.

Unless there was more than one Mabel at Sunnyside, I assumed this woman was Mabel "can't satisfy a man" Shapiro.

"Is it true?" she demanded, planting her bedazzled walker inches from my toes. "You gonna make that pain-in-everyone's-patootie famous?"

Kara turned to me. "What's this all about?"

"Seeing Lyndella's work gave me an idea for a feature article on Sunnyside's crafting residents."

"You think her stuff is good?" asked Mabel. "Hon, you don't know *good.* Take a look at my work. Or Berniece's work. Or Estelle's work. Or anyone else for that matter. The last thing we need around here is for that bitch Lyndella Wegner's head to swell any fatter than it already is. We'll never hear the end of it."

"I plan to feature several crafters," I said in my defense, "not just Mrs. Wegner."

"See that you do," said Mabel. "And think about editing Lyndella out. You'd be doing the rest of us a huge favor." With that she rolled around to return to the table.

"Wow!" I said under my breath.

Kara laughed. "Welcome to Sunnyside's version of *Jersey Shore.* I should write a book about this bunch while I'm out on maternity leave."

"Are you trying to talk me out of taking the job?"

"Just preparing you for an interesting experience."

"Was that Mabel Shapiro?"

"The one and only. No one likes Lyndella, but the rivalry between her and Mabel makes the New York Giants and Dallas Cowboys look like bosom buddies. When Lyndella and Mabel collide, dull moments take off for parts unknown."

Given my life the past five months, I craved any dull moments I could snare. However, the thought of all those Benjamins nixed the idea of turning down the Sunnyside gig before Shirley even offered it. I needed the money far more than I needed a few dull moments. Besides, if I could deal with Lucille and Mama, I could deal with any geriatric antics Sunnyside threw my way. Bring 'em on.

By this point Mabel had made her way back to the table, and began bickering again with Lyndella. I decided now was a perfect time to cut out. "I've got to get to work," I told Kara.

"We should keep in touch," she said. "Maybe get together for dinner at some point and catch up."

"Absolutely!" As soon as that leprechaun with the pot of gold arrives on my doorstep. The way I calculated my current finances, I might just be able to swing dinner at the Golden Arches around the time I reached Lyndella's age.

A perk to arriving nearly three hours late for work is not having to put up with bumper-to-bumper rush-hour traffic on Routes 24, 78, and 287, especially in an eight-year-old rattletrap of a car with temperamental air conditioning. However, by the time I arrived at work, even zipping along at this hour of the morning, I was thoroughly baked. To a crisp.

Not yet noon and less than two weeks into summer, and the mercury had already climbed into triple digits for the third day in a row and the seventh time so far this year. If this wasn't a sign of global warming, I didn't know what was.

American Woman used to be headquartered in Lower Manhattan, a short train commute for me. After Trimedia forced a hostile takeover of Reynolds-Alsopp Publishing, we moved to the middle of a corn field in Morris County, New Jersey. Other companies were supposed to follow. Then the bottom fell out of the real estate market. We remain the single building in the planned business park. Our only neighbor besides the corn fields is the train station built specifically to handle the influx of commuters that never materialized.

I entered the building and made my way up to the third floor. No one seemed to have noticed my absence. I found the usually bustling halls eerily quiet. That sent a shiver coursing from my toes up to my scalp, reminding me of the last time I found myself alone in the building. Alone with a dead body hot glued to my desk chair.

I stopped and strained to hear some sounds of activity. Today was the last day of work before the Fourth of July three-day weekend, and it appeared many of my coworkers had taken a vacation day.

I was concentrating so hard on trying to hear something, that I didn't hear Cloris come up behind me. I nearly jumped out of my skin when she placed her hand on my shoulder. "Jeez! You scared the shit out of me!"

"Sorry. You looked like you were in a trance. What's going on?"

"It's so quiet here. I was having a Marlys flashback." Marlys, AKA our former fashion editor Marlys Vandenburg, AKA the afore-mentioned dead body.

"That would creep anyone out. Lucky for you, I've got just the cure." She wrapped her arm around my shoulders and led me into the break room.

Cloris is the food editor at *American Woman*, but more importantly, she's played Watson to my Sherlock twice now, helping me solve three murders among the ranks of Trimedia employees. I could always count on Cloris to have my back. And something chocolate.

She didn't disappoint. As soon as we entered the break room, I spied today's bounty sitting on the counter next to the coffee maker: brownies. "What kind?" I asked, helping myself to one. Cloris never featured plain old brownies in our magazine. Our food editor was the Michelangelo of baked goods, crafting decadent master-pieces, her raw materials of choice: flour, sugar, and eggs.

"Caramel Marshmallow." She poured us coffee while I savored my first bite. "What do you think?"

I let the flavors send my taste buds into gastronomic heaven before answering. "I think you're going to be responsible for me having to buy a new wardrobe. How many gazillion calories are in one of these suckers?"

"Let's just say this is definitely not for one of our diet spreads." She picked up the plate and held it under my nose. "Have another. You look like you need it."

I didn't argue with her, rationalizing to myself that I'd make up for all the calories by eating celery and carrot sticks all weekend. *Right.*

However, before I polished off the first brownie, my cell phone rang. "Sunnyside," I said, frowning at the display.

"You think Lucille has whipped the proletariat masses into rebellion already?"

"With Lucille anything is possible." I flipped open my phone, expecting the worst. "Hello?"

"Mrs. Pollack, this is Shirley Hallstead. I understand you're interested in the temporary part-time position we have open for an art therapist. When can you start?"

"When can I start? Don't you want to interview me first? See a résumé?"

"No need. Kara vouches for you, and after all, it's arts and crafts, not rocket science.

You're more than qualified from what Kara told me. How's tomorrow sound? Nine-thirty? That will give us half an hour for paperwork before your first class begins."

"Uhm, sure. Nine-thirty sounds great."

"I'll see you then." And with that she hung up.

I pocketed my phone and looked up to find Cloris staring at me. "Are you quitting?"

"Of course not."

"Could have fooled me. That certainly sounded like a job offer."

"It was." I proceeded to tell her what had transpired at Sunnyside. "That was the director. She wants me to start tomorrow morning."

Cloris placed her hand on my forearm. "I know you're desperate for money, sweetie, but are you sure about this? You're going to burn yourself out."

I sank down into one of the molded plastic chairs surrounding the break room table and stuffed the remainder of the brownie into my mouth. "The money's too good to pass up," I said, talking around chocolate, caramel, and marshmallow. "It's only for a few months. I'll manage." Somehow.

"Famous last words. I'll start researching asylums for loony craft editors."

48

"Make sure you pick one that allows care packages from sarcastic food editors."

Since God saw fit to make women the multi-taskers of the species (really, have you ever met a man who could do more than one thing at a time?), why didn't He see fit to endow us with the ability to thrive on a mere three or four hours of sleep a night? Or create longer days for us? Or more than seven days in a week?

When you come right down to it, it would have been nice if the Big Guy had thought things through a little more before going on a creation tear. Sort of a Biblical spin on *measure twice, cut once.* After all, no one forced Him to get it all done in six days. He certainly wasn't in competition with anyone else at the time. Think of all the kinks He could have worked out beforehand had He simply taken eight or ten days. Or a couple of weeks.

For example, let there be light, but hold off on the ones that cause melanoma. And we really could have done quite nicely minus the bed bugs and cockroaches. Not to mention the head lice.

I pondered this and more as I inched my way home from work. How do I juggle a second job on top of my already more-than-forty-hours-a-week primary job without going totally bonkers from sleep deprivation?

Or sacrificing my multiple responsibilities as a single parent?

Yet something else I could blame on my selfish Dead Louse of a Spouse. Thanks to Karl, one kid now never had a parent standing on the sidelines or sitting in the bleachers, cheering him on when both boys had games at the same time. And given their sports fanaticism, rarely was there a Saturday or Sunday that Alex and Nick weren't both playing in separate games on opposite ends of town. Or in some other town.

While I continued to ponder and cast blame, my stomach grumbled, reminding me that I'd skipped both breakfast and lunch in my mad dash to move Lucille from the hospital to Sunnyside and squeeze a day's worth of work into half a day at the office. Woman cannot live by coffee and Cloris confections alone, as much as I try.

As I sat in bumper-to-bumper evening rush-hour traffic, tepid air blowing on me, I took a mental inventory of my refrigerator and pantry, hoping I'd discover enough leftovers to serve for dinner since I'd forgotten to defrost something that morning. The last thing I felt like doing at six o'clock on a Friday night was making a run to ShopRite before heading home.

Hell, if all else failed, I made a mean mac and cheese. I'm sure if I looked hard enough, I'd find a bag of frozen peas hiding in the deep recesses of the freezer. Cheese, pasta, veggies. Major food groups covered. But could I sell mac and cheese to the starving masses in the middle of a blistering heat wave?

However, when I finally arrived home, the moment I opened the front door, all thoughts of mac and cheese — with or without peas — flew from my thoughts.

THREE

I may have suffered a lollapalooza of a triple whammy when Karl permanently cashed in his chips in Las Vegas, but there is one bright spot in the chaos that has become my life — photojournalist and to-die-for stud, Zachary Barnes.

The apartment over our garage used to house my studio. It now houses Zachary Barnes, my tenant. Zack entered my life within days of Karl's funeral, after I ran an ad to rent out the apartment.

Even though attraction sparked from the beginning, fanned in no small part by the none-too-subtle maneuverings of Mama, Alex, and Nick, protocol dictated a platonic relationship. Karl's deceit not withstanding, I was still newly widowed. For all I knew, those sparks shooting through my body could have been a reaction to the anger stage of my grief — anger directed toward Dead Louse of a Spouse.

However, two near-death experiences in less than five months made me realize I'd mourned Dead Louse of a Spouse long enough. Zack and I went on our first and only date so far three weeks ago. Where this blossoming relationship eventually leads is anyone's guess, but right now I've given myself permission to enjoy the journey.

Who would have thought that a guy who looks like Pierce Brosnan, George Clooney, Patrick Dempsey, and Antonio Banderas all contributed to his gene pool would be interested in a pear-shaped, cellulite-riddled, slightly overweight, more than slightly in debt, middle-aged widow? Certainly not me. But there Zack was in my life. And if that weren't enough, the guy can out-cook Jamie Oliver, Bobby Flay, and Emeril Lagasse. All together. With one hand tied behind his back.

Yeah, he's that good. And his cooking doesn't hold a candle to his kissing. I can only imagine his other talents at this point. We haven't taken our relationship to that level yet.

Zack had spent the last two and a half weeks on assignment in Madagascar. I didn't even know he'd returned until I saw his Porsche Boxster parked in the driveway, and the aroma of something taste bud—

seducing hit me the moment I walked into the house.

Mama's never met a recipe she didn't mutilate, and peanut butter and jelly sandwiches are about the extent of Nick's and Alex's culinary skills. So unless the food gods had sent me my own personal chef, those tantalizing aromas wafting toward me meant Zack was creating gastronomic magic in my kitchen.

"Hey," I said as I entered the kitchen. Zack stood stirring something on the stove. Ralph, my African Grey parrot, perched on his shoulder. "When did you get home?" I asked.

"Where the devil should this Romeo be? Came he not home tonight?" squawked Ralph. *"Romeo and Juliet.* Act Two, Scene Four."

Did I mention Ralph spouts Shakespeare? Only Shakespeare. And always circumstance-appropriate quotes, thanks to decades of residing in Great-aunt Penelope Periwinkle's classroom. When Aunt Penelope died two and a half years ago, I inherited Ralph. There are times I would have preferred inheriting her cameo collection, but those went to Mama. At least Ralph is potty trained.

"A couple of hours ago." Zack abandoned

the sauté pan and greeted me with one of *those* kisses. He ended the kiss before I was ready and turned his attention back to the sauté pan. Mushrooms in a wine reduction sauce if my olfactory sense was any judge of such things.

"And after flying halfway round the world, you felt the need to cook a gourmet dinner?"

"I slept most of the flight."

"First class, no doubt."

Zack shrugged, which caused Ralph to abandon his shoulder for mine. "A perk of the job."

Zack freelances for the Smithsonian and World Wildlife Federation, among others, and always negotiates first class accommodations into his contracts. He says it makes up for the days he spends camped out in jungles and deserts.

"Flora and the boys mentioned you were moving Lucille to rehab today. I figured you might need a little bit of TLC tonight."

I glanced around, straining to hear any other activity from within the house. Aside from the unmistakable roaring snores of Mephisto, coming from the direction of the den, silence greeted my ears. "Speaking of Yenta, the Matchmaker, and her two matchmakers-in-training, where are they?

The house is too quiet."

Zack poured a glass of wine from the open bottle of Sauvignon Blanc sitting on the counter and handed it to me. "I sent them out for pizza and a movie."

"My kind of TLC." One of the first casualties of my recently acquired single-parent status had been *me* time. My life now revolved around everyone else 24/7. Having Mama and Lucille living with me only made matters worse. Both were high maintenance, each in her own way.

Zack tossed a bowl of raw shrimp into the sauté pan. The ensuing sizzle sent up a cloud of steam infused with intense aromas that sent my tummy into growl mode and Ralph into squawk mode.

"And you even made a supermarket and wine run?" The last time my fridge contained shrimp or my wine rack contained anything other than dust bunnies, I was still living under the false delusion of the American dream.

"If you'd prefer hot dogs —"

I held up a hand to stop him mid-sentence. "I'll suffer through the shrimp."

"Smart choice. You're all out of hot dogs."

I opened the refrigerator and took a quick inventory. Damn if he wasn't right. The man knew more about the contents of my refrigerator and freezer than I did.

"So how was Madagascar?" I asked as we sat down to dinner. "Safe?" After Zack flew off, I ran a Google search, knowing little about the country except for the eponymous DreamWorks version. What I discovered — an unstable political situation with travelers being warned to exercise extreme caution — made me wish I hadn't looked.

Zack is always flying off to iffy locales. For a while I suspected he used the photojournalism gig as a cover for his real work as a government agent. He assures me that's not the case, but I'm not totally convinced. Spies never admit they're spies, right? It's against the spy code.

"Noisy," he said. "Did you know there's a lemur that sounds exactly like a police siren?"

"I'll take your word for it."

"How did Lucille take to rehab?"

"Like a duck to an oil slick." I expected the quick change of subject. Other than shortly after we met, when Zack regaled Alex and Nick with a tale set in the Guatemalan jungle, he never talks much about his work. Yet another indicator that sends my skepticism barometer soaring.

"I did meet some interesting old ladies, though, and bumped into a college roommate I haven't seen since freshman year." I proceeded to tell Zack about Lyndella and Mabel, and Kara and the job offer.

Zack placed his knife and fork on his plate and stared at me for a long moment before saying anything. Then in an extremely serious tone he asked, "Have you discovered a way to go without sleep?"

"You sound like Cloris. I'll manage. It's only for a few months, and the money is too good to pass up."

"You could raise my rent."

"By over a thousand dollars a month? You might as well buy your own house for what you'd be paying me."

"I don't want my own house. I travel too much. This setup is ideal for my needs, and I don't mind paying more to keep it that way."

It was my turn to employ a serious tone. "I appreciate the gesture, Zack, but I'm not taking any handouts. Not from you. Not from anyone. But especially not from you."

"And why is that?"

I didn't want to have this conversation. Not now. Maybe not ever. I'd gotten into my current financial predicament by putting too much trust in a man who supposedly cared about me. I couldn't dig my way out by depending on another man who

58

cared about me. What if he, too, someday stopped caring?

I stood to clear the table and didn't answer until I'd turned toward the sink, shielding my face from Zack's view. "I think you know."

The next morning Alex and Nick took the news of my weekend job with little complaint, probably because neither had football/soccer/baseball/basketball practice this time of year. Having recently turned seventeen, Alex had secured a job at Starbucks. Nearly fifteen-year-old Nick was spending the summer stocking shelves and bagging groceries at Trader Joe's.

Both boys had expected to go on a month-long teen tour of Arizona, Colorado, and New Mexico this summer, followed by a family trip to Cambridge in late August to visit Harvard. I'd paid the deposit on the teen tour last December but was forced to ask for a refund in February.

As for Harvard, that dream had died with Karl. Unless Alex received a fully paid scholarship (and how realistic was that?), he'd be attending Union County Community College a little more than a year from now and continuing to work at Starbucks part-time to cover tuition, books, car payments, and insurance.

That was my next financial hurdle. At some point this year I'd have to allow Alex to get his license and would have to purchase a second car before next September.

"How will we get to and from work?" asked Nick as he scarfed down a bowl of cereal.

"Same way you get to work during the week. Pedal power."

"What if it's raining?"

"You wear your rain slickers."

"Ah, jeez, Mom! You ever try to bike in a thunderstorm? We could get fried by lightning."

"He has a point," said Alex. "You know how fast summer storms pop up around here."

"They can just as easily pop up during the week."

"This was supposed to be such a cool summer," grumbled Nick.

"Life sucks," I said. "Consider how much more it would suck if you lived in Haiti."

"Is that supposed to make me feel better?"

"No, it's supposed to make me feel better."

I had to keep reminding myself that at least we still had a roof over our heads, and

I still had a job. Most of the people in the world were a lot worse off than the residents of *Casa Pollack*. Most didn't go on summer teen tours or attend Ivy League colleges. Most would be happy to trade places with us. I knew all this.

But I'd worked damn hard to give my kids the American dream. Karl had not only robbed our bank accounts, he'd robbed Alex and Nick of their futures. Alex deserved to go to Harvard. He'd worked his butt off, and I'd sacrificed being a stay-at-home mom so my kids could be whatever they wanted to be. That was the pact. They worked hard at school; their father and I worked hard to pay for their college educations. Someone didn't hold up his end of the bargain.

When Karl and I wed, I agreed to have and to hold, to love and to cherish, for better or for worse, for richer or for poorer, in sickness and in health. Nowhere did those vows mention to trust blindly and without question.

Ay, there's the rub, as Ralph would squawk.

If only I'd taken the least bit of interest in our family finances. Had I not been so trusting, maybe I would have noticed that two plus two no longer added up to four. My trust in my spouse had made me his unwitting accomplice. I'd carry that guilt around with me for the rest of my life.

"Does Grandma know about this new job?" asked Alex.

I tossed back the last swig of my coffee before answering him. "Not yet. She's still sleeping. I'll tell her later." I got up and carried my dishes to the sink. "I'm leaving. I walked Mephisto earlier, but one of you should walk him again before you leave for work later."

"Your turn, bro," said Nick.

"How do you figure that?" asked Alex.

"I walked him last."

"Mom walked him last."

"I mean last night."

I grabbed my purse and keys, leaving the house and their bickering behind, and headed for Sunnyside.

Shirley Hallstead was waiting for me in her office, the door ajar. She once again wore a power suit, this one navy with brass buttons, and once again not a hair on her head dared stick out of place. I also noted the Prussian blue Birkin bag prominently displayed on her desk. Most working women place their purses in a desk drawer or file cabinet while at work. Then again, most working women don't carry around handbags that cost thousands of dollars.

I knocked on the jam, and she turned her attention from her computer screen, waving me in and directing me to the chair adjacent to her desk. "Give me a minute to finish this up," she said.

While she clicked away, I surveyed the room. Dozens of awards and commendations — some for Shirley, others for Sunnyside — hung on the walls, along with framed newspaper clippings about Sunnyside and Shirley. There was also an assortment of framed diplomas. Shirley held a bachelor of science degree in nursing as well as masters degrees in nursing, social work, and business administration from Rutgers University.

Framed photos of her with various past and present local and state politicians dotted the shelves of a wall unit and lined the top of a bookcase. Not a single family photo in the mix. No husband. No kids. Not even a snapshot of a pet. It seemed Shirley Hallstead's entire life revolved entirely around her career.

"I don't usually work on Saturdays," she said, finally turning her attention to me, "but I figured as long as I was waiting for you, I'd catch up on some paperwork."

Was she blaming me for forcing her to give

up part of her weekend? Hadn't she requested we meet this morning? And if she'd only come in today for me, what was with the power suit? She hardly needed to dress up to have me fill out the requisite paperwork.

Speaking of which, she reached across the desk and handed me a clipboard of papers. "However," she continued, "I'm happy to be here today if it means I've filled our staffing vacancy. I had someone all lined up, but she found a full-time position and bailed on me yesterday morning. You can imagine how thrilled I was when Kara told me you'd agreed to take the job."

I guess she wasn't blaming me. "But you have someone for the rest of week?"

"Yes."

I was a bit puzzled by the urgency attached to filling a few extra hours of a non-critical staff position. "Surely, you could go for a few weeks without holding arts and crafts classes on the weekends."

Shirley sighed. "If only it were that simple. I need the program staffed forty hours a week. Normally, that would be Mondays through Fridays, but the person I was able to hire to replace Kara can't give me that many hours each week. The additional person I hired for the remaining hours is the one who quit on me."

I placed the clipboard on the edge of Shirley's desk. "Before I start in on paperwork, I need my responsibilities outlined. I don't know what Kara told you, but I have no training as an art therapist."

"You went to art school, right?"

"Yes."

"And I know you must do crafts, given what you mentioned yesterday. Any teaching experience?"

"Prior to working at the magazine, I taught art in the public school system for several years."

She clapped her hands together. "What could be more perfect? As far as I'm concerned, Mrs. Pollack, you're abundantly qualified. Think of this as running a school arts and crafts program. Except instead of kids, you've got geriatric students. You give them projects, supervise them, help those having trouble."

"That's it?"

"In a nutshell. Most of the men and women who will take advantage of weekend classes have worked with their hands throughout their lives. They know what to do, but now because of advancing age, they often have trouble completing tasks that were once second nature to them."

"Lyndella Wegner and the other women I saw in the needlework class yesterday must be the exceptions. Those women needed no help."

"To some extent, but even they have their good days and bad days. They mostly need praise, guidance, and encouragement, but just wait until it rains and their arthritis acts up. They become very frustrated and depressed."

"So I'm more a proctor than anything?" Or babysitter.

"Your job will be to help when needed. Propose new projects when current ones are completed. Demonstrate techniques to those interested in trying something new.

"I'd also like you to get them more interested in crafting for various charities like Caps for Kids. We get great PR for Sunnyside out of that, and I'd like to see more of it."

Translation: Shirley wanted her picture in the newspaper more often.

"Finally," she continued, "you'll need to organize rotating exhibits of our residents' art works in the lobby and commons areas."

"I'm assuming these exhibits are G-rated? Nothing from Lyndella Wegner's *Blue* Period?"

Shirley's face hardened. "Definitely not."

"And Lyndella's okay with that? She strikes me as a woman who likes to call the shots rather than take orders."

"She has no choice in the matter. We have children who come to visit their grandparents. I don't need a lawsuit on my hands because someone's five year old was traumatized by a six-foot penis."

"I hope that was hyperbole."

Shirley gave a sigh of frustration. "So far, but with Lyndella one never knows."

She leaned forward, resting her elbows on a neat stack of file folders. Her business-like demeanor returned, and her voice grew serious. "As people age, tasks that once seemed simple become difficult, even for those without any underlying medical conditions. Self-esteem often plummets. These classes and the exhibits are a form of creative social work, a way of making our residents feel useful and appreciated."

"Where does the therapy come in?" I had college friends who went on to do masters programs in art therapy. There had to be more to an art therapy major than what Shirley Hallstead just described.

"You don't need to worry yourself about that. We have the trained therapist, Kara's replacement, on staff during the week for those who need such services. You'll work with those who want to avail themselves of the arts and crafts room on the weekends, the full-time residents in independent housing and assisted living, not our rehab patients."

I could do that. Then again, so could most seventeen year old day camp counselors. Maybe Kara had been mistaken about the pay. "Kara mentioned thirty-five dollars an hour?"

Shirley changed the subject. "Have you noticed the watercolors hanging in the lobby and hallways throughout Sunnyside?"

I had, but I didn't see how they connected to a thirty-five dollars an hour salary. When I nodded, she continued. "They were all painted by Mildred Burnbaum, a retired art teacher and deceased Sunnyside resident. Mrs. Burnbaum left Sunnyside the collection as well as a yearly grant for the express purpose of staffing art classes with qualified personnel. As a former teacher, she realized the importance of such programs, especially for the elderly. The bequest stipulates the number of hours a week and the salary, adjusted each year to the cost of living index."

"Generous woman."

"Indeed." Shirley gave me another tight-lipped smile. "It's one of the reasons that

Sunnyside has such an excellent reputation. Our residents don't sit around watching television all day. However, if we don't comply with the terms of the grant, we lose the money. Permanently. We're back to staffing a part-time art therapist a few hours a week and no one to run an arts and crafts program for the non-rehab residents."

Sounded exactly like the public schools statewide. I couldn't go back to teaching had I wanted to. School districts no longer had money for the arts in their budgets. "That would be a shame," I said.

Shirley agreed with a nod. "The overseer of the trust, Mildred's oldest son, is a greedy, anal bastard, prone to surprise visits. He's hoping to catch us in noncompliance one of these days so he no longer has to share his mother's estate with us. That's why I need the program staffed forty hours a week without interruption and why I was put in such a bind yesterday."

This explained Kara's high octane sales pitch. She must have just learned that she'd have no job to come back to after her maternity leave if Shirley didn't find a last-minute replacement for the teacher who'd bailed on her. Chad might be making big bucks with the Giants, but Kara wasn't about to give up her shop-till-you-drop funds without pulling out every available stop. Lucille's stint at Sunnyside turned out to be a bit of financial serendipity for both of us.

I was having trouble reconciling the two sides of Shirley Hallstead. Yesterday she tried to nix my article, saying she didn't want Sunnyside looking like Kitsch Central. Now she was taking pride in the same programs that produced those projects, milking them for all the PR she could. Maybe she was fine with crafts as long as they didn't extend beyond knitted baby caps for preemies and sweaters for the homeless, as long as she got something out of it.

Then again, we all have our good days and bad days, no matter our age. I'm certainly not above unleashing my inner bitch when I get overwhelmed. Maybe yesterday was just one of Shirley's bad days, given what she'd just told me, and she overreacted to the magazine article.

I redirected the conversation back to soliciting the answers I needed. "Kara wasn't certain about the number of hours. She said between eight and twelve."

"I need ten from you. Kara's replacement was going to work twenty-eight hours a week, but she agreed to increase to thirty yesterday. How you break those ten hours up over the weekend is your decision, but if at all possible, try not to start before nine-thirty or finish after five-thirty."

"Why is that?"

"Our residents often have trouble getting up in the morning and many like an early dinner."

"I can work around your request."

"Thank you." She lifted the clipboard from the corner of the desk and handed it back to me. "As soon as you fill out those forms, you can get yourself situated. For today you'll have to follow the posted schedule." She handed me a separate sheet of paper. "You can make any changes you want for the remainder of the weekend and thereafter. Just let the receptionist at the front desk know before the end of today so she can notify the residents of any changes."

I scanned the schedule. The next two days included classes in painting and drawing; pottery; sculpture; needlework, quilting, and sewing; scrap crafts; decoupage; beadwork and jewelry; and paper crafts and scrapbooking. "This will work out fine," I told her.

"Great. Just leave the paperwork on my desk when you're finished. I'm going to head out." She stood to leave. "Oh, one other thing. Can you also work six hours on

Monday this week? Kara's replacement won't be starting until Tuesday because of the long weekend."

"Sure." Who needs a day off when working means another dent in the debt monster?

"Great." She grabbed her Birkin. "Then I'll see you Monday."

"Before you go —"

"Yes?"

"My mother-in-law really misses her dog. Would it be okay if I brought him to visit with her on the weekends while I'm here?"

"She's not capable of walking him yet, is she?"

"I'm really not sure what she's capable of at this point. She doesn't want to be here, so that's a huge incentive to take the rehab seriously, but I'll walk him before we arrive and again during my lunch break."

Shirley shrugged. "I don't see why not as long as he doesn't bother any of the other residents or their pets. She can't let him run loose around the facility."

"Mephisto's more a lummox than a dog. He'll spend most of his time sleeping on her bed."

"Mephisto?"

"Long story."

"Another time, then." And without so much as a wave of her arm, she exited her office, leaving me with a clipboard full of blank forms.

I glanced at my watch. No way would I ever finish before my first group of students arrived. I tucked the clipboard under my arm and headed for the arts and crafts room. The forms could wait until lunchtime.

Since I passed Lucille's room on the way, I decided to pop in to tell her that I'd bring Mephisto to visit her tomorrow. As I pushed the door open, it flew from my hands. Reggie, the anorexic-looking aide from yesterday, froze in front of me, her face drained of color, her eyes huge with fear.

"She . . . she's . . . she's dead!"

FOUR

"Who's dead?" When Reggie didn't answer, I grabbed her toothpick thin arms as delicately as possible, afraid that I'd break a bone, and gently shook her. "Focus, Reggie. Who's dead? Lucille?"

"You wish," came my mother-in-law's booming voice from within the room.

Reggie shook her head. "Lyn . . . Lyndella. I came to check on her because she never showed up for breakfast."

I stepped into the room and found Lucille dressed in her lime green and orange paisley pantsuit, sitting upright in the recliner next to her bed. She had accessorized the outfit with her usual scowl. "At least I won't have to listen to that woman's incessant prattle any more," she said. "You wouldn't believe what went on here last night."

I'm sure I'd hear about it whether I wanted to or not but not now. I hurried across the room and pulled back the curtain separating Lyndella's half of the room from Lucille's half. On her back with the quilt pulled up to her chin, Lyndella appeared to be sleeping peacefully. I placed my fingers alongside her neck, searching for a pulse. Nothing. I pulled back the quilt and tried her wrist. Still nothing. Lyndella Wegner was definitely dead.

Reggie still stood in the doorway, still looked scared out of her mind. "Shirley Hallstead just left," I told her. "See if you can catch her in the parking lot."

Reggie nodded, but her feet remained planted.

Oh jeez! "Haven't you ever seen a dead body before?"

She shook her head.

How on earth had she gone through a nurse's aide program without coming in contact with at least a few dead bodies? Hell, I'm a magazine editor, and I'm averaging a dead body every few months lately.

I tossed my purse and the clipboard onto Lucille's bed and dashed out of the room. If Shirley had stopped to use the restroom or chat with someone on her way out, she might still be in the parking lot. I raced down the hall to the information desk. "Where's the employee parking lot?" I shouted, startling the receptionist. Her hand flew to her overly abundant chest emblazoned with a silver glitter *Jerseylicious* spelled out across a turquoise T-shirt.

"Out back."

"Is that where Shirley Hallstead parks?"

She nodded vigorously, causing her enormous chandelier earrings to keep swinging back and forth long after the nod ended.

Crap! No way would she still be around by the time I made my way to the back of the sprawling complex. "Do you have her cell number?"

"I'm only supposed to call her in an emergency."

"Is a dead resident considered an emergency?"

She grabbed the handset and began pushing buttons. "Who died?"

"Lyndella Wegner."

"About time."

I spun around to find Mabel Shapiro leaning on her rhinestone festooned walker. "That good-for-nothing Southern hussy's been a thorn in everyone's patootie from the moment she moved in twenty years ago. Swore she'd outlast us all." Mabel chuckled. "Guess we got the last laugh, huh? And now the self-proclaimed Empress of Everything won't be in your magazine article. That's what I call divine justice, hon."

Wow! Few things ever leave me speechless, but I had no idea how to respond to Mabel. I needn't have worried. As I stood there with my mouth gaping open, she spun around and shuffled her rotund, squat self down the hall.

The clock in the lobby told me I'd be seriously late for my first class if I didn't hustle. So I headed back to Lucille's room. Both she and her wheelchair were gone, probably off to therapy of some sort. I grabbed my purse and the clipboard and headed for the arts and crafts room. I'd tell Lucille about Mephisto later. Or maybe I'd just surprise her tomorrow.

I arrived in the arts and crafts room to find a dozen elderly men and women crowded around Mabel and her walker as they all reveled in having outlived Lyndella Wegner. "I'm going to throw a party," said Mabel, "and you're all invited."

"A wake?" I asked, horning my way into the crowd of nine women and four men.

"A celebration." She beamed like the newly crowned Empress of Everything. The woman was definitely enjoying Lyndella Wegner's demise a tad too much, even for diehard, longtime rivals.

"Isn't that a bit harsh?"

"You didn't know Lyndella," said another

woman in the group. "That two-bit strumpet made everyone's life a living hell."

"Damn right," said a third woman. "She had a way of yanking the happy out of everyone." She then broke out in an off-key rendition of *Ding Dong the Witch Is Dead*, only she substituted *bitch* for *witch*. Everyone joined in.

"Wasn't there anyone who liked her?" I asked when the singing had died down. "Did she have any friends or family who came to visit?"

"No one cared about that old floozy except the old floozy herself," said Mabel. "If she had any family, they never bothered to visit."

"She never mentioned any family," said another woman. "All she ever talked about was herself."

If Lyndella had no friends or family, with whom had she been speaking on the phone Friday morning?

"Good riddance," muttered one of the men under his breath. "Hell's too good for that one."

"As for friends," said a fourth woman, "Lyndella only knew how to hurt and annoy people. Who wants to befriend someone who takes pleasure in making everyone else miserable?"

"Nothing anyone did was ever good enough or up to her high standards," chimed in another woman. "As far as she was concerned, we were all inferior beings. In every way."

That's where the similarities between Lyndella and my mother-in-law ended. As nasty as she was to just about everyone, Lucille did have her fellow Daughters of the October Revolution. Those women worshipped at the feet of their glorious leader, even if their worship didn't extend to offering her a place to live.

"Who are you, anyway?" asked a second man who appeared several years younger than the others. He sported a lame gray comb-over and a huge blue and purple shiner under his right eye. Beyond those two defining features and the paint-splotched smock he wore, *nondescript* best described him, a run-of-the-mill average old guy — average height, average weight, average looks — someone who left no lasting impression.

However, he had provided me with the opening I needed to change the subject and start the class. "I'm Anastasia Pollack. I'll be running the arts and crafts program on weekends for the next few months."

"That's the one who's going to put us in

her magazine, Dirk," said Mabel.

"That so?" he asked.

"If you'd like," I said.

"We getting paid?" asked a third man.

"No."

"Then what's in it for us?" asked the man who'd commented on hell being too good a place for Lyndella Wegner.

"We'll be celebrities, Murray," said Mabel.

"Celebrities get paid," he said. "You want me in your magazine, you pay me."

"Can't do that, Murray. We'll have to leave you out of the spread."

Murray muttered something under his breath as he shuffled off to one of the pottery wheels.

"Don't pay him no mind," said the woman who'd started the singing. "Like all of us, Murray's on a fixed income. The economy has really taken a bite out of our savings. Some of us are having a hard time staying at Sunnyside. Many have already downsized from apartments to single rooms. Others have traded in singles for doubles in order to remain here."

"We could all use a little extra cash," added one of the other women.

"Murray's a sweetheart, though," said Mabel. "There isn't anything he wouldn't do for us. Right girls?" The other women all nodded in agreement.

Mabel jabbed me in the ribs with her elbow. When I turned toward her she whispered, "Not to mention a cutie-patootie, if you know what I mean."

I glanced over at Murray and saw no evidence of a cutie, patootie or otherwise, only a slightly hunched and more than slightly balding elderly man with a scruffy beard, hair sprouting from his ears, a bulbous nose, wiry unibrow, and threadbare chinos belted far too high above his waist. To each his own. Or judging from the male/female ratio, maybe beggars couldn't be choosers at Sunnyside.

I smiled at Mabel before addressing the group. "Why don't you all show me what you've been working on?"

By the time three-thirty rolled around, exhaustion had invaded every tendon and muscle of my body. My feet burned from standing, and my head throbbed. My facial muscles ached from keeping a friendly smile plastered across my face even though I wanted to give the residents of Sunnyside an extremely large piece of my mind. I hadn't seen such relish over the demise of another human being since the SEAL Team 6 put a bullet through the head of Osama bin Laden.

On my way out, I handed the receptionist at the front desk the clipboard of forms that I'd filled out during my lunch break. "Sorry I startled you earlier." I extended my right hand. "I'm Anastasia Pollack, by the way. I'll be working here on the weekends for the next few months."

"April May. Nice to meet you." When I raised my eyebrows, she shrugged and added, "My parents had a warped sense of humor."

"I know what you mean. I've got a mother who thinks she's a Russian princess."

She gave me a puzzled look. "Is she?"

"Highly unlikely." I guess she'd never heard of Grand Duchess Anastasia. April appeared to be in her early twenties. Maybe they were no longer teaching the Russian Revolution wherever she'd gone to school. "Your name certainly makes you stand out in a crowd," I added.

She pointed to her *Jerseylicious* boobs, a minimum triple D cup on what was otherwise a size four body, and offered up a huge belly laugh. "Girl, these make me stand out enough!"

Her boobs, as well as her head of dreadlocks and enormous earrings, bobbed in tempo with her laugh. April had obviously inherited her parents' sense of humor.

However, I was surprised that Shirley Hallstead allowed such a lax dress code for her receptionist, given her own obvious penchant for power suits. After all, April was the official Sunnyside greeter, the first person people encountered as they stepped into the lobby, and Shirley struck me as someone decidedly averse to nose rings, dreadlocks, and billboard chests.

Maybe she was eye candy for prospective male residents. It didn't matter to me. I asked her to see that Shirley got the forms, then waved good-bye and told her I'd see her around. I didn't bother checking in on Lucille. My body couldn't tolerate a pain in the ass on top of all the other pain.

Less than two miles separated Sunnyside from my house. Even though the mercury had hovered in the high nineties all day, I didn't bother turning on the air conditioning in my rust-bucket Hyundai. The engine would only blow hot air for that short distance. I rolled down all four windows, settled into the oven on wheels, and headed home, stoked by thoughts of soaking in a cool tub once I arrived.

The Karma gods had other plans for me.

FIVE

The moment I entered the house, I kicked off my sandals, leaving them where they landed askew on the foyer floor. A definite do-as-I-say-not-as-I-do moment, but I was too tired to care. Besides, the boys weren't home. I'd pick up my sandals and move them to my closet way before Alex and Nick ever discover their mother's transgression.

"Mama?" I called as I headed for the kitchen.

"Downstairs, dear."

Uh-oh. As much as I'd appreciate some help around the house, the last time Mama did laundry, she'd tossed a red T-shirt in with the white wash. Alex and Nick swore they'd sooner go commando than wear pink jockey shorts, and who could blame them? They'd never survive gym class.

The interior temperature of my home was only slightly cooler than the Saharan temps of outside. Air conditioning only works up to a certain point. Once the mercury soars above that point, the AC unit can chug nonstop without producing further benefits. I anticipated an electric bill in the triple digits for inside air not much below triple digits. Still, it was better than nothing. We'd all die of heat prostration without the minimal relief the unit provided. May it continue to chug for years to come.

I'd just filled a glass with ice water and was holding it against my forehead, my eyes closed, when I heard Mama climbing up the basement stairs. "Where have you been all day, Anastasia?"

"Working."

"On a Saturday?"

"I'll tell you all about it in a few minutes."

"Well, I'm glad you're home, dear. How can you work with such dangerous tools?"

My eyes sprang open. Mama looked like she'd walked into an enormous cobweb. Strings of glue clung to her hands and arms and hung from her chin. A large glob covered the top of her left Ferragamo. Good thing she wasn't wearing sandals. I grabbed the glue gun from her hand and began de-stringing her. "Did you burn yourself?"

"Only every finger."

"What were you doing?"

"Fixing your father."

Harold Periwinkle, my father, had drowned while SCUBA diving seventeen years ago. I sent up a silent prayer to the God of Dementia, begging him to keep his stinking mitts off my mother. "Mama, Daddy's dead."

"Well of course he is, dear! I was there, you know."

"But you just said —"

"Honestly, Anastasia! I was dusting my Dear Departeds when that Satanic communist mongrel startled me and I knocked Harold off the shelf. He spilled onto the dining room floor, and the porcelain band around his urn broke. I was trying to glue it back in place."

Flora Sudberry Periwinkle Ramirez Scoffield Goldberg O'Keefe had outlived each of her five husbands plus Lou Beaumont, her recently murdered fiancé. All except Lou now resided in a row of bronze urns on a shelf in my dining room. By some miracle, Ricardo had overlooked the urns when he trashed my house five months ago. Or maybe they'd spooked him enough that he'd left them undisturbed. I suppose even Mafia loan sharks have their share of superstitions.

As for Lou, still too upset over his deceit, Mama had relegated him to a shelf in the basement when she couldn't pawn his remains off on any of his ex-wives. I called the dining room shelf Flora's Dead Husbands' Shrine. Mama called the urns her Dear Departeds. "Where's Daddy now?" I asked.

She pointed to the far corner of the kitchen floor where a green plastic dustpan held the ashy remains of my father. "I wanted to fix the urn before I poured him back into his resting place."

"I'll fix the urn. You pick up Daddy before Catherine the Great uses him for a litter box."

"She wouldn't dare! She's too well trained."

Right. As if on cue, Catherine the Great sauntered into the kitchen, looked around, then headed straight for Daddy. I grabbed the dustpan just as she was about to paw what remained of my father. "Let's not tempt her. Pour Daddy into a plastic bag until I fix his urn."

"You'll do it right away, won't you, dear? The thought of my darling Harold sealed up in a plastic bag is more than I can bear."

She preferred Daddy sitting in a dustpan? "After I get rid of this headache."

I collapsed into a kitchen chair and placed the now tepid glass of water back on my forehead. A second later the doorbell rang. I contemplated ignoring it, except that one of the boys may have forgotten his key. So I took a quick sip of the water and dragged my exhausted butt back to the foyer while Mama carefully spooned Daddy into a Ziploc.

On my way through the living room, I glanced out the window and found a gray minivan parked at the curb in front of my house. Before opening the door, I checked the peephole. A tall, thin man with a head of shaggy brown hair in need of a trim stood on my stoop. He wore a pair of wrinkled khaki trousers and an equally wrinkled blue and white pencil-striped, short-sleeved sports shirt. Something about him struck me as vaguely familiar, but I couldn't place him.

"Is this the home of Lucille Pollack?" he asked when I opened the door.

I checked his hands before answering. No envelope. Hopefully, that meant he wasn't a process server. Lucille had keyed a Beemer prior to her stroke. The owner threatened to sue her. Not that she had anything besides her monthly social security check and a meager pension from her days as the editor of *The Worker's Herald,* the weekly newspaper of the American Communist Party.

"Yes, but she's not here."

"Are you Anastasia Pollack?"

"I am." The Beemer owner couldn't sue me, could he? "And you are?"

He held out his hand. "Ira Pollack. Your half-brother. I'm so very happy to meet you."

I stared at his extended hand, then his face. Finally, it hit me. Give the man a haircut, add a few years and a dozen pounds or so, and Ira Pollack could be a not-so-dead ringer for Dead Louse of a Spouse. How could I not have noticed immediately? "I believe you've made a mistake," I said.

"Isidore Pollack was your father, wasn't he?"

"Of course Isidore Pollack wasn't her father!" Mama strode across the living room to join me. "I should know who fathered my only child."

Ira stared at Mama, a look of total confusion spreading across his face. "*You're* Lucille Pollack?"

"I should say not!"

"I'm sorry, ma'am, I —"

I grabbed Ira Pollack's still extended hand, his sweaty palm making me immediately regret my action. "As I was about to say, I'm not Lucille's daughter. I'm her daughter-in-law, and this," I nodded toward

89

Mama, "is my mother, not Lucille. My mother-in-law recently had surgery and is currently in a rehab facility."

"That's too bad. I would have liked to speak with her."

I doubted Lucille would feel likewise. "Maybe once she returns home."

"I have a half-brother, then?" asked Ira. "I guess that makes you my half-sister-in-law." His sweaty palm still gripping my hand, he vigorously pumped my arm. "I'm so very happy to meet you, and I can't wait to meet your husband. Is he home?"

"Perhaps you should come in." I slipped my hand from his and led him into the living room. With my left hand I motioned him toward one of the two overstuffed easy chairs that flanked the bay window while I surreptitiously swiped my right hand dry across my denim skirt. "Would you like a cold drink?"

"I wouldn't mind a glass of ice water if it's no trouble. Kind of brutal outside today."

"No trouble at all." I turned to Mama. "Would you mind getting Mr. Pollack —"

"Ira," he interjected. "After all, we're family."

Were we? He certainly looked like Karl, although younger. Karl had claimed Isidore

Pollack walked out on Lucille shortly after she became pregnant with him. The way my mother-in-law tells it, J. Edgar Hoover abducted Isidore. She also believed the feds disposed of his body under the goalposts at Giants stadium. If I had money to bet, I'd go with Karl's more plausible explanation. How could I take seriously a woman who confused her husband with Jimmy Hoffa?

I revised my request. "Mama, would you mind getting Ira a glass of water?"

"Of course not, dear, but don't you dare continue this conversation until I get back. I certainly don't want to miss anything juicy."

Mama returned with Ira's water. While he guzzled down the entire glass, she nestled herself into the opposite corner of the sofa from where I sat. Catherine the Great jumped onto Mama's lap and hunkered down.

Ira placed the empty glass on the floor by his feet, then leaned forward, resting his forearms on his thighs, and said, "I suppose I should start from the beginning."

"Always a good place, young man," said Mama. "Take your time, and don't leave anything out."

"Isidore Pollack was my father," he began.

"Was?" I asked.

"He passed away recently."

Mama and I both murmured the requisite *so sorry to hear that.*

"After he died," continued Ira, "I discovered a secret from his past while sorting through his possessions."

"That he'd had a child before you?" I prompted.

Ira nodded. "I don't even think my mother ever knew. If she did, she never let on. At least not to me. She passed away three years ago."

Once again Mama and I murmured an *I'm sorry.*

"What did you find?" I asked.

He pulled an envelope from his pocket and handed it to me. "Dad owned a huge collection of 45s from the fifties and sixties. This was squirreled away in the dust sleeve of Little Richard's *Lucille.* "

The envelope was addressed to a Mrs. Edith Pollack at an address in Queens. Underneath the address, an additional note stated, "Please forward to Isidore Pollack."

"Read it," said Ira.

I pulled the one sheet of thick pale lavender stationery from the envelope and unfolded it. A small deckle-edged black and white photo of a young man and a woman dropped onto my lap. I recognized the hard set of the woman's mouth. The man looked very much like Karl at that age. I handed Mama the yellowed snapshot.

She turned the photo over and read the inscription written on the back. *"Lucille Trachtenburg and Isidore Pollack, Ban the Bomb rally. Greenwich Village 1957."*

"Several years before Karl was born," I said. "Maybe the photo was taken shortly after they met."

"Read the letter," said Mama.

I scanned the text. "Oh, dear."

Mama scooted closer to me. "What does it say? Read it out loud, for heaven's sake, Anastasia."

Dear Isidore,

I hope this letter eventually reaches you. The return name and address are obviously fictitious, and I took a bus to New Jersey to mail it. I even spent good money on some decadent perfumed stationery to complete the ruse, hoping your mother would believe the letter came from an old high school or college flame. I know she'd trash any letter from me, the "evil pinko" she believes nearly corrupted you.

I won't apologize for who I am or what

I believe in. You once said that was what first attracted you to me, that you loved my passion for a cause I believed in more than anything or anyone. And you once shared that passion, or so you claimed.

The suburban home with the white picket fence is Madison Avenue propaganda. That life will suck everything that's good and unique and special out of you and turn you into a mindless machine. You've been brainwashed by your parents and others like them. I cannot in good conscience subject any child of mine to that numbing way of life.

I have complete faith that you will eventually realize your mistake. I await your return. Lucille

The letter only raised more questions about Lucille's past. For one thing, I never knew her maiden name, and I'm not sure Karl did, either.

"She doesn't mention the photo," said Mama, "and the handwriting on the photo doesn't match the handwriting on the letter."

"The photo may have belonged to my father," said Ira. "I have no way of knowing whether it was sent with the letter or not."

"Probably his," I said. "Lucille's not the sentimental type. To my knowledge, she's never kept any family photos."

I glanced at the envelope. "This letter isn't dated, and the postmark is too smudged to read. Lucille doesn't say she's pregnant with Isidore's child. She could be referring to any future children they might have together. How did you make the huge leap from this letter and photo to my doorstep?"

"Through a bit of unbelievable co-incidence," said Ira. "Three weeks ago I saw a news story about a group of elderly women protesters blocking an intersection in Westfield. The reporter interviewed the ring leader, one Lucille Pollack. The news clip also showed footage of you arriving home and refusing to speak to the press. I'd discovered the letter and photo about a week earlier."

"I would imagine there's more than one Lucille Pollack in the world. What made you think you'd discovered the right Lucille? The photo gives her maiden name."

"From the background information mentioned by the reporter. I knew Dad briefly flirted with communism in his youth and that for a short time he worked as a stringer for *The Worker's Herald*, the same paper where your mother-in-law worked. And the age fit. When I compared the snapshot to the news footage, I was convinced I had the right woman. That's why I was so confused by your mother a few minutes ago."

"Why did you wait so long to contact us?" I asked.

Ira ran his fingers through his hair, then took a deep breath and slowly released it. "I needed time to work up the courage. At first I wasn't sure I should intrude and possibly dig up a past that your mother-in-law might want to keep buried. However, the pull of connecting with a sibling won out. I never had any brothers or sisters."

I understood Ira's dilemma. As an only child, I had often wished for a brother or sister. At times I still do. "If your father knew about the baby, he walked out on Lucille while she was pregnant."

"The letter doesn't say Ira left Lucille," said Mama. "She may have kicked him out."

I quickly perused the letter again. Lucille had little tolerance for anyone who disagreed with her. Mama could be right.

"Dad loved kids," said Ira. "He always regretted that he and mom couldn't have more than one. Even if he and Lucille broke up, I think he'd want to have a relationship with his son. If he knew that a son existed."

I had absolutely no doubt that the Lucille

of the letter and photo was Karl's mother. I also had no doubt that Ira was Karl's half-brother. The proof sat across the room from me, written in his DNA. "Did you know about your father's previous marriage?"

Ira shook his head. "That's another mystery. I found no evidence of a previous marriage. Believe me, after finding this letter, I searched high and low. No marriage license, no divorce papers. Nothing referring to alimony or child support. He and Lucille may never have married."

"Or he was a bigamist," said Mama.

"Dad was an attorney. He'd never jeopardize his practice by breaking the law."

Not that the two are mutually exclusive. Especially in New Jersey where our prisons have been home to many a lawbreaking lawyer. I kept that thought to myself, though. "So either he and Lucille married, then divorced, and he didn't keep any proof of it," I said, "which would be very odd for an attorney, or —"

"They never married," added Mama.

"But she took his name," I reminded her. "For both herself and Karl. Why would she do that if she and Isidore never married?"

"For the sake of propriety," suggested Mama. "Consider the stigma of a child born out-of-wedlock back then. It's not like today where young people start families, then eventually get around to marrying. Or not."

"We're talking about Lucille here, Mama. When did she ever do anything for the sake of propriety?"

"Maybe your husband can shed some light on all this," said Ira. "When do you expect him home?"

I took a deep breath before answering. "Actually, Karl won't be coming home, Ira."

"He's away on business?"

"He died this past winter."

Ira's mouth dropped open, but no sounds came out. Poor man. He'd spent weeks working up the courage to contact a sibling that he'd never meet. I didn't know how to comfort him. An awkward silence settled over the room with Ira fighting to hold back his emotions and Mama and I at a loss for words.

When the phone rang a moment later, I was glad for the excuse to leave the room, if only for a minute. Maybe I'd think of something to say by the time I returned.

"Hello?"

"Mrs. Pollack?"

"Yes."

"This is Officer Harley from the Westfield Police Department."

Officer Harley and I had history. Thankfully, neither he nor his partner, Officer Fogarty, have leaked my trials and tribulations stemming from Dead Louse of a Spouse to the town newspaper. "How are you?" I asked, hoping he wasn't calling for a donation to the Police Benevolent Association.

"Can you get over to Sunnyside right away, ma'am?"

"Of course. Has something happened to my mother-in-law?"

"We may have to book her."

"Book her?" What sort of trouble could Lucille have gotten herself into already? "On what charges?"

"Murder."

Six

I grabbed my keys, dashed out the back door, and slammed smack into Zack's chest.

"Whoa! Where's the fire?"

"I've got to get to Sunnyside. Harley wants to charge Lucille with murder."

"Who'd she kill?"

"He didn't say. Crap!"

"What?"

"I ran out without saying anything to Mama and Ira."

"Who's Ira?"

"Karl's half-brother."

"Huh?" Zack grabbed my arm as I started for my car. "You're not making any sense. I'll drive."

I didn't argue with him. As much as I never again wanted to rely on any man, I wasn't above accepting Zack's knight-in-shining-armor offer at the moment. Besides, the air conditioning worked far better in his Porsche Boxster than it did in my Hyundai.

With the mercury still hovering close to triple digits, I'd compromise my scruples for a cooling blast of AC.

As Zack sped out of the driveway, I pulled my cell phone from my purse and called home.

Mama answered on the third ring. "Hello?"

"Mama, I —"

"Anastasia! Where in the world are you?"

"On my way to Sunnyside. Something's happened —"

"What? Did that Bolshevik cow finally get what's coming to her?"

"Mama!"

"Whatever happened, I'm sure she deserved it."

"Just make my apologies to Ira, please? I'll be home as soon as possible."

"Don't worry about Ira, dear. I'll take very good care of him."

That's what I was afraid of. By the time I returned, Ira, no doubt, would be armpits deep in family dirt and wishing he'd never rung my doorbell, but maybe that was a good thing. It would save me the trouble of having to explain that he hadn't missed much by being five months too late to meet his half-brother. Not to mention that he'd most likely saved his bank accounts from

Karl's raiding fingers.

"None of this makes sense," I said as we zipped through downtown Westfield. "Lucille is many things — annoying, mean, strident, and a pain in everyone's tush. But a killer? I don't believe that for a minute."

"I don't know," said Zack. "She can wield a mighty nasty cane."

"But only as a threat. She's never used it as a weapon on anyone."

"Didn't she smack Flora with her cane once?"

"The jury's still out on that one. You know how Mama's prone to hyperbole, and she's certainly not above an occasional fib if it suits her purpose."

"Maybe whatever happened at Sunnyside was an accident," suggested Zack.

"Harley mentioned murder, not manslaughter." I shifted in my seat to confront him. "What if something went horribly wrong with her brain during the surgery and caused her to become homicidal?"

"Wouldn't the doctors have seen some signs of that earlier?"

"Who knows? Maybe not. Maybe whatever happened needed some sort of trigger to manifest itself."

Zack turned into Sunnyside's driveway, bypassed the guest parking lot, and pulled right up to the front door. "I guess we'll soon find out."

"They're all waiting for you in the library," said April when Zack and I rushed into the lobby. "Down that hall, last door on your right. Never had a murder here before," she added, "but, girl, your mother-in-law couldn't have chosen a finer pain in the ass to eliminate. Some of the residents want to pin a medal on her."

I stopped short. "Are you saying Lyndella Wegner was *murdered*?"

"Apparently."

"But I saw her this morning. She died in her sleep. I reported her death to you."

"Rumor has it the medical examiner claims otherwise. The Union County crime unit is doing their CSI thing in her room right now."

I sprinted the rest of the way down the hall to the library. Zack sprinted alongside me. Officer Fogarty stood in the hall, blocking the library entrance, but stepped aside to allow me and Zack entry.

Bookshelves lined the walls of the library. A circular seating area with burgundy leather upholstered chairs and two sofas filled the Oriental carpet in the center of the small room. Lucille sat ramrod straight in her wheelchair alongside one of the sofas.

Shirley Hallstead, still dressed in her navy power suit, was perched on the edge of one of the chairs but jumped to her feet as I entered the room. Officer Harley stood off to one side.

A rotund man in a pair of light brown trousers, white dress shirt, and dark brown solid tie stood towering over my mother-in-law. His shirt sleeves were rolled to just below his elbows, his tie loosened.

"Well, look who's here," said my mother-in-law, jutting her chin in my direction. "This is all your fault, Anastasia."

"What's going on?" I asked.

Shirley pointed an index finger at Lucille and in a voice filled with anger said, "Your mother-in-law killed Lyndella Wegner."

"I did no such thing," said Lucille. "You're all trying to frame me."

"We have a witness who heard you threaten to strangle her," said Shirley. "Now Lyndella's dead. Strangled. Explain that, why don't you?"

"Lies!" said Lucille.

"That's enough," said the stranger. "I'll do the questioning if you don't mind, Ms. Hallstead." He turned to Harley. "Escort Ms. Hallstead to her office. I'll be with her shortly."

"I have a right to stay here," said Shirley.

"Sunnyside is my responsibility."

"And murder is mine," said the man. "Now leave or I'll arrest you for interfering with an investigation."

Shirley jerked away from Harley when he reached for her arm. With her head held high, her lips pursed tightly, she stalked out of the room, Harley following closely on her heels. The stranger closed the door behind them. Then he turned to me. "Mrs. Pollack?"

I nodded. "And you are?"

He flashed a badge. "Detective Spader. Union County." He nodded in Zack's direction. "This here your mother-in-law's lawyer?"

"He's nobody," said Lucille. "Just someone she's taken up with to sully my son's memory."

I glared at her. "You might want to dial down the insults a bit, Lucille. It looks like you need all the help you can get right now."

"I don't need your help."

"You didn't have Officer Harley call me?"

"Why would I do that?"

"I don't know. Maybe because the detective here wants to charge you with murder?"

"He doesn't have a shred of evidence. My lawyers will make mincemeat out of him."

"What lawyers?"

"The ones my sisters will hire for me."

"Are those the same sisters who offered you a place to live after your apartment building burned to the ground?"

She had no quick retort for that. However, knowing the Daughters of the October Revolution, I wouldn't be surprised to learn they kept some old geezer of a commie lawyer on retainer. Lucille and her fellow sisters had faced many a judge over the years. At this very moment the other Daughters were probably fumigating the mothball stench from the guy's fifty-year-old suit.

Detective Spader turned to Zack. "I'm going to have to ask you to step outside, sir."

"You okay with that?" Zack asked me.

"Sure."

As soon as Zack left, I confronted Detective Spader in as non-confrontational a manner as I could muster. "Exactly what happened here, Detective, and why do you think my mother-in-law had a hand in it?"

He answered my question with one of his own. "Am I correct that you reported Mrs. Wegner's death, ma'am?"

I outlined the events of the morning for him. "She appeared to have died in her sleep. She looked quite peaceful, lying on her back, eyes closed, the quilt pulled up to her chin. I even remember a hint of smile on her face."

"No signs of a struggle?"

"Absolutely not. At first I thought she was sleeping. It wasn't until I felt for a pulse that I realized she was dead. Why do you believe she was murdered?"

"The funeral director found bruising on her neck. As the law requires, he called in the medical examiner, who ruled her death a homicide and contacted the police."

"You think she was strangled?"

"She was definitely strangled. With the scarf that was tied around her neck."

"Not by me," said Lucille.

"I remember the scarf," I said. "The ends were draped on top of her quilt."

"You didn't think it odd that she'd wear a scarf to bed when it's so hot in this place?"

"Not really. It wasn't the kind of scarf you wear for warmth, more as an accessory. Besides, from the little I'd gotten to know her, Lyndella loved to show off. The scarf was one I saw her crocheting yesterday. She probably tried it on when she finished it and forgot to take it off before going to bed."

"Or the killer grabbed it and tied it around her neck," he said.

"I don't think the killer is my mother-in-law."

"And why is that?"

"She doesn't have the strength to cut her own food right now, let alone strangle someone as strong as Lyndella."

Detective Spader's bushy salt and pepper eyebrows rose up toward what was left of his hairline. "The deceased was ninety-eight years old. What makes you think she was strong?"

"She shook hands like a politician."

My explanation elicited a chuckle he tried to cover up with a cough. "Your mother-in-law's infirmity aside, you'd be surprised at the strength adrenalin can produce under the right circumstances."

"Do you have any evidence pointing to Lucille as the killer?"

"All we have right now is one of the other Sunnyside residents who claims hearing your mother-in-law shouting yesterday morning that she was going to strangle Mrs. Wegner if she didn't shut up."

I turned to Lucille. "I told you to lower your voice, didn't I?"

Lucille harrumphed. "If you'd taken me home like I demanded, he'd be out searching for the real killer instead of trying to railroad me."

"Are you confirming your mother-in-law threatened Mrs. Wegner yesterday?"

"Not exactly."

The detective let loose a deep sigh and loosened his tie further. "Explain."

I did. When I finished, I asked, "Are you arresting Lucille?"

"Not yet. I don't have enough evidence."

"And you won't find any," said Lucille, "because there's none to find. You're harassing an innocent citizen. I'll have your badge before this is over."

Detective Spader glared at Lucille. Another strangulation might occur at any moment if she didn't keep her mouth shut. "Is she always this combative?" he asked.

"You mean you don't know?" With her record I figured the Westfield PD had Lucille's image plastered over their firing range targets.

"I recently transferred over from Essex County. Docs told me the stress would kill me sooner than a bullet. I've got another year before I can retire and figured I stood a better chance of making it here in Union County."

"There are plenty of homicides in Elizabeth and Plainfield," I said, reminding him that although Westfield might be considered a bucolic oasis, other parts of Union County certainly weren't.

He shrugged. "Nothing's perfect. Still beats the streets of Newark. I just never

109

expected my first homicide investigation to be in Westfield. There hasn't been a murder in this town in more than a dozen years."

I imagined the stress of working in Newark would suck the life out of anyone. Those ruptured capillaries on the detective's nose told me he drank too much. His girth certainly didn't help. With a paunch that hung well over his belt buckle, he looked either nine months pregnant or like a heart attack waiting to happen. I also took note of the pack of cigarettes poking out of his shirt pocket and wondered if he'd live to enjoy that retirement.

"Have Harley and Fogarty fill you in about my mother-in-law," I said.

"Those two? They're out to get me," said Lucille. "It's all one huge conspiracy to frame me because of my political views. Freedom of speech in this country is laughable."

"And what might those political views be, ma'am?" asked Spader.

I answered for Lucille, figuring short and sweet trumped her going off on one of her anti-government rants. "She's a communist."

In a *sotto voce* voice Spader asked, "Anybody ever clue her in about the Berlin Wall falling and the Soviet Union dissolving?"

"Don't speak as if I'm not in the room, and don't you dare imply I'm crazy," said Lucille. "I'm saner than you are! And I know far more about what's going on in this country than you and the rest of your mindless blue brethren."

Short and sweet obviously hadn't worked. "Lucille, I don't think this is the time or place for —"

"It's always the time and place. That's the trouble with you, Anastasia. With all of you. Does anyone really care that some prattling dimwit is dead? There are far more important things going on in this country that should be investigated instead of wasting taxpayer money on some slutty trollop."

Talk about a non sequitur. Spader again raised those bushy salt and pepper eyebrows of his, this time even higher than before, and directed his question to Lucille. "Is there something you'd like to tell me, ma'am?"

Lucille once more jutted her chin toward me. "I tried to tell you this morning, but you weren't interested."

I remembered Lucille saying something about how I wouldn't believe what had gone on in her room last night, but I didn't have time to listen to another one of her complaints. "Tell us now, Lucille."

"This place is a den of iniquity. I was awake most of the night, thanks to that floozy, her bouncing bedsprings, and all the moaning and groaning going on."

Spader stared in utter disbelief. "Are you saying the victim, a ninety-eight-year-old woman, had a sexual encounter last night?"

"No," said Lucille. "I'm saying she had more than one."

SEVEN

"I agree with the detective," said Zack on our ride back to the house. "Lucille probably dreamed the whole thing up. Didn't they give her a sleeping pill last night?"

Even though Detective Spader had asked Zack to leave the room, he and Officer Fogarty, as well as Officer Harley when he returned from depositing Shirley in her office, were able to hear every word of our conversation. No wonder some passing resident overheard Lucille threaten to strangle Lyndella yesterday.

"I'd have to ask about her meds. I've heard some sleeping pills can cause extremely vivid dreams. Right now, I don't know what to believe. Her roommate did brag about sex keeping her young."

"But all night long?" Zack laughed. "No way!"

"Not to mention at her age. If it's true, she's like those little old lady nymphomaniacs in *The Producers*."

"Those characters sprang from the extremely fertile imagination of Mel Brooks. I doubt women in their nineties have any sex drive at all, let alone an insatiable one."

Zack had a point. A woman's sex drive stems from hormone production. At her age, Lyndella's body couldn't possibly be producing estrogen, could it? Her body most likely hadn't produced any estrogen for at least forty years. No estrogen, no urges.

"Maybe Lucille only thought the sex went on all night. If it even happened at all. She either dreamed it all up, or she drifted in and out of sleep and didn't have an accurate grasp of the passage of time."

"Lucille doesn't have an accurate grasp of many things," said Zack, "especially reality."

"I don't believe she had anything to do with Lyndella's death, though. Do you?"

"No."

"And she might be a huge albatross around my neck, but I can't sit back and watch her convicted of a crime she didn't commit."

Zack slowed for a red light, turned toward me, and placed his hand over mine. "Please tell me you're not going to get involved in another murder investigation."

"If I don't, who will?"

"Let the police do their job. That's why you pay those exorbitant taxes. Besides, do I need to remind you that you were nearly killed last time you decided to play Sherlock Holmes? *And* the time before that?"

"I'll be careful."

"Famous last words," he muttered. "I'm not going to be able to stop you, am I?"

"Probably not."

"Will you at least let me help you this time?"

"Actually, there is something I'd like your help with, Zack."

"Name it."

"Do you think Patricia would do a little record digging for me?"

Patricia Tierney is Zack's ex-wife and an assistant DA in Manhattan. She'd have access to all sorts of documents, including New York City marriage certificates and divorce records.

Zack and Patricia have the friendliest divorce I've ever come across. Her twin daughters call him Uncle Zacky. Patricia also thinks I'm the best thing to happen to Zack since the last time the Mets won a World Series.

"What kind of records in Manhattan would help prove Lucille didn't commit murder?"

"None that I know of, but there's another mystery brewing, and I think it's beyond time I learned the truth."

"About what?"

"Lucille's past."

"Does this have anything to do with Karl's half-brother showing up at your door? And speaking of which, when did you find out he had one?"

I checked my watch. "About two hours ago."

"You sure the guy isn't trying to scam you?"

"Not unless he's found a way to replicate Karl's DNA. The resemblance is uncanny."

Zack chuckled. "That ought to freak Lucille out."

"In more ways than one." I recapped my brief encounter with Ira, telling Zack about the letter and photo. "Lucille has always claimed that Isidore was abducted. Looks like she fabricated the entire story."

"She probably talked herself into believing it a long time ago because she couldn't accept the truth."

"Especially if she kicked him out, hoping he'd come groveling back to her. She's the reason Karl grew up without a father."

If Karl had been raised in a typical two-parent household, would his life have turned out differently? Would Lady Luck, that demanding and financially draining mistress of his, ever have entered his life? I'd never know, and speculating would only drive me crazy.

When we turned down our street, I saw Ira's gray minivan still parked in front of my house. Didn't the guy have a wife and kids who expected him home for dinner? And speaking of dinner . . .

I guess I could forget about that relaxing soak in the tub. The two bikes leaning up against the garage doors told me Alex and Nick had arrived home.

I turned to Zack as he parked the car. "When you rooted around in my freezer yesterday, did you find any hamburger patties and bags of rolls? I have a feeling Mama invited Ira to join us for dinner."

"Should be enough," he said. We both reluctantly exited the comfort of the air-conditioned car for the brutal outdoor heat. "Want me to fire up the grill?"

"You don't have to join us."

He laughed. "Are you kidding? And miss out on the entertainment?"

"Very funny."

Zack grew serious, grabbed my hand, and squeezed gently. "You look like you need a buffer tonight."

"What I need is a week in Aruba."

"That can be arranged."

I closed my eyes, and envisioned a white sandy beach, gently lapping waves, and a brilliant blue sky. I wish. "No it can't," I said, reluctantly opening my eyes. "I've used up all my vacation for the year, and now I don't even have my weekends free for the next several months."

"Then you're just going to have to settle for the next best thing."

"What's that?"

"A burger flipper tonight."

Zack could flip my burgers any time he wanted, but I bit down on my tongue to keep from saying so. I'd vowed not to rely on any man ever again. How many times did I have to remind myself? So instead, I smiled, squeezed his hand back, and headed into the house.

I found Mama, Alex, Nick, and Ira gathered around the kitchen table, all munching from a large bowl of popcorn. Catherine the Great batted a popped kernel around the floor. Ralph perched on Alex's shoulder. I assumed Mephisto was snoring somewhere, hopefully not on my bed.

"Hey Mom, we've got an uncle," said Alex as he tossed another piece of popcorn to

Ralph. "And three cousins. Cool, huh?"

"When's dinner?" asked Nick. "We're starving."

I tossed my purse on the counter. "Did anyone walk Mephisto?"

"Done," said Alex.

I raised my eyebrows at that. "Without a single nag from me?"

"He's not such a devil dog with Grandmother Lucille gone," said Nick. "All he does is eat, sleep, and poop."

I'd noticed that, too. Mephisto hadn't uttered a single growl at anyone, not even Catherine the Great, since Lucille's emergency trip to the hospital. That made me wonder if Mephisto had even been in the dining room when Mama dropped Daddy earlier today. "Maybe he's just getting old, and his devil dog days are behind him."

"Unlikely," said Mama. "I don't trust that vicious mutt, not after the way he scared the living daylights out of me earlier today. Neither should any of you. That dog is up to something. Lulling you all into a false sense of security before he strikes. Look at what happened to my dear Harold today, thanks to that mongrel."

"Mephisto, the Ninja Bulldog?" I asked.

Ira chuckled. I realized I'd totally ignored him since entering the house. My bad.

119

Chalk it up to sheer exhaustion and not wanting another mouth to feed tonight. "Ira, don't you need to get home to your family?"

Subtle, Anastasia.

"The kids are at summer camp, and my wife is out of town, visiting her sister. Flora was kind enough to invite me to join all of you for dinner this evening. If you don't mind, of course."

I forced a smile and began pulling food from the fridge and freezer. "Not at all. As long as you don't mind burgers."

"I'm happy to cook them for you," he offered. "I wield a mean spatula."

"Thanks but it's taken care of."

"Is Zack joining us, dear?" Before I could answer her, Mama turned to Ira. "Zack is Anastasia's boyfriend. I'm sure you'll like him."

"He's not my boyfriend," I said. "He's my tenant."

"He's her boyfriend," said Mama, Alex, and Nick, all in unison.

Heat seared my cheeks. What did that say about my relationship with Ira's half-brother that only five months after his death, I already had another man in my life? Even if we'd only had one official date so far. I turned toward the sink and began scraping

120

carrots. Furiously. "It's not what you think," I muttered.

"That's okay," said Ira. "Flora told me about my brother. I understand."

Not at all comfortable with Mama spilling the Karl beans to a total stranger, even a quasi-related total stranger, I turned to face her. "Everything?"

"He's family, dear. I thought he had a right to know what that man did to you."

Great. Blabbermouth Flora strikes again. I'm glad I never told her how Karl tried to mow down his mother and wound up killing three innocent people when he torched her apartment building. Alex and Nick didn't need to know the gory details about the seamier side of their father's life. They already knew more than I wanted to tell them, but what choice did I have? When your life plummets from the heights of comfortably Middle-classdom to one step away from living out of a cardboard box, you have to offer your kids some explanation for the downward spiral.

I suppose my expression told Mama she'd better change the subject because she did. "You haven't told us what that commie rabble-rouser did this time, dear. What was so serious that you had to rush out without saying a word? I certainly raised you to have better manners than that. Especially with a guest in the house."

Zack picked that moment to open the back door. His expression told me he'd heard Mama. Mine told him this was a conversation I didn't want to have right now. "You might as well tell her now and get it over with," he said. "You know she's not going to give up."

I closed my eyes and took a deep breath, counting silently to five as I exhaled. While I did so, Mama introduced Zack to Ira. As I opened my eyes, I caught a glimpse of the two men, hands clasped in vice-like grips, sizing each other up in that way only men do.

All those quotes about the measure of a man? They really only mean one thing: mine's bigger than yours.

I broke up the testosterone standoff by blurting out, "Lucille's roommate was murdered last night."

That got everyone's attention.

"Holy shit!" said Alex, then added a hasty, "Sorry, Mom," before my reprimand made it past my lips.

"Did that crazy Bolshevik kill her?" asked Mama.

"I think she's at the top of the suspects list," I said, "but she claims she's innocent."

"Like hell," says Mama. "I always worried she'd murder me in my sleep one of these nights. Looks like I had good cause for concern."

The next morning, another scorcher of a day already under way, I packed Mephisto into the rust-bucket sauna on wheels and headed back to Sunnyside. Since Shirley hadn't assigned me a spot in the employees' parking lot out back or even mentioned the existence of such a lot, I parked in the closer visitors' lot in front and decided to continue to do so unless instructed otherwise. Ignorance in this case was the bliss of subjecting my body to a minute less of blistering heat and oppressive humidity as I made my way into the building.

Once inside, I was surprised to find the crime scene tape gone and Lucille ensconced back in her room. She greeted Mephisto with such a smothering hug that the poor dog whined and struggled for breath.

"Mother's missed you so much," she crooned into his fur, oblivious to the poor pooch's discomfort. No wonder devil dog had dropped his satanic ways at home. With Lucille gone, he didn't have to submit to constant *s'mother* love.

I waited, hoping for at least a thank you

for bringing him, but in typical Lucille fashion, she ignored me. "I'll come walk him during my lunch break," I finally said.

No response. She didn't even ask why I'd be hanging around Sunnyside all day, or maybe she thought I intended to go home, then come back at lunchtime to walk her dog. Who knows? I may as well have been invisible for all the acknowledgement I received from her. Maybe she thought the dog magically appeared on his own.

Given the way Lucille had always treated me, why did I even care whether or not the police arrested her for Lyndella's murder? With Lucille out of my life, I'd have one less problem. However, even a woman who cared more about her dog than her daughter-in-law deserved justice. Someone had to give a damn about the truth, even for an ingrate like my pain-in-the-tush mother-in-law.

Lucille epitomized *all bark and no bite.* She didn't kill Lyndella Wegner. I knew that. The real killer lurked somewhere in the halls of Sunnyside. With no one else stepping up to the plate to ferret him out, I became the designated batter by default.

I was about to head to my first class when I heard a rustling coming from the other side of the floral curtain that separated the two halves of the room. Curious, I peeked around the curtain's edge and found Reggie bagging up Lyndella's clothing. "Hi," I said.

She yelped, stumbling backward and nearly tripping over a desk chair.

"Sorry. I didn't mean to startle you."

Her teeth trembling, she gnawed at her lower lip. "I . . . I didn't hear you."

"Are you getting the room ready for a new resident?" I asked.

Reggie shrugged her emaciated shoulders. "I guess. Ms. Hallstead said to pack up all of Mrs. Wegner's stuff, so that's what I'm doing."

"What will happen to her possessions?"

"The clothes and furniture get donated."

"And the rest?"

She frowned at the hundreds of crafts covering nearly every horizontal and vertical surface. "Ms. Hallstead told me to toss them in the Dumpster out back."

I couldn't let that happen, not to such exemplary craftsmanship, even X-rated ones. "Don't do that. Bring them to the arts and crafts room, okay?"

Reggie shrugged again. "Sure. Less lugging for me."

My first class of the morning consisted of pottery and sculpture. Four men and two

125

women hunched over the six potter's wheels while a dozen other men and women worked with polymer clay, fashioning everything from chess pieces to earrings. I sat at my desk, reading the directions for firing the kiln, something I hadn't done since my sophomore year of college. Baking polymer clay in a standard kitchen oven was much more my speed.

My mind kept wandering, though. I needed to figure out a way to clear Lucille. To do that, I had to learn more about Lyndella and why everyone hated her so much. I got that she was a hard-to-please, know-it-all pain in the ass, but that hardly seemed like justification for murder. What had Lyndella Wegner done that caused someone to strangle her?

In order to find out more about Lyndella, I needed to make friends with the Sunnyside residents, and the best way to do that was to give them something they needed — money. Not mine, of course. I didn't have any to give.

Trimedia would never agree to pay them for interviews, though. I saw no point in even asking, not for a crafts spread. I was a bottom feeder in the magazine's pecking order and worked with an almost non-existent budget. Most of my supplies came gratis from manufacturers hoping for free publicity for their products. The bean counters expected me to make do with very little beyond that.

I closed the kiln manual and circulated around the room, checking on the progress of my students. With few exceptions their skill and craftsmanship amazed me. These were incredibly talented senior citizens.

That's when inspiration struck. Why not organize a gallery showing? Not an exhibit in the Sunnyside lobby but a real exhibit in a real gallery where people bought artwork and crafts.

I crossed the room to the pottery area. Murray had just finished throwing a perfectly formed hourglass-shaped vase. He grabbed a needle tool and with a steady hand deftly trimmed the top edge.

Not bad for a guy in his eighties. I never could master that trimming technique when I took my one and only mandatory class in pottery. My hands would shake too much, causing at best a lopsided cut or more often, a total cave-in and collapse of the wet clay.

"You're very good at that," I told Murray. "The vase is perfectly symmetrical. And the walls are so incredibly thin! Have you been throwing pots for a long time?"

He shrugged. "Long enough to know what

I'm doing."

"I took a pottery course in college, but I was a total failure at it. I guess I lacked the necessary hand/eye coordination."

"Always been good with my hands. And my eyes."

"What did you do before you retired?"

Murray scowled. "Why do you want to know?"

Now it was my turn to shrug. "I was wondering if you worked at something that required precise and intricate skills. Like a surgeon or a violin maker."

Murray greeted my suggestions with a snort. "I fixed things for a living."

"You were a repairman?"

"Yeah, a repairman."

I moved the conversation along to my main reason for chatting with him. "What do you do with all your completed pottery pieces?"

Another shrug. "Keep a few. Give most away."

"Ever think of selling them?"

That caught his attention. "For money?"

"What else?"

"You really think people would pay for my pots?"

"Absolutely. I was thinking about what you and the others said yesterday about money, and I think we should set up a show to sell your work."

"Here? Who's gonna come here to buy stuff?"

"Not here. In an art gallery."

"We get to keep all the money?"

"Minus the gallery commission."

He thought about that for a moment, then nodded. "Okay. Sounds good."

And with that Murray dipped his head and went back to work on his vase, sculpting on the first of a series of three-dimensional petals. However, I noticed that gruff Murray, man of few words, now had a smile on his face. I'd made my first friend.

Flush with the success of winning over Murray, I headed for my polymer clay sculptors and presented my idea to them.

Estelle, the woman who'd led everyone in that rousing rendition of *Ding Dong, the Bitch is Dead,* asked, "What about Shirley?"

"What about her?"

"She has to approve all Sunnyside-sponsored activities," said a woman who'd introduced herself earlier as Pearl.

"Why?"

"Cause she says so," said Estelle.

"She'll only agree if the money goes to one of her pet charities, not to us," said a woman named Martha.

129

"For the publicity," muttered Dirk from across the room where he worked on a still life acrylic painting at one of the easels. I had learned yesterday that some of my students spent as much time as possible in the arts and crafts room, no matter what class was scheduled or whether or not an instructor was present. "The woman's a damn publicity whore."

I'd come to that same conclusion after viewing the numerous photos plastered across Shirley's office walls. Publicity for Shirley at the expense of Sunnyside's residents didn't sit well with me. I didn't see where Shirley Hallstead had any say in what the Sunnyside residents did with their artwork and crafts.

These men and women needed extra cash, and at the appropriate venue their work would bring them that extra cash. What right did Shirley have to deny them an exhibition of their work? She was the director of an assisted living facility, not a prison warden.

The more I learned about Shirley "Control Freak" Hallstead, the less I liked her. "Leave Shirley to me," I told my students. "Meanwhile, I'd like each of you to start rounding up your best pieces."

■ ■ ■ ■

Shortly after I'd had the same discussion with my next class, the needlework women from Friday, minus Lyndella, Reggie tripped into the room. Literally. The top box of the two cardboard cartons she carried tumbled from her arms onto the floor. Fabric yo-yos spilled across the room.

"I . . . I'm so . . . sorry!" She trembled inside her Winnie the Pooh scrubs, her scrawny arms still clutching the one remaining carton to her chest.

The poor kid looked like she expected a horse whipping. I took the remaining carton from her and set it down on a table. "No problem. Fabric doesn't break."

She cowered in front of me. I placed my hand on her forearm. "Reggie, it's okay. Really."

What the hell had happened to this kid? The mother in me knew something was seriously wrong. Now that we stood toe-to-toe I took a good look at her for the first time. I noted chewed fingernails, patches of thinning hair, and sparse eyelashes. Coupled with her anorexic frame, I didn't need a degree in psychology to tell me this kid abused herself. If I pulled up the legs of her pants, I was convinced I'd find evidence of cutting.

Given all the diplomas hanging on Shirley Hallstead's wall, how could she not see that this child needed help? Or did she see and not give a damn?

Reggie dropped to her hands and knees. "I'll pick everything up."

"There are more cartons, right?"

She nodded as she scooped up handfuls of yo-yos and deposited them back in the box. "Lots."

"I'll finish here. Why don't you get the rest of the cartons? Do you need help with them?"

She paused mid-scoop and thought for a moment. "No, this is m . . . my fault. I'll pick these up, then get the rest of the boxes for you."

I decided to let her do as she wanted. I grabbed the carton from the table and headed back to my desk to sort through Lyndella's treasures.

"Whatcha got there?" asked Mabel as I passed the table where she and several other women worked on various embroidery projects.

"Some of Lyndella's crafts."

"Why would you want those here?"

"Shirley planned to toss them out. I didn't

want that to happen."

"You should let her trash them," said Mabel. "We don't need any reminders of that hussy and her pornographic crafts around here."

I placed the box on my desk and walked over to Mabel's table. "Maybe you can help me," I said. "I'm trying to understand why everyone hated Lyndella so much."

"Why?" asked Mabel.

"Because right now my mother-in-law is the prime suspect in her death, and I know she didn't kill Lyndella Wegner."

"You think one of us did?" asked a woman working on a Bargello pillow.

"I'm not accusing anyone. I'm merely trying to understand why you all hated her."

"Because she spread her legs for every man living at Sunnyside," said Mabel.

EIGHT

"None of us stood a chance with Lyndella Wegner around," said a woman knitting a baby sweater.

Maybe Lucille hadn't been dreaming. "You're telling me Lyndella had sex with all the male residents living at Sunnyside?"

"Every last one of them," said Mabel. "She'd pounce the moment new blood crossed the threshold. A one-woman Welcoming Committee."

"Hardly give them time to unpack," added Bargello Lady.

I really needed to find a way to remember all these women's names. Maybe I could plead a mild case of aphasia and ask them all to wear name tags.

"Worse than that," said a blonde woman working on a fisherman knit sweater, "she went after our husbands."

Mabel patted her hand. "Tell her what happened to George, Sally."

Sally set her knitting down and folded her hands on the little bit of lap that stuck out beneath her expansive girth. Her eyes filled with tears. "We had a good marriage. Fifty-two years. Then George and I moved to Sunnyside and that Lyndella Wegner started filling my George's head with all sorts of X-rated nonsense, telling him she could make him feel like a teenager again."

Sally's floodgates gave way at that point. I placed my hand on her plump shoulder, unsure what else to do as she sobbed.

"She killed him," said Bargello Lady. "Lyndella killed Sally's husband."

"How?" I asked.

"Those damn little blue pills," said Sally between gulping sobs.

"Viagra?"

"Lyndella talked George into getting a prescription," said Mabel, "but Sally —"

"We hadn't had sex in years," said Sally. She pulled a tissue from her pocket, dabbed at her eyes, and blew her nose. "It hurt. Lyndella knew this would happen. She lured George into her bed, and he had a massive heart attack."

"I'm sorry," I said.

"Now you know," said Mabel. "We didn't kill that whore, but we'll throw a party for the person who did."

At that moment Reggie reentered the room. She carried another couple of cartons, the top one shifting precariously. The needlework women stopped talking the moment they saw her and resumed their stitching. I hurried to meet Reggie and grabbed the top carton before it fell.

With a loud *oomph,* Reggie placed the remaining box on the nearest table. "Do you want her books, too?" she asked.

"Shouldn't they go to the library?"

"I suppose."

She didn't seem too happy with my answer, probably because the library was situated farther from Lyndella's room than the arts and crafts room. "Why don't you bring them here?" I suggested. "I'll sort through them."

"Okay." Reggie headed back for another armload of boxes.

As soon as she left the room, I returned to my group of needlework women. "One thing puzzles me," I said.

"What's that?" asked Mabel.

I hesitated, unsure how to broach such a delicate question without offending anyone.

"Spit it out," said Mabel. "None of us is getting any younger."

I inhaled a deep breath, then took the plunge. "A woman of Lyndella's advanced years, how did she . . . I mean, I didn't think it was even possible —"

"For her to have sex?" asked the baby sweater knitter.

I nodded.

"Hormones," said Mabel. "The rest of us were too scared of cancer, especially after that women's health study came out a few years back. Those of us who'd been on HRT got off it at that point. Not Lyndella."

"No hormone replacement therapy means no libido for many women," said Sally. "You dry up in more ways than one."

"Try explaining that to the Viagra generation," said Mabel. "Those randy lotharios want a hell of a lot more than hand-holding and cuddling nowadays."

"And they got what they wanted from Lyndella," said Bargello Lady. "Any time, night or day."

Holy TMI! But I'd asked, and these women certainly weren't shy about dishing all the lascivious details. I had to admit, though, part of me was totally fascinated by the late Lyndella Wegner. In a macabre sort of way.

By the end of the needlework class, Reggie had deposited fifteen extra-large cartons in the room, eight filled with Lyndella's crafts and seven containing an assortment of craft

137

books, fiction, and loose-leaf binders. I decided the arts and crafts room should have a library of its own.

After walking Mephisto, I took the remainder of my lunch break to sort and shelve the craft books while scarfing down a cup of store-brand cherry yogurt I'd brought from home. Maybe the yogurt would balance out the Cloris-fueled calories I'd gobbled up Friday.

A set of built-in bookcases ran the length of the room under the windows. I straightened out the various items on one section of shelves to make room. Then I separated Lyndella's books, placing the craft titles on the shelves and stacking the fiction and the loose-leaf binders on a table.

After sorting the books, I picked up one of the binders and began flipping through the pages, which turned out to be a crafts journal. The pages contained notes, drawings, and photos for many of Lyndella's craft projects. What a treasure trove for a crafts editor! I placed all the binders back into cartons and moved the cartons to the floor near my desk to study them more at length later.

Lyndella's taste in fiction matched her taste in artwork. I suppose her collection of erotic novels shouldn't have surprised me, but I still had difficulty wrapping my head around a ruffles and lace-bedecked, ninety-eight-year-old woman reading the Marquis de Sade.

I wondered if I should bring the novels to the library but quickly decided against doing so. What if some resident's grandchild pulled Anne Rice's *The Sleeping Beauty Trilogy* off a shelf and began reading? I didn't want to be responsible for introducing a ten year old to the world of BDSM. So I began placing the novels back into one of the cartons. Although I hated to trash any books, Lyndella's fiction collection probably belonged in the Dumpster.

The question remained what to do with Lyndella's various craft projects. I decided to discuss the subject with my next class of crafters — after I told them about my gallery idea. First, though, I quickly cut up squares of colored construction paper.

"For those of you who haven't met me yet," I said after they'd all entered the room and seated themselves at various tables, "my name is Anastasia Pollack. I'm the craft editor at *American Woman* magazine, and I'll be filling in on weekends for the next few months while Kara Kennedy is out on maternity leave."

I then passed around the colored paper,

markers, and safety pins I'd found in the supply closet. "Unfortunately, I'm really terrible with names," I continued. "So I'd appreciate it if you'd make yourselves name tags until I get to know all of you better."

"Getting old like us, huh?" said a tall, thin woman with ginger-colored hair pulled back into a low ponytail. She laughed. "Hate to tell you, dearie, but it only gets worse the older you get."

The others chuckled and nodded in agreement. I laughed along with them, although on the inside I worried. With all I juggled and all the stress, my brain had already begun to turn to mush. I hated to think what it might be like fifteen or twenty years from now.

"Construction paper?" said a woman with red-framed glasses and a thick head of obviously dyed, midnight-black hair that hugged her head like a helmet. When she turned up her nose and pushed aside the supplies I'd passed out, not a hair moved, thanks to a thick coating of hairspray. "We're not in kindergarten. You want name tags? We'll make name tags we'll be proud to wear. Right, girls?"

Everyone agreed. I should have known. These were my paper crafters and scrapbookers. Much like their younger counterparts I'd come across over the years, they had a near obsessive love for their particular craft of choice. They set about pulling supplies off shelves and from the closets — rubber stamps and pads, decorative papers, paper punches, specialty scissors, stickers, and assorted trims.

Like the classes before them, they needed no help from me, so as they worked, I told them about my gallery idea. Everyone loved the idea, but once again someone brought up Shirley Hallstead.

"You'll have to clear it with her," said a woman I assumed was named Barbara from the *BAR* she'd so far rubber stamped onto her name tag.

"So I've been told," I said. Then I brought up the subject of Lyndella's crafts. "Shirley told Reggie to throw them out. That seems like such a waste. Anyone have a suggestion as to what to do with them?"

"Do as Shirley said."

"Use them for target practice."

"Burn 'em."

"Smash them to smithereens."

Wow! I've known people who weren't well-liked by others. My own mother-in-law headed the list. But the anger these women felt toward Lyndella Wegner bordered on rage. After what my last class had told me, I

141

suppose I couldn't blame them for not wanting any reminders of the woman hanging around Sunnyside.

"There's an enormous assortment of fabric yo-yos," I continued. "Would any of you want them to decorate your card and scrapbooking projects?"

"Did Lyndella make them?" asked the woman who'd suggested burning Lyndella's crafts.

"Most likely. They came from her room."

"Hell no," she said. The others nodded in agreement.

I certainly wasn't going to toss a perfectly good crop of yo-yos. If no one at Sunnyside wanted them, I'd take them home with me. I hadn't featured any yo-yo crafts in the magazine in several years. With hundreds of pre-made yo-yos at my disposal, now seemed as good a time as any for a fresh batch of yo-yo projects.

LYNDELLA'S YO-YO EMBELLISHED CARDIGAN

What's old is new. Give retro life to an old cardigan by adding a decorative yoke of coordinating yo-yos.

Materials
cardigan sweater

basic yo-yo supplies to sew approximately 20–30 coordinating yo-yos made from 5" circle template

equal number of coordinating or contrasting 7/8" buttons

straight pins

invisible thread or fabric glue

Directions
The number of yo-yos needed will depend on the size of the sweater. Make the yo-yos following the Basic Yo-yo directions (pp. 32–34). Stitch a button over the center hole of each yo-yo.

Lay the sweater flat, front side up. Place the yo-yos along the neckline of the front of the sweater, overlapping the yoyos slightly. Pin in place. Turn the sweater over. Continue placing and pinning yo-yos along the back neckline.

Using invisible thread, slipstitch the yo-yos onto the sweater or attach with a small amount of fabric glue at the middle back of each yo-yo. Note: if using glue, slide a piece of waxed paper inside the sweater so you don't accidently glue the front to the back.

The remainder of my classes were much like the earlier ones. Everyone loved the idea of a gallery show; no one wanted anything to do with crafts or supplies that had belonged to the late Lyndella Wegner. Since the craft books all had her name written on the inside cover, I suspected they'd remain where they sat on the shelf, gathering dust for years to come.

After my last class, I carried the boxes of yo-yos and notebooks to my car, having to make one trip for each of the cartons due to the weight of the notebooks. The triple digit temperature had turned the asphalt parking lot spongy, and heat waves radiated from the cement sidewalks. By the time I'd finished, I had just enough room left in the Hyundai for me and Mephisto. The cartons of crafts would have to wait until tomorrow.

Because the elderly are always cold, Sunnyside's air conditioning didn't cool enough to satisfy me. I spent a good deal of the day fanning myself. (Not to mention offering all sorts of inducements and bribes to the menopause gods to target someone else. I was so not ready for that stage of my life and prayed I was merely reacting to the warmth of Sunnyside and not experiencing my first hot flashes.) Meanwhile, many of the residents walked around in long sleeves

144

and sweaters.

Still, Sunnyside felt like Siberia compared to the wall of heat that hit me each time I stepped outside the building. By the time I headed back for Mephisto, I felt like I'd spent an hour in a sauna. While wearing a parka. I needed to wring out my entire body.

I found both Lucille and Mephisto deep in siesta mode, each loudly snoring away on the bed. I decided to duck into the bathroom, hoping Reggie hadn't thought to clean out Lyndella's toiletries when she bagged her belongings. Sure enough, the medicine cabinet held a tube of vaginal estrogen cream and a package of hormone replacement patches, both prescriptions in Lyndella's name and from separate mail-order pharmacies, one located in Canada, the other in Mexico. The meds, along with a certain battery-operated device filling up the remainder of the shelf, left no doubt about the tales I'd heard today.

I closed the cabinet, walked back into the bedroom, and grabbed Mephisto's leash from Lucille's dresser. He woke as soon as I clipped the leash to his collar but instead of growling at me, he wagged his tail.

In all the years I'd known him, Mephisto had never wagged his tail at me. He must have had one s'mothering of a day at Sunnyside.

"Let's go, you big lummox."

He lumbered off the bed as Lucille continued to snore. Instead of waking her and running the risk of a leash tug-a-war, I jotted a quick note, to inform her no one had dognapped her precious pooch.

As I stepped from Lucille's room, I heard yelling coming from the direction of Shirley's office. "What! How dare you disobey me? When I tell you to do something, you do it. I don't give a damn what anyone else says. Do you understand me?"

I couldn't hear a reply. Either Shirley was reaming out someone over the phone, or the subject of her wrath hadn't answered her. A few members of the staff lurked in the hallway, obviously eavesdropping. Shirley should learn to close her office door and lower her voice.

"This is my facility," she continued. "I make the rules. No one else."

I wondered what Shirley was even doing here today. Maybe it had something to do with Lyndella's murder, but I had a sneaking suspicion Shirley Hallstead had no life beyond Sunnyside. Contrary to her comment about not working on weekends, I suspected she spent a good portion of her weekends at Sunnyside. Her entire self-worth seemed tied to her job. Something told me the woman had few, if any, friends. Part of me felt sorry for her. However, that didn't excuse her acting like a tyrant.

"I've had enough of you. Get out of my building. You're fired."

A moment later those of us lingering in the hallway saw Reggie Koltzner run out of Shirley's office and make a beeline for the back of the building. Poor kid. However, she'd be much better off without Shirley in her life. Maybe she'd even stop abusing herself.

I gave a tug on Mephisto's leash and headed for the front entrance. Mephisto hesitated as a brutal wall of heat hit us. He yelped as he stepped from the walkway onto the parking lot asphalt and immediately yanked me toward a patch of burnt grass at the edge of the curb. Once he planted all four paws on the dead grass, he held his ground, refusing to budge, no matter how hard I tugged at his leash.

Finally, I understood why. The temperature of the black parking lot surface had to be a good twenty degrees higher than the hundred and two degrees beating down on us. Sandals protected my feet, but Mephisto wore no doggy foot coverings on his paws.

The only way I was going to get him into the car was by hauling him into my arms and carrying him. Ugh! Nothing like lugging twenty-odd pounds of hot, panting dog in triple-digit heat.

"You owe me," I said as I deposited him in the passenger seat of the rust-bucket sauna on wheels. I cranked down all four windows, then settled in behind the steering wheel. Mephisto rode home with his head hanging out of the car, doggie slobber blowing in the breeze.

We arrived home to an empty house. I filled a fresh bowl of water for Mephisto and a glass of ice water for myself. He lapped up all of his water before I took my first sip. I'd have to remember to bring a water dish for him when I brought him back to Sunnyside. After his second bowl, he waddled over to the nearest air-conditioning vent and planted himself directly under it. "Not a bad idea," I told him.

According to the message board next to the phone, Alex and Nick planned to attend a pool party after work, then head over to Clark for the fireworks. Westfield never has fireworks. We have more highbrow summer entertainment like concerts in Mindowaskin Park and downtown street corner jazz. So laden down with blankets and folding chairs, we hike over to the next town for our yearly dose of rockets' red glare and bombs bursting in air. Tonight I'd forego the fireworks for a long soak in a cool tub.

The message board also contained a short note from Mama: *Be back late. Don't wait up.* Unfortunately, that could only mean one thing with my mother — she'd set her sights on Husband Number Six.

To verify, I checked her room. Sure enough, cast aside Chanels (Mama's designer of choice) were strewn over her bed and Lucille's. A sea of cardboard shoeboxes, tissue paper, and designer heels covered the floor. The evidence screamed loud and clear that Flora Sudberry Periwinkle Ramirez Scoffield Goldberg O'Keefe was once again in full husband-hunting mode.

I pitied the poor guy. Except for my own father, Mama's husbands never lived long after the wedding. The last sucker hadn't even made it to the altar before someone thrust one of my knitting needles into his heart.

The good news was that I had the house entirely to myself for the next several hours. I drew myself a cool bath. Knowing if I started to read a novel, I'd never find time to finish it, I grabbed the cartons filled with Lyndella's notebooks and placed them on the floor next to the tub. The craft editor in me was dying to peruse them.

After setting the caddy across the edge of the tub, I grabbed the top loose-leaf from the carton nearest to me, settled into the water, and flipped open to the first page. Lyndella took meticulous notes on each of her projects. In a very tight, neat, flowing script she had recorded materials, directions, and cost, plus her start and completion dates. She included sketches, diagrams, fabric and yarn swatches, directions, patterns, and photos of both the finished projects and the inspiration pieces where applicable. A sheet protector held the contents of each page.

Although I hadn't realized it earlier, almost all of Lyndella's work contained some element of the erotic or pornographic, even the appliquéd quilt on her bed. It was just far less in-your-face than her lint David, the X-rated elements hidden among floral motifs.

I would have loved to examine the quilt closer, but I didn't remember seeing it in any of the boxes. Reggie must have bagged it up with Lyndella's clothes. I hoped someone shopping at Goodwill didn't mistakenly buy it for a little girl's bedroom.

As I read the various notations written on

one page, I realized that these notebooks were not only journals of Lyndella's crafting history but of her life. Mostly a certain part of her life. Hidden within the various notes were other notes — the who, what, where, and when of her numerous sexual encounters, among other things.

This particular notebook began shortly after Lyndella arrived at Sunnyside twenty years ago. On a page dated August twenty-ninth, along with directions and patterns for an appliquéd wall hanging depicting one of the acts described in the *Kama Sutra,* she'd written:

Never met so many prudes in my life. The women act like nuns. The men have no imagination. Missionary position is all they've ever known. These people need an education, and this place needs a good shaking up. I'm just the person to do both. And won't that piss off a certain someone?

A clue to Lyndella's killer — perhaps the person she wanted to piss off — might hide in the pages of this book or one of the other journals. Shouldn't the police have taken them as evidence when they did their CSI thing?

Yesterday Detective Spader had given me his card, telling me to contact him if I remembered anything further. I probably should get out of the tub and call him immediately, but my curiosity had other ideas. I wanted to read through all the journals first.

Did this constitute obstruction of justice? I didn't think so. After all, the CSI team had the chance to grab the journals yesterday and didn't. The crime scene tape had been removed from the room. Lucille had moved back in; Reggie had been in the process of disposing of Lyndella's possessions. Besides, I didn't know if the journals contained anything pertinent to the investigation and wouldn't know that until I read through all of them.

Would such an excuse hold up in court? Unbidden, a vision of Zack's ex-wife came to mind. Patricia stood in front of me, shaking her head and muttering, "Naughty Anastasia" as I was led away in handcuffs.

I checked the date on the last page, then set the binder on the tile floor and reached for another. Each thick loose-leaf appeared to span numerous years. If one of them contained a clue to the identity of the killer, chances were, I'd find that clue in the most recent notebook.

The second binder dated back to before Lyndella moved to Sunnyside. I set that one aside and grabbed a third binder. This one dated back to the nineteen thirties, but it wasn't a craft journal. This book was an accounts ledger.

For The Savannah Club for Discerning Gentlemen.

NINE

Oh. My. God.

That certainly explained Lyndella Wegner's obsession with sex. Not to mention her Southern accent. I started skimming the pages and couldn't believe what I was reading. Good grief!

"Hello? Anyone home? Anastasia?"

I heard Zack calling from the kitchen. Why hadn't I locked the door? "Be right there," I yelled back. No way was I ready for Zack to see me butt naked in broad daylight. Hell, I wasn't sure I wanted him *ever* to see me butt naked in broad daylight. Mood lighting was an overweight middle-aged gal's best friend.

I stepped out of the tub and grabbed a towel. After quickly drying myself, I dashed into my bedroom, closed the door, and threw on a long cotton sundress, the better to conceal hairy legs in desperate need of a sit-down with a razor.

Before joining Zack, I dashed back into the bathroom and grabbed the carton of binders containing the accounts ledger, then padded barefoot into the hall.

"Hey," I said, finding him in the kitchen. "You'll never believe what I discovered."

Zack had Ralph perched on his shoulder and was feeding him chunks of apple. "I hope it's a solution to global warming. I can't believe how hot it is out there."

"Sorry, I lack the requisite science-specific genes."

"Too bad. The guy who figures that one out will make a fortune. What did you discover?"

"Something a lot hotter. In a matter of speaking." I set the carton on the kitchen table. Then I pulled out the accounts ledger, flipped it open to the first page, and handed him the open book.

Zack stared in disbelief. "The woman killed at Sunnyside was a ninety-eight-year-old madam?"

"Until she semi-retired and moved to Sunnyside."

"Semi-retired?"

"Apparently, once a call girl, always a call girl. According to some of the other Sunnyside residents, Lyndella slept with any and all residents in possession of a Y chromo-

155

some." I indicated the carton. "And the proof is written in these notebooks. And several dozen others."

Zack flipped through some of the ledger pages. "She certainly kept detailed records. This ledger dates back over eighty years. Did you read through it?"

"I quickly skimmed the first few pages, then flipped randomly. What I've learned so far is that she started out as one of the *girls* when she was still in her teens, then bought out the owner before she turned thirty. Looks like she kept detailed records of all her *clients* and payment from Day One, noted what she paid for the operation, then kept account of each girl's johns — numbers and first names to indicate clients, along with dates, payment, and preferences. So far I haven't found any mention of her selling the business. I was looking for that when I heard you come in."

"Maybe the bordello is still in operation, and she gets a cut of the action."

"I thought about that, but I don't think so. She moved to Sunnyside twenty years ago, and she didn't have enough money for a single, or at least she hasn't for some time. Maybe she did in the beginning."

"So what's your theory, Ms. Sherlock?"

"I think her operation was shut down, possibly raided by vice. She grabbed her liquid assets and fled, moving where nobody knew her, and bought herself a spot at Sunnyside."

"You have to admit, she was one damned enterprising woman for her day."

I raised both eyebrows. "Really?"

"Think about it. There weren't many opportunities for women back then. Most didn't finish high school, let alone go to college. She probably had the choice of working in a sweat shop or working up a sweat."

"There were other options."

"Other than marriage? Not many. For all we know, her parents sold her. Or she may have been kidnapped."

I shuddered at the thought.

"White slavery is still very much alive," he continued. "Even in this country."

I'd heard that, seen the occasional news articles. "If she bought out the business, it's unlikely she started out as a sex slave," I said.

"True." Zack closed the ledger and placed it back in the box. "From the looks of things, I'd say Lyndella Wegner enjoyed her work immensely."

"And was still enjoying it up until sometime Friday night or early Saturday morning. With or without companionship."

"How do you —"

Heat rushed to my cheeks. Me and my big mouth.

"What else did you find?" prodded Zack. "A dildo?"

Busted. "In the medicine cabinet. Battery operated and rather life-like."

"You sure it doesn't belong to Lucille?"

Could it? My mother-in-law had been without a man in her life for many years. We both pondered the question for a moment, then simultaneously said, "No way!" and burst out laughing. Besides, I unpacked Lucille's suitcase. I definitely would have noticed any sex toys. Still, I made a mental note to do a bit of snooping through her drawers before she returned home.

"I spoke with Patricia," said Zack, changing the subject. "She said this sounded like a perfect assignment for her pain-in-butt summer intern. Records that old haven't been digitized yet, so she can exile him to the bowels of the building to dig through musty files. If she's lucky, he'll take most of the summer to find anything."

"Tell her I said thank you."

"It's going to cost you. Big time."

"A Manhattan assistant district attorney is blackmailing me?"

"Actually, I think she's blackmailing both

of us. She said I have to bring you up to Westchester for dinner if you want the information."

"That's going to have to wait until I'm done working at Sunnyside. I don't have a spare day until then."

"Which should be about the time it takes her intern to comb through all those records."

"Then she's got herself a deal."

"Now," said Zack, "I noticed you're all alone tonight. How about if we have that second date?"

"Braaack!" squawked Ralph. "*Now we are alone, wouldst thou then counsel me to fall in love? Two Gentleman of Verona.* Act One, Scene Two."

Zack laughed as he handed Ralph another apple chunk. "I stand corrected. Since you're *nearly* alone —"

"I wondered when you'd get around to asking. What did you have in mind?" And it better be something that doesn't involve baring my legs, I thought to myself. If I ever have any discretionary money again, I'm treating myself to laser hair removal.

Monday morning started out even hotter than Friday, Saturday, or Sunday. The thermometer outside my bedroom window read ninety degrees at seven o'clock. How was that even possible? We live in New Jersey, not the Mojave Desert!

Every blade of grass on my lawn had withered and died. The hydrangea, rhododendron, and azalea bushes surrounding the house drooped from lack of hydration. I couldn't afford to water anything; my water bills were high enough, but neither could I afford to replace the landscaping. Talk about a catch-22! I prayed for rain but saw not a cloud in the sky as Mephisto and I left the house and headed for Sunnyside.

Devil Dog seemed reluctant to hop in the car. I suspected he knew our destination. The dog possessed more brains than I'd given him credit for in the past. Separated from his mistress, Mephisto was nowhere near the pain in the mutt he was with Lucille around. I don't know why that should come as a surprise to me.

"Be a good doggie, and you don't have to go visit her again until next weekend." I hoisted the big lummox up into the back seat. He'd made it clear he wasn't going on his own volition. Mephisto whimpered. Normally, he growls at me. I guess that said it all.

Once we arrived at Sunnyside, Lucille greeted Mephisto with open arms. "There's mother's precious! Did you miss me?"

If she only knew. "I'll be back to walk him during my lunch break."

"Why are you here?" she asked. "Isn't it Monday?"

"I've taken a temporary weekend job teaching arts and crafts here. Today is the Fourth of July. Independence Day," I added, not sure whether the commie curmudgeon recognized the significance of the date.

"So that's what all the racket was last night."

"Fireworks. Yes."

"Gave me a blinding headache."

"Are you sure the headache was from the noise? Did you tell the nurse on duty? After all, you recently underwent brain surgery."

"I'm not a fool, Anastasia. I know they cut open my head and poked around in my brain three weeks ago. A headache that begins right after the noise started and ended a few minutes after taking a couple of Tylenol, is a headache from the noise. Nothing more. But thank you for your concern. If that's what it was."

A first! Lucille had never thanked me for anything. Even though her gratitude came with a disclaimer, this was definitely progress. Did I dare hold out hope that an attitude adjustment waited in the wings?

Right! Talk about wishful thinking on my part. "That's exactly what it was," I said. With that I exited the room before she had a chance to respond.

I was surprised to see Shirley Hallstead as I headed toward the arts and crafts room. Once again she wore a power suit, this one salmon colored. The woman must not have sweat glands. How could she wear a suit in this weather?

"I didn't think you'd be in today," I said.

"Why is that?"

"It's a legal holiday."

"It's Monday. This place doesn't run by itself. I have a new extended stay patient arriving shortly. She'll be rooming with your mother-in-law. Aside from the fact that I now have a public relations nightmare on my hands, thanks to Lyndella's murder."

"I do hope you don't believe my mother-in-law had anything to do with that."

"If I believed your mother-in-law was the killer, she'd be sitting in a jail cell, not taking up one of my beds," she snapped.

I suppose my startled look gave her pause because she took a deep calming breath, then continued, "No, the truth of the matter is, when murders occur in nursing homes and assisted living facilities, the killer

162

usually turns out to be a member of the staff."

"Really?" I needed an advanced degree in psychology to figure out Shirley Hallstead's mood swings. I wondered how many of those murders were committed by the facilities' directors and administrators.

"They're called mercy killings," she continued.

"I've heard of those occurring in hospitals, but aren't the victims usually terminally ill?"

"Not always. But as you can see, I have a lot on my hands right now." She crossed her arms over her chest and began tapping her foot. "Is there something you need, Mrs. Pollack, or are we just shooting the breeze here?"

And yet another whiplash-inducing mood swing. I needed a scorecard. "Actually, I did want to discuss something if you have a few minutes to spare me."

Shirley glanced at her watch. "I can give you a minute or two."

I plunged right in. "I want to organize an arts and crafts exhibition for my students."

"We do those all the time. I told you Saturday that it was one of your responsibilities."

"At an outside art gallery. Where they'll benefit from the proceeds of the sales."

"What? If there are any sales, the proceeds should go to Sunnyside to offset the cost of the supplies they use."

"Aren't the supplies covered by the grant you receive from Mildred Burnbaum's estate?"

"No, just the teachers. The supplies come out of my budget."

"Which is funded by the residents' monthly fees, right?" As much as I wanted to, I refrained from saying *exorbitant* fees. "Just like their meals and all other services provided to them, they're already paying for their supplies."

"The money should still go to Sunnyside. The work is created here."

Talk about grasping at straws! "Shirley, this isn't a business with the residents as your employees. This is their home. They have the right to do what they want with their artwork, and they want — no, they need — the extra income. The way the economy's been the last few years, many of them have little cash left after they pay Sunnyside each month. They're excited about this opportunity. It gives them an additional cash stream."

Shirley's eyes bugged out. "You've already spoken to them about this?"

"Yes. I needed to know if they were interested before speaking with you."

Her face grew an unflattering shade of red that clashed with her salmon power suit; a huge purple vein bulged along her neck and began to throb. "You had no right!" She spoke through gritted teeth, apparently trying to keep from yelling to avoid a scene. Too bad she hadn't thought to do that yesterday when she reamed out Reggie.

"You're turning out to be a real trouble-maker, Mrs. Pollack. I never should have hired you."

What a control freak! Didn't I bail her out, allowing her to keep her precious grant money? Made me wonder if she was cooking the books and pocketing some of that grant money for herself.

I fought to control my temper. In as modulated a tone as I could muster, I said, "I fail to see how an art exhibit causes trouble. No one is asking you to do anything or fund anything. And the residents certainly don't need your permission to take part."

"I run Sunnyside. *I* control what the residents can and can't do."

"Really? I believe the Board of Directors might see things quite differently."

That caught her off-guard. "Fine! Have your stupid art show. No one is going to buy any of that crap, anyway."

165

With that she spun around and stormed off toward her office.

"Told you so." I turned around to find Mabel Shapiro standing behind me, leaning on her rhinestone-studded walker. "That one's a piece of work, isn't she?"

"She certainly is, Mabel, but I learned a lot from that little altercation."

"I'll bet you did, hon."

"Bottom line, we're going to have our gallery show. With or without her blessing."

Mabel and I headed for the arts and crafts room. We arrived to find several of the other women gathered at the entrance to the room. "What's going on?" I asked.

They stepped aside to show me.

TEN

"Who did this?" I asked, staring at the mess covering the floor. All of the boxes containing Lyndella's crafts and novels had been upended, the contents dumped. But not just dumped. Dumped. Stomped. Shredded. Shattered. Pulverized. Thoroughly and irreparably broken and destroyed.

The vandal or vandals hadn't spared a single item, and they'd taken their sweet time in doing so. Every fabric craft had been cut up into hundreds of small scraps. Every paper craft and all the novels had been torn into confetti. The floor was covered with slivers of glass, splinters of wood, and shards of clay from stained glass, decoupage, and sculpting projects.

I scanned the room. Nothing else had been touched. The greenware drying on a shelf in the pottery area still stood all intact. Same for the canvases in the painting area and the quilt on the quilting frame. No

167

paintings or fabric slashed, no stretchers or frames broken. The vandal had targeted only Lyndella's work.

I glanced over at the bookcases under the windows and found the craft books still there. The vandals must not have been aware of them, which exonerated all the residents who'd been in the classroom while I was sorting through the books and shelving them.

"Someone didn't want Lyndella's porn left lying around," said Mabel.

Indeed. "Aside from setting her work on fire, this is exactly what many of you suggested doing with her possessions yesterday," I reminded them.

"We didn't do it," said Sally.

"If we had, we wouldn't have left the mess for you to clean up," said Estelle. "We like you."

"Thanks." I think. However, no one seemed all that upset about the destruction except me. "Anyone know where the janitor hangs out?"

Mabel gave me directions, and I headed out in search of someone to clean up the mess. Janitorial duties didn't fall under my job description.

When I turned a corner at the end of the hall, I nearly collided with an empty wheelchair pushed by a nurse. I recognized her as one of the staff who'd been eavesdropping outside Shirley's office yesterday afternoon.

"Sorry," she said. Then, when she realized who she'd nearly crashed into, she said, "You left too soon yesterday. You missed the finale." She held out her hand. "I'm Carla, by the way. Carla Fitzhugh."

I shook her hand. "Anastasia Pollack. What do you mean I missed the finale?"

"After Reggie ran out, Shirley called that detective who'd questioned all of us on Saturday."

"Detective Spader?"

"Right. She told him Reggie killed Lyndella."

"That makes no sense," I said. "I saw the way Reggie looked when she discovered Lyndella's body. That poor kid was totally freaked. What proof does Shirley have?"

"None that I know of. Besides, Reggie isn't capable of stomping a bug, much less strangling a human. No, Shirley wanted her pound of flesh. She knew the cops would pick up Reggie for questioning, maybe even lock her up for a few hours before they realized she had nothing to do with Lyndella's murder."

"That's sick."

"That's Shirley for you. As vindictive a

169

bitch as you'll ever meet."

"I'm beginning to see that."

"How dare you disobey me? When I tell you to do something, you do it. I don't give a damn what anyone else says."

Everything began to make sense. Shirley fired Reggie because Reggie gave Lyndella's craft projects to me instead of trashing them.

"This is all my fault," I said. "I'm afraid I got Reggie fired."

"How do you figure that?"

I told her about finding Reggie packing up Lyndella's clothes and how I told her to bring me her crafts instead of tossing them in the Dumpster as Shirley had directed.

Carla patted my shoulder. "Don't beat yourself up. Shirley was itching to fire Reggie. It was bound to happen sooner or later."

I remembered Shirley's earlier comments about Reggie. *"That girl's already on probation after the stunt she pulled last week. One more strike and she's out of here."*

"Shirley mentioned something on Friday about a stunt Reggie pulled. Something to do with one of the other residents. Do you know anything about that?"

She thought for a moment. "Must have been last week when Reggie accompanied

several of the residents into downtown Westfield. Some of the men took off to have a
few beers at a local pub."

"So? Why wouldn't they be allowed to do
whatever they want?"

"They can."

"Then why did Reggie get in trouble?"

"Dirk tripped climbing back on the bus.
Gave himself a shiner. Shirley blamed Reggie."

"For what?"

"Letting Dirk get drunk."

"Was he?"

"Hell, no. I checked him out when they
arrived back at Sunnyside. I doubt Dirk had
more than one beer. Two max. But that
didn't matter to Shirley. Like I said, she's
been looking for excuses to fire Reggie."

"Makes you wonder why she hired her in
the first place."

"I don't have to wonder; I know."

I raised my eyebrows at that. Carla continued. "Reggie is the daughter of the girlfriend
of one of Sunnyside's board members.
Shirley was ordered to hire her. The only
way she'd be able to get rid of Reggie was
to prove her incompetent. She's been docu-
menting all of Reggie's supposed screw ups.
I guess Shirley figured she finally had
enough proof to fire Reggie without jeopar-

171

dizing her own job."

All I could think to say was, "Wow."

"Watch your back, Mrs. Pollack."

"Are you threatening me?"

She held up both her hands, palms outward. "Heavens, no. I'm warning you to tiptoe lightly around Shirley Hallstead, that's all."

"Thanks, but I think your warning might be too late."

I headed off in search of the janitor. I'd had my suspicions before, but after hearing what Carla had to say, I'd bet what little money I had that Shirley was my vandal. I'd dared to countermand an order she gave, so she got even.

Hauling the cartons out to the Dumpster after I left yesterday or telling someone else to do it wouldn't have been enough for Shirley. The mess in the arts and crafts room was meant to leave a message. Nobody messes with Shirley Hallstead and gets away with it. Apparently, not even members of the Board of Directors.

Should I confront her? Chances were, she'd deny knowing anything about the vandalism. I'd already had enough confrontations with her; I didn't need another. The damage was done. She'd made her point loud and clear. I was better off ignoring

172

what had happened. I decided not to mention anything to her. Let her stew in her own rage. I'd choose my battles. This was merely a temporary gig to raise some much-needed extra cash. I wouldn't let it get to me.

And what about Reggie? Should I call Detective Spader? What would I tell him? That I knew Reggie wasn't Lyndella's killer? I had no proof. Just as I had no proof that Lucille didn't kill Lyndella. Having a feeling or a hunch didn't sit well with cops unless it was their feeling or their hunch. Reggie would have to hope that Detective Spader was a keen enough student of human nature to realize Shirley was manipulating him and his investigation for her own purposes. As much as I wanted to help Reggie, there really wasn't anything I could do.

I found the janitor in his closet of an office and asked him to clean up the mess. When I returned to my classroom, all my students were busy with their projects, the mess on the floor having no further interest to them.

Although I offered, no one needed my help, advice, or suggestions. So I settled in at my desk, pulled out Lyndella's accounts ledger, which I'd brought with me, and started reading again from the beginning. This time I didn't skim. I read each line item, word for word, marking important milestones with a yellow highlighter.

"Whatcha reading?" asked Mabel after I had my nose buried through two classes.

"Just something I brought from home that I need to go over," I told her. "Financials. Extremely dull reading." I didn't want anyone to know what I had, not after the trashing of Lyndella's crafts and books.

Mabel didn't press further. She turned her attention back to fastening sequins and studs onto a pair of jeans she was blinging up for her granddaughter.

At lunch I slipped the ledger into my tote and brought it with me while I walked Mephisto. I didn't trust leaving it behind in the empty room while I was gone.

When I arrived at Lucille's room, I saw that her new roommate had arrived. One look at Mrs. Edna Crowley told me my mother-in-law should find no fault with the woman. Given her full-body cast and wired jaw, she'd neither talk incessantly nor entertain gentleman callers throughout the night.

"Would you like to get some fresh air?" I asked Lucille as I snapped Mephisto's leash onto his collar.

"Anything to get out of this place." She then surprised me by hoisting herself out of her wheelchair and standing without so much as a teeter or a wobble. "Hand me that walker," she said, nodding in the direction of the apparatus.

"You're making excellent progress," I said as we headed out of the room. I walked slowly to keep pace with her even though Mephisto strained at the leash. Devil Dog's bladder demanded a quicker pace, but I hesitated to leave Lucille shuffling down the hall on her own. What if she became dizzy or her legs gave way suddenly?

"I have tremendous incentive," she said, stepping up her pace. I gave Mephisto free rein and hustled to catch up with her.

The heat hit us full blast the moment the doors swooshed open, but Lucille didn't seem to mind. She shuffled her polyester pantsuited self over to a bench under a dogwood to the side of the entrance and plopped down while Mephisto sniffed, then baptized the tree.

"I want you to take me home today," said Lucille. "As you can see, I'm functioning quite well on my own."

"I'll speak with your therapist. If he gives his okay, I'll bring you home."

"I don't care what he says. You can't keep

me here against my will."

I sat down beside her. "All right, Lucille. I'll take you home today but only if you can feed yourself, dress yourself, and go to the bathroom without help. Otherwise, you're staying here whether you like it or not. There isn't anyone home during the day to help you."

She let forth with a loud *harrumph.* "Maybe tomorrow."

"Maybe tomorrow," I agreed.

We headed back inside, Lucille a bit less frisky, Mephisto and I both glad for the welcoming rush of air conditioning that hit us the moment we stepped into the lobby.

One of the aides met us at Lucille's room. "Time for your water therapy, Mrs. Pollack."

"I'm going home tomorrow," said Lucille.

"That so?" The aide positioned the wheelchair behind Lucille and guided her into the seat.

"Tomorrow," said my mother-in-law to me as she was wheeled away. "Don't you forget, Anastasia."

The remainder of my day went by much as the morning had with my students having little need of my assistance. I spent the bulk of my time pouring through Lyndella's ledger. By the end of the day, I'd uncovered some very intriguing facts about her life. I couldn't wait to get home to cross-reference the dates of various line items in the ledger with any personal notations she'd written in her craft journals around the corresponding times.

When I arrived home, I found a note from the boys.

Spending "quality time" with Uncle Ira. Be home after dinner. Love ya, Mom! Alex and Nick.

Uncle Ira was sure making up for lost time. I suppose I couldn't blame either him or my sons for wanting a relationship. I just hoped Ira had no ulterior motives. Although what those ulterior motives might be, eluded me. Part of me wanted to take him at face value and believe all he'd said. Another part of me, the part that had lived through his half-brother's deceit, no longer believed that what you see is what you get.

Bottom line? I didn't want my sons hurt by another Pollack male.

I swept aside my doubts, though, to concentrate on a more pressing matter — proving the innocence of a certain Pollack female. To that end, after giving Mephisto fresh water and releasing Ralph from his cage, I gathered up all of Lyndella's journals and set up camp on the dining room table with the journals, the accounts ledger, a legal pad, a pen, and a stack of multi-colored sticky note flags.

Mephisto parked himself under an air-conditioner vent, and Ralph perched on top of the dining room breakfront. Within minutes Mephisto was snoring away. Ralph seemed intent on following my investigation.

Lyndella had assigned her *clients* numbers alongside their first names, probably because she never knew their last names. Or if she did, she protected her clients' privacy. A vice raid that seized her ledger as evidence could unleash a mess of trouble for those clients, especially any who were public figures, had she included their last names.

The first line item in the ledger read: *February 12, 1931 — John #1 — $2.00 tip — likes to suck my toes.* Unless Lyndella's birthday fell within the first few weeks of the year, she had only been fifteen when she entered the world's oldest profession.

I found the earliest craft journal. No sheet protectors preserved these pages. Lyndella had glued lined writing paper and her samples to sheets of heavy black paper, the kind used in old photo albums. The pages were brittle, and the glue had partially discolored the lined paper and samples. Envelopes glued to the back of each black sheet held patterns.

The first page, dated two months prior to John #1, featured directions for a long white nightgown with cerulean blue forget-me-nots embroidered across the bodice. There was no photo, as I'd expect for that early date. Back then, any camera sophisticated enough to capture a close-up of the embroidery would have cost more than most people earned in a week.

Instead, Lyndella had illustrated the page with a detailed sketch of the finished garment and included a scrap of the batiste fabric with a couple of embroidered flowers as a sample.

The sketch showed a nightgown more virginal than risqué, with a high neck and long sleeves gathered at the wrists.

I pulled the full-size embroidery pattern from the envelope. Unlike the crafts that decorated her room at Sunnyside, nothing erotic hid among the embroidered flowers.

Much of the writing had faded over time. With great difficulty, I read every word of the directions, hoping to find more information. In the margin she'd written, *"Something blue."*

Was the nightgown for her hope chest or

an upcoming wedding? For herself or a gift for someone else?

The next page, dated three weeks later, contained information on a crocheted granny squares baby afghan in pale yellow, mint green, and white wool. Lyndella had included one sample square. I found nothing sexual about that project, either. A lone note at the bottom of the page read, *"For the baby,"* but gave no indication as to whose baby.

I marked both pages with red sticky note flags on which I wrote BC to indicate the crafts were made prior to the start of Lyndella's *career.* Before I could flip to the next page, Mama arrived home.

"What's all this?" she asked as she dropped half a dozen shopping bags onto the table and began nosing around the binders.

"I'm trying to find out who had a motive to kill Lucille's roommate."

Mama laughed. "You mean besides the pinko commie?"

"Lucille is many things, Mama, but I refuse to believe she's a murderer."

"Are you one hundred percent certain of that?"

"I can't be a hundred percent sure of anything, but —"

"Butt out, Anastasia. Let the police handle things. This new hobby of yours is not very ladylike."

"Hobby?" It's not like I'd made a conscious decision to become an amateur sleuth. "Might I remind you that if I'd previously followed that advice and left things to the police, both you and I might now be dead?"

Mama shuddered. "Don't remind me, but those were different circumstances. No one is out to kill either of us. Besides, you're certainly not going to find your next husband by spending your spare time snooping around murder suspects at a nursing home."

"My next husband? What makes you think I want a *next* husband?"

"Don't be silly, dear. Of course you want a next husband. You're far too young to live out the rest of your life like that spinster great-aunt of yours." She glared at Ralph. "Maybe if Penelope Periwinkle had spent more time with eligible men and less time with that filthy bird of hers, she wouldn't have died an old maid."

Ralph squawked. "*You would be another Penelope. Coriolanus.* Act One, Scene Three."

"Traitor. Remember who supplies your sunflower seeds," I told him.

I turned back to Mama. "In case you hadn't noticed, I've given birth to your two grandsons. So unless you're under the deluded impression that a couple of immaculate conceptions occurred, I'm definitely not an old maid and can't possibly become one. Besides, I thought you'd already picked out my *next* husband."

"You need to keep your options open, dear. Just in case things don't work out between you and Zack."

I nodded in the direction of the shopping bags. "Speaking of future husbands, is that what your shopping spree is all about? New man, new wardrobe? You had a date last night, didn't you? Who is he this time, Mama?"

"Mr. Lord and Mr. Taylor. You can't expect me to pass up a 70 percent-off sale." She scowled at my faded navy tank top and khaki cargo pants, both hovering this side of stretched out and threadbare. "As a matter of fact, you could use a bit of wardrobe updating. Tear yourself away from whatever it is you're doing. The sale ends this evening."

"When Mr. Lord and Mr. Taylor decide to have a 100 percent-off sale, let me know. Until that day, I'm not interested."

Mama let loose a huge sigh as she gathered

up her shopping bags. "Honestly, Anastasia, I don't know what I'm going to do with you."

"Buy me a winning Powerball ticket, and I promise I'll shop till I drop," I muttered to her departing back as she headed toward her bedroom. Then I turned my attention back to Lyndella's journal.

Baby items filled the next several entries in the journal — knitted sweaters, booties, and caps, all decorated with duplicate stitched ducks and teddy bears; an assortment of bibs and burp cloths embroidered with nursery rhymes; and a yo-yo doll. With great difficulty, I strained to read every word of Lyndella's tight, faded handwriting but again found no clue as to the baby's identity.

Then I discovered a note written at the bottom of a page featuring the yo-yo doll. The ink on this page was not only faded but blurred, as though Lyndella had been caught in a sudden downpour as she wrote. Much of the page was indecipherable, but at the bottom I made out the following: *What am I going to do now?*

The page was dated one week prior to the first ledger entry for John #1.

YO-YO DOLL

NOTE: Yo-yo dolls contain small components that are choking hazards. Never give a yo-yo doll to a baby or toddler. Use only as a decorative item in a nursery or as a toy for older children who don't put things in their mouths.

Materials

basic yo-yo supplies to sew 61 yo-yos made from a 5" circle template
buttonhole thread
quilting thread
four embroidery needles
four 3/4" jingle bells
8" × 8" muslin
compass or 8" diameter plate
small amount of fiberfill
sewing needle
black and red embroidery thread
three 2-hole buttons
1/2-yd. 2" wide gathered lace
4-ply yarn for hair (your choice of color)
fabric glue or glue gun

Directions

Thread two yards of buttonhole thread through an embroidery needle. Knot ends together. Thread the needle through the top of a bell, then insert the needle through the doubled thread and pull to secure the bell.

String 14 yo-yos onto the thread by inserting the needle into the bottom (ungathered side) of the center of each yoyo, pushing the yo-yos down toward the bell.

Leave the thread and needle attached for the first leg. Construct a second leg in the same manner.

Repeat this process for the two arms, using 10 yo-yos for each arm.

Using a compass or a plate as a template, trace an 8″ circle on the muslin for the doll's head. Cut out the circle. Using the quilting thread, sew a running stitch 1/4″ from cut edge. Place fiberfill in the center of the circle. Gather the muslin around the fiberfill, adding more fiberfill if needed to make a firm head. Gather the opening closed and knot the thread.

With the black embroidery floss, make French knot eyes. Straight stitch a mouth with the red embroidery floss.

To assemble the doll, pass one leg needle through one hole of a 2-hole button. Pass the other leg needle through the second hole. Tie the two lengths of thread together, knotting several times.

Passing both needles through each yo-yo, string twelve yo-yos for the body. Pass one needle through one hole of a second 2-hole button and the other needle through the other hole.

String the arms through the same button, one arm through each hole. Knot the arm threads to the body threads.

Pass all four needles through the remaining yo-yo for a neck. Pass two needles through one hole of the remaining button and the other two needles through the other hole. Knot the threads. Stitch the head to the neck over the button.

Using the quilting thread, sew a running stitch around the gathered edge of the lace. Place the lace around the bottom of the head and tie off at the back of the head to form a ruffled collar.

To make the doll's hair, cut yarn into 4″ lengths. For each section of hair, knot three lengths together at the center of the yarn. Glue knots to head along hairline, then in horizontal rows across the back of the head.

ELEVEN

The next craft page, one featuring a crocheted baby bunting, was dated two weeks after John #1. In the margin Lyndella had written, *"Had doubts at first but an amazingly enjoyable way to earn a living. Preacher be damned. Not looking forward to having to stop for several months."*

I consulted the ledger. In those two weeks Lyndella had *entertained* Matthew #1 three times, James #1 twice, William #1 twice, William #2 twice, John #1 four additional times, and John #2 three times.

Mama came back into the dining room. She'd changed into a sleeveless pink seersucker sundress which she accented with a white coral necklace, a white straw hat, and white sandals. "Going somewhere?" I asked.

"Out to dinner."

"With Mr. Lord and Mr. Taylor?"

"Of course." She pirouetted to show off the halter back of her dress. Not many sixty-

187

five year olds can wear a halter without eliciting stares and snickers. I had to admit, Mama looked damn good for a woman of her age. Probably a hell of a lot better than I'd look in that same outfit. Sometimes life is so not fair.

"Like it?" she asked.

"It's lovely. Will anyone else be joining you for dinner this evening?"

"Of course, dear. You don't think I'd get all dressed up to dine alone, do you?"

"And would this person have a name?"

"Doesn't everyone?"

I waited for more information, but Mama spun around and headed for the front door. "Don't wait up, dear."

Not only does Flora Sudberry Periwinkle Ramirez Scoffield Goldberg O'Keefe have a better body than her much younger daughter, she's also got a far better social life.

I pulled a yogurt out of the refrigerator and returned to the puzzling life of Lyndella Wegner. As I ate, I read through the next several months of Lyndella's crafting life and the few personal comments she made from time to time. The pieces began to fall into place. I kept reading, eager to view the complete picture.

But was I reading too much between the lines? All of Lyndella's notes so far were more cryptic than definitive. I needed to bounce my ideas off someone, and the only someone who knew enough about the situation to be of any help was a certain guy living above my garage.

The silver Porsche Boxster parked in my driveway told me Zack was home. I headed out the back door and up the outside staircase that led to his apartment.

The sign hanging from the doorknob read, "Darkroom in use," a warning not to open the door. The apartment consisted of one large, combined living room/kitchen, and two bedrooms with a Jack and Jill bathroom between them. Zack had converted the smaller bedroom into a dark room.

Even though he used digital cameras for most of his photography, Zack still shot with film for certain projects and did his own developing and printing. He gave up his Manhattan apartment to live above my garage five months ago due to a pair of geriatric neighbors who confused his darkroom for a meth lab and continually called the cops. After a raid that destroyed three days worth of location work, Zack decided he needed a more private space, one where he didn't share walls with paranoid neighbors.

I hesitated before knocking. If Zack was

working, I didn't want to interrupt him. I turned to head back downstairs when the door swung open.

"Hey," he said, "I was just thinking of you. Come see what I finished." He reached for my hand and pulled me inside.

"I don't want to disturb you," I said. "I can come back later."

"You're not disturbing me. I was just about to take the sign off the knob."

He walked me over to the large worktable set up at the far end of the living room. "Madagascar lemurs," he said, pointing to the array of photos spread out on the table.

"Which is the one that sounds like a police siren?"

He reached for a photo of an animal that resembled a panda, except for the pointy black snout. "This one. The indri lemur. They're very rare because they only reproduce once every two to three years. Took me forever to get these shots."

"Camped in a jungle in Madagascar?"

"Unfortunately, the lemurs don't frequent The Four Seasons."

Surreptitiously shooting lemurs with a camera didn't prove Zack wasn't also surreptitiously shooting humans — with a camera or something a lot deadlier. No matter how many times he denied it, I still couldn't shake the suspicion that Zack was also involved with one of the alphabet agencies. Didn't all spies deny they worked for the government? After all, James Bond's business card claimed he worked for Universal Imports, not MI6.

"So what have you been up to today?" he asked.

I shoved my worries over Zack's real job to the back burner of my brain to simmer more. Maybe I had too active an imagination for my own good. If so, I could also be totally off-base about Lyndella. "I think I know why Lyndella became a prostitute."

A few minutes later, Zack leaned over my dining room table as I pointed out the various crafts and notes. "I think Lyndella got knocked up when she was fifteen. Either the guy promised to marry her and bailed, or something happened to him before the wedding took place."

"Or they married and something happened shortly afterward," suggested Zack. "You did say she went by *Mrs*. Wegner, right?"

"That's another possibility. But for whatever reason, Lyndella was left alone and pregnant. Maybe she ran away; maybe her family kicked her out. Who knows? Either way, she wound up at a whorehouse and began earning a living on her back." And in a multitude of other positions, given the notations concerning client preferences.

"Makes perfect sense. Does she mention the baby?"

"I haven't gotten that far yet, but she does mention how she's not going to be able to work for several months, and the ledger bears that out." I pointed out the gap in dates on the ledger page. "Here. See. Nearly five month between *clients.* The corresponding period in her crafts journal shows she did quite a bit of intricate sewing and needlework. I think she continued to work throughout her pregnancy, but she was working as a seamstress, probably for the other girls and the madam. She mentions the recipient by name on each page."

I flipped back several pages and pointed out the names to him. "For Millie. For Evelyn. For Rebecca. For Madam Abigail. And so on."

"Fascinating, but how does any of this prove Lucille didn't strangle Lyndella?"

"It doesn't. So far. However, my gut tells me if I keep digging through these binders and the ledger, I'm going to find clues pointing me to Lyndella's killer."

Zack pulled his phone out of his jeans

pocket. "Looks like we're in for a long night. What toppings would you like on your pizza?"

Having two sets of eyes made sifting through the journal and ledger much easier. Zack and I continued reading and taking notes.

Mama arrived home alone well-past ten o'clock. Her date may have walked her to the door, but he didn't come in.

"How was your dinner?" I asked.

"Lovely dear. Hello, Zack. If you two will excuse me, I'm exhausted." With that, she headed for her room.

"I may have to start spying on her," I said. "She's up to something."

"Listen, *Harriet,* she's a grown woman and shows no signs of senility. Let her have some fun."

"Letting her have fun usually means I wind up with another stepfather."

"Would that be so bad?"

I thought for a moment. "No, I suppose not. I'd just like her to find one who sticks around for a bit before kicking the proverbial bucket."

"Maybe six is her lucky number."

"Lou Beaumont was supposed to be Husband Number Six. Look how that turned out."

"He never made it to the altar. Lou doesn't count."

Before I could say anything else, Alex and Nick barreled into the house with Ira following close behind. "Have a good time?" I asked.

"Uhm . . . sure," said Alex.

"Yeah," said Nick.

They certainly didn't sound very enthusiastic. "Where'd you take them?" I asked Ira.

"Up to the Catskills. My kids' camp had parents' visitation. I thought I'd surprise them by bringing their new cousins with me."

Alex rolled his eyes. Nick mouthed, "Brats." Since all three of them were looking in my direction, Ira didn't notice.

I smiled. "How nice. Next time I'd appreciate a bit more information, though. Especially if you're going to be gone so long."

"Right," said Ira, looking a bit embarrassed. "I should have thought to leave you my cell phone number."

Actually, he should have thought to ask my permission before taking my sons out of state, but I decided to bite my tongue. Something told me this wouldn't be a problem after tonight.

"I didn't realize the boys don't have their

own phones," he added.

"We used to," said Alex.

"Can't afford them any more," said Nick.

Ira looked even more embarrassed. "Well, I'd better get going. I have to pick up my wife at the airport in less than an hour."

We all said good-night, and when I gave the boys my *Mom Look,* they remembered their manners and thanked Ira for taking them.

"So," I said after closing the front door, "not such a great day, huh?"

"His kids are the most obnoxious spoiled brats," said Nick. "Eleven-year-old twin girls who think they're the next Miley Cyrus —"

"Except neither of them can carry a tune," said Alex. "We had to sit through a talent show and listen to them yowl like cats. And then listen to Uncle Ira gush over them like they're already superstars. The guy must be tone deaf."

"They totally pretended we weren't even there," said Nick. "But their nine-year-old brother was worse. He's convinced he's headed to the majors."

"Not that he can hit or field a ball worth a damn," added Alex. "He struck out all three times at bat and committed two fielding errors."

"When I tried to give him some pointers,"

said Nick, "he told me to go fuck myself."

"Did Ira hear him?" I asked.

"Yeah. Not that he did anything. Told the little shit to apologize, but when he refused, Uncle Ira just kind of shrugged and gave me a lame smile."

"Ira's pretty much a wimp, Mom," said Alex. "His kids treat him like crap, and he let's them get away with it."

"I was really excited about having cousins," said Nick. "What a bummer."

"That's the trouble with family," said Zack, who'd listened quietly up until now. "You can't pick and choose."

"It's not fair," said Nick. "We're already stuck with Grandmother Lucille."

"You're not stuck with Ira and his kids," I said. "You can choose how much of a relationship you want to have. Or you can choose not to have any relationship with them. I'm certainly not going to force you to see them, but you might want to give them a second chance."

"Why?" Alex and Nick asked together.

"Because Ira sprang this on his kids without warning. Maybe they were acting out because they were jealous."

"Jealous?" asked Nick. "They're like totally loaded; we've got nothing."

"You had their father," said Zack.

196

"Huh?"

"Zack's right," I said. "Put yourselves in their shoes for a minute, Nick. How would you feel if one of your parents didn't show up for visiting day and the other brought along a couple of strange kids who were spending time with their father while you were off at camp."

"Could be they didn't even want to go to camp," added Zack. "What if they've been homesick?"

Alex and Nick mulled. "Yeah," said Alex. "Ira didn't use the best judgment, did he?"

"Definitely not," I said.

The grandfather clock in the hall chimed eleven o'clock. As much as I wanted to continuing investigating Lyndella's life, I knew I needed to put aside her journals for the night. I still had to pull together a presentation for tomorrow's staff meeting, something I had planned to do over the three-day weekend, back when I thought I'd have a three-day weekend.

Hopefully I'd have some time to continue reading through the journals during the week.

By next weekend Detective Spader might have enough circumstantial evidence to arrest Lucille, and I couldn't let that happen. Sitting in a jail cell for protesting without a permit or for compulsive jaywalking was one thing. Murder was quite another.

"Time to call it a night," I said. "We all have to work in the morning."

"And I've got to get up at the crack of dawn to catch an early train to D.C.," said Zack.

"Meeting at headquarters?" I teased.

"The Smithsonian."

Or so he claimed.

TWELVE

On the last Monday of each month at the *American Woman* offices we hold staff meetings to present progress reports on the various issues in the works and begin planning the issue five months out. However, with so many people taking vacation last week, Naomi Dreyfus, our editorial director, had pushed the meeting back to today.

Thanks to the traffic gods smiling down on me this morning, I arrived at work in time to head into the conference room with the other editors and editorial assistants. We poured ourselves coffee, grabbed blueberry oat bran muffins — compliments of Cloris — then settled into our usual seats around the battered and chipped walnut conference table. Crafts, food, health, travel, finance, and the one editorial assistant we all shared sat on one side of the table. Fashion, beauty, decorating, and each of their assistants sat across from us.

A few minutes later Naomi and her assistant Kim O'Hara entered the room and took seats at the head of the table. I'm convinced that one of these days Naomi's picture will illustrate the words *cultured* and *elegant* in the dictionary. A product of Swiss boarding schools, she looks years younger than her actual age of fifty-nine and bears a striking resemblance to the late Grace Kelly. More importantly, Naomi is a great boss. She treats all of her editors with respect and continually goes to bat for us.

She'd gone to bat for me recently to the tune of fifty thousand dollars after another Trimedia employee tried to kill me. Naomi convinced the Board of Directors that it was in their best interests to make me an offer for all my pain and suffering to avoid a lawsuit, a lawsuit that had never even crossed my mind. Thanks to Naomi's quick thinking and her powers of persuasion, I'd made a sizeable dent in the debt left by Dead Louse of a Spouse. In addition, I'd moved my family out of the Stone Age by reinstating our wireless account. Not that I needed another monthly bill, but being without a home Internet connection severely limited my ability to work from home.

"Hugo won't be joining us today," said Naomi. "He's at another meeting."

A dozen pairs of eyebrows simultaneously headed northward. It was no secret that Hugo Reynolds-Alsopp rued the day Trimedia had gained control of his family-owned publishing company. Hugo remained publisher in title only, confined to a closet of an office on the fourth floor where the corporate bigwigs and bean counters routinely ignored him. Other than attending our monthly staff meetings, which were more due to his long-standing romantic relationship with Naomi and less about editorial input, Hugo rarely attended any Trimedia meetings.

"Don't get your hopes up," said Naomi. She didn't have to be a mind reader to know what we were all thinking. Naomi spent half her days battling with the parsimonious Trimedia Board. Whenever belts needed tightening, *American Woman* became the sacrificial waist of choice. I think in great part that's why Naomi decided to wheedle that fifty grand out of the board for me. Watching the head bean counter write that check must have given her a huge vicarious thrill.

"Not even a little?" asked Cloris.

We all held onto the pipe dream that Hugo might someday secure enough financial backing to buy back *American Woman* and the four other remaining magazines once part of the Reynolds-Alsopp Publishing Company.

"No comment."

That in itself spoke volumes. We all knew if Naomi was privy to any information, she'd be unable to divulge a word until all parties had signed on the dotted lines. Her "no comment" comment gave us all hope.

She opened the folder in front of her, indicating the subject closed. "Shall we get on with the meeting?"

By the time each editor gave her updates on the status of various issues in production, lunch arrived. Unbeknownst to the bean counters upstairs, Naomi tapped into her miscellaneous expenditures budget to pay for our monthly deli perk. Someday they'd find out, and we'd wind up pigging out on whatever Cloris whipped up in the test kitchen, but for now we lunched on club sandwiches and sides of potato salad and coleslaw as we turned our attention to the November issue.

"Of course, as usual, Thanksgiving and a Christmas preview will be our main themes," said Naomi, "but I'd love for us to come up with something different from what all the other monthlies will be doing. Ideas, anyone?"

"I have one," I said.

When Naomi nodded for me to continue, I told her and my fellow editors about the crafting residents of the Sunnyside of Westfield Assisted Living and Rehabilitation Center. "Their work is so good that I'm going to contact a gallery owner I know to see about arranging a show. I'd love to do a feature story on them," I concluded.

"What about craft projects?" asked Naomi.

"Fabric yo-yos."

As I suspected, blank stares greeted my statement. I pulled out some of Lyndella's yo-yos I'd brought with me and passed them around. "They're made from small scraps of fabric. Yo-yo quilts were very popular in the nineteen-thirties and forties, and yo-yo vests gained popularity with hippies in the early nineteen-seventies. They have lots of other uses, though."

"Such as?" asked Jeanie Sims, our decorating editor and a garage sale aficionado.

I had printed out some photos from the Internet last night. Pulling them from my file folder, I passed them around the table. "As you can see, decorative embellishments on clothing and accessories, pillows, placemats, dolls —"

"Yes," said Sheila Conway, our finance editor. She held up the photo of a yo-yo doll. "I remember a doll just like this from a baby shower I attended years ago."

"It's a simple, portable craft," I said, "and since it's a craft that our readers' mothers and grandmothers might have done, it ties in with the multi-generational aspect of Thanksgiving. I thought I'd feature a series of yo-yo Christmas ornaments."

Naomi studied the yo-yo in her hand and thought for a minute. "I like Anastasia's ideas. Now, how do the rest of you piggyback on the seniors slant?"

"Seniors are outside our targeted demographic," said Kim. "Our readership is women in their early thirties to late forties, mostly stay-at-home and working moms, not AARP members. How do we make this work without alienating our core readership and pissing off our advertisers?"

"Most of our readers deal with elderly parents," said Janice Kerr, our health editor. "I think featuring seniors for our Thanksgiving issue is brilliant. I could do an article on warning signs to look for when aging parents should no longer live on their own."

"And my focus could be on how to help those aging parents and their children pick the right assisted living facility," said Sheila.

"How about recipes handed down from

generation to generation?" asked Cloris. "Maybe I can get some of you to give me recipes from your parents and grand-parents."

"That's a brilliant idea," said Naomi. "Our readers always want to know more about our editors. I'm sure they'd love for all of you to each share a recipe." She turned her attention to the remaining editors who hadn't yet contributed any ideas. "What about travel, fashion, and beauty?"

"How about an article on family reunion vacation spots?" asked travel editor Serena Brower.

Naomi nodded and turned to Kim. "Are you getting this all down?"

Kim typed furiously on her iPad. "Still need beauty and fashion."

Naomi turned to beauty editor Nicole Emmerling and fashion editor Tessa Lisbon. "Ladies?"

Nicole wrinkled her pert, twenty-something nose. "I don't know. Maybe an article on the best products for getting rid of age spots?"

Sheila held her hands out in front of her. At sixty-two, she was our oldest editor. "I'd be interested in that. I'm already starting to get some."

"See if you can tie it into a broader piece

about taking care of your skin, no matter your age," said Naomi.

Nicole breathed a sigh of relief. "I can do that."

"Fashion," said Kim.

We all directed our attention toward Tessa, every inch the prima donna of her predecessor, but scoring way below the late Marlys Vandenburg on the Bitch-o-meter. As fashion editors went, Tessa was somewhat tolerable. Sometimes.

Tessa picked up one of the yo-yos. I think she tried to scowl at it, but too many Botox injections — and Lord only knew why someone as young as Tessa needed Botox — had robbed her of much of her ability to form facial expressions. She then flung the yo-yo across the table at me. "None of the designers are featuring kitsch in their spring collections."

"So what do you propose for your spread?" asked Naomi.

"You want me to showcase off-the-rack polyester separates?" She folded her arms over her silicone-enhanced cleavage and attempted a mini pout with her collagen-enhanced lips, but once again her facial muscles refused to respond. "I don't do Walmart and Kmart."

Cloris leaned over and whispered in my

ear, "Remind you of anyone?"

"She's a featherweight compared to Marlys," I whispered back, "but I think she just climbed a few points higher on the Bitch-o-meter."

Tessa glared across the table at us. "What are you two whispering about?"

Cloris and I offered her identical looks of innocence. "Nothing," we said in unison.

"Cloris, Anastasia, do either of you have an idea for Tessa?" asked Naomi.

"She's a bright girl," said Cloris. "I'm sure she'll come up with something suitable."

"There is nothing suitable," said Tessa. "Old people and fashion are as compatible as feed sacks and Prada."

"Have something on my desk by the end of the day," said Naomi.

Tessa pushed away from the table and stood. "I will not showcase fashion for stooped-over, wrinkly old people. It's obscene!" She then stalked out of the conference room, slamming the door behind her.

"Now *that* sounded like Marlys," said Cloris.

We all laughed. Even Naomi.

With Naomi green-lighting my interview of the Sunnyside crafters, I now had the freedom to spend Trimedia's dime interviewing them. Which meant I wouldn't have to wait until Saturday to continue my onsite investigation into Lyndella's murder. First though, I had to arrange for a gallery show. If I didn't keep my promise to the residents, I couldn't expect their continuing co-operation as I nosed around.

Back when I taught art in the public schools, the parents of one of my students owned a crafts gallery in Hoboken. A quick Internet search showed me that the gallery still existed, a feat in itself, given the economy. Art sales always took the first hit during an economic downturn, and al-though the economy continued to creep back toward pre-recession numbers, art sales would be the last indicator of a full-fledged recovery.

I dialed the number for Creative Hearts & Hands, hoping the Hulons still owned the gallery. Three rings later I heard, "Creative Hearts & Hands, Clara speaking."

Bingo! "Hi, Clara. This is Anastasia Pol-lack."

"Hey, stranger! I haven't seen you in ages. How are things?"

I had no idea whether she knew about Karl's death. If she did, she'd offer her condolences. If not, I'd keep mum. That wasn't a conversation for a phone call between acquaintances after the years-long gap since last speaking. Even if she knew of my widowhood, she certainly wouldn't know about the ensuing chaos brought about by the demise of Dead Louse of a Spouse. I planned to keep that information a closely guarded secret for as long as possible to avoid having to deal with behind my back gossip, prying questions, and pity stares.

Instead, after some pleasantries, I told her about the crafting residents of Sunnyside, stressing the quality of their work and finishing my pitch with, "I'd love to organize a gallery show for them, Clara, and I thought of you and Ronnie first."

"Had anyone else pitched me this idea, I would have dismissed it immediately, but I know it takes a lot to impress you, Anastasia."

"So you're interested?"

"Crafty old crones and geezers? Hell yes! And as luck would have it, we had to postpone a pottery exhibit set to open a week from Friday. The artist took ill and won't have a sufficient number of new pieces completed in time. Do these seniors of yours have enough work for me to choose from now?"

"Definitely."

"Great! How soon can you get me some photos?"

"I'm headed over there now to start the interviews for my article. I'll email photos to you later this evening."

"Too bad the magazine works so far in advance. It would have been nice to tie in the show with the article."

Thinking back to what Kara had mentioned on Friday, I realized the odds were against all of my crafters still being alive in November, but I didn't mention that to Clara. Instead, I said, "At least we'll be able to run photos from the show in the issue, and it will hit the newsstands right before the holidays."

"True. Let's see what sort of response we get from the show. If it's good enough, we might carry some of the crafts and artwork on an ongoing basis or at least bring some in again for the holidays."

Murray and the other cash-strapped Sunnyside crafters would love that. This gallery show could lead to a steady income stream for some of them.

When I hung up from Clara, I called Mabel Shapiro and filled her in on my progress.

"So this show is really going to happen?" she asked. "Some of us had our doubts."

"Not only is it going to happen, but it's going to happen much sooner than I expected. I need you to round up the other crafters and their work. Find a place where we can meet. I have to photograph all of your pieces for the gallery owner to choose which ones she wants."

"You mean we don't get to include whatever we want?"

"I'm afraid not. Space is limited."

"Why does she get to choose?"

"It's her gallery, Mabel. Besides, she'll know which pieces have the best chance of selling."

"I suppose that makes sense, but what if she doesn't choose work from all of us? You can't let her leave anyone out. It wouldn't be fair."

Mabel wouldn't have had any qualms about leaving Lyndella out of the show, had Lyndella still been alive, but I didn't mention that. "I'll do my best to see that everyone is represented, but you'll all have to accept that the gallery has the final say."

"Better do more than your best, hon. You don't want to piss off anyone."

Was that a threat? As much animosity as there had been between Lyndella and Mabel, I hadn't considered the possibility of Mabel being Lyndella's killer. Mabel hardly

211

seemed capable of strangling Lyndella, but maybe the strangulation took place more through surprise than strength.

Lyndella showed no signs of a struggle, but the killer may have struck while Lyndella slept. Or maybe Lyndella was first drugged. Then again, if Mabel had murdered Lyndella, why now? Why after so many years of putting up with Lyndella's verbal abuse? What had changed?

Maybe Mabel had finally reached her breaking point and just snapped. If that were the case, I probably wouldn't find any clues combing through Lyndella's old journals.

Instead of driving directly to Sunnyside, I first stopped home to change clothes and walk Mephisto. After the mutual animosity that had defined our relationship from the onset, the dog and I were now bonding. I wondered how Lucille would deal with that once she came home.

Neither my mother-in-law nor Sunnyside had phoned me concerning her imminent departure. I had no intention of making my presence known once I arrived. Lucille's progress on her feet yesterday boded well for her eventual total recovery, but by her own admission, she wasn't anywhere near ready to take care of herself on her own. No matter how much she complained, she'd remain at Sunnyside for now. I held the medical power of attorney papers to make sure of that.

I arrived home to find the stereo blaring, Ralph squawking, and Mephisto holding his paws over his ears. When I lowered the volume to a non-ear-bleeding decibel level, I heard a sound that made me want to cover my own ears.

THIRTEEN

No mother should ever have to hear her offspring having sex. Standing in the living room, I debated my next move. Do I walk in on the randy duo, running the risk of embarrassing the culprits to death and causing one son never to speak to me again? Would knocking on the bedroom door be any less embarrassing? Or should I just leave?

Once they were done making all their noise, they'd notice the lowered stereo volume. We could pretend nothing had happened, even though we'd both know exactly what had happened. And I'd know which son had been doing it by the way he'd avoid making eye contact with me.

No, that didn't seem like the responsible parental move. I couldn't ignore this. If nothing else, it was obviously past time to have *the protection talk.* I had no idea whether or not Karl had fulfilled that responsibility. Even though he'd told me he had, since he'd bailed on all his other family duties, why should I believe he'd ever had *the protection talk*? Since I was way too young to become a grandmother, I couldn't take Karl at his word, recent experience having proved his words less than worthless.

Loathe as I was to do so, I marched down the hall toward the boys' bedroom, only to stop short and issue a quick prayer of thanks to whichever of the gods looks out for mothers of teenagers. The sounds of passion emanated from Mama's room, not Alex's and Nick's.

The mother in me sighed a huge sigh of relief, but that relief was short-lived. What if my sons had arrived home instead of me? Mama's actions were nothing short of irresponsible.

Mama's bedroom no longer contained an entry door. After Lucille repeatedly locked Mama out of their shared bedroom, Zack came up with the ingenious idea of taking the door off its hinges and replacing it with a curtain rod and curtain. I stepped in front of the curtained doorway and called out to her. "Flora Sudberry Periwinkle Ramirez Scoffield Goldberg O'Keefe!"

The bouncing springs and moans of passion abruptly ceased. "I'm a bit busy right now, Anastasia."

"I can hear that, Mama. Toss on a robe, and meet me in the kitchen."

"Can't it wait, dear?"

"Now, Mama!"

When she joined me in the kitchen, nearly five minutes later, Mama showed no signs of remorse. She sat down opposite me, an irritation-filled expression plastered across her face. Catherine the Great appeared from the dining room and jumped onto her lap. Mama stroked the cat's fur for several seconds before finally asking, "Well? I'm here. What's so important that it couldn't wait?"

"How could you, Mama? What if one of the boys had walked in on you?"

"They would have acted a lot less aggrieved than their mother. I don't see what's got you in such an uptight snit, dear."

"You don't?"

"Of course not."

"Mama, you were having sex! In my home. On your grandson's bed!"

"I wanted to use your bed, dear. Two people on a twin is rather uncomfortable, but then I realized I might not have time to launder your sheets before you came home."

"How thoughtful of you."

"Sarcasm isn't becoming, Anastasia."

"My *faux pas,* Mama. Now let's discuss yours."

"The only thing to discuss is how I wound up with a prude for a daughter. You must get it from the Periwinkle side of the family."

Was she that dense? "You really see nothing wrong with your behavior?"

"Of course not, dear. Why should I? I'm a grown woman with a grown woman's needs." She stood. "Now if you'll excuse me, I was in the middle of something."

She turned and sashayed from the kitchen. I called after her. "Who is he, Mama?"

"If we're both lucky, your next stepfather."

"Really? Why should he bother buying the cow when he's getting the milk for free?"

Mama shook her head and muttered, "Definitely the Periwinkle side of the family."

I grabbed Mephisto's leash, clipped it to his collar, and rushed outside. How could my mother twist this situation around to make me the one at fault? I wasn't a prude, but the *ick* factor in all of this flew off the charts. A vision of Mama morphing into Lyndella Wegner thirty years from now refused to leave my mind, no matter how

217

much I shook my head to dislodge the image.

When I brought Mephisto back inside, the two horny lovebirds were going at it once again. I filled the dog's water bowl and left without changing my clothes. No way did I want to walk past her bedroom, let alone undress to the sounds of a senior citizen mattress tango going on down the hall.

I arrived at Sunnyside to find Mabel cooling both her heels and her walker's rhinestone-studded wheels in the lobby. "About time you showed up," she said. "I've got everyone assembled and waiting in the solarium. Figured the light there would work best for you."

She led me down the hallway that took us past Shirley's office. Luckily, the door was closed. The last thing I needed after my altercation with Mama was a run-in with Sunnyside's director, especially since I'd segued from savior to rabble-rouser in her eyes.

Eleven Sunnyside residents awaited me in the solarium, their various works gathered on the bistro tables set up around the room with paintings lining one wall. The afternoon sun filled the space with light perfect for shooting the assembled artwork and

218

crafts. A combination of air conditioning and whirring ceiling fans kept the glass-enclosed room from turning into an oven.

I had asked Mabel to tell the other crafters to bring their six best pieces for the shoot. Either Mabel had forgotten to convey my message, or she'd deliberately ignored me. My money was on the latter.

Having spoken of a possible gallery show to all my classes, I was also now surprised to see so few students from the arts and crafts program in the solarium. Many more had shown interest. "Where's everyone else?" I asked.

"This is the best of the best."

"No, it's not. I don't see Irene here. Her embroidery work is museum quality, and I know she was interested in taking part. And what about Bonita's watercolors? Jerome's stained glass? Maxwell's —"

"You said space was limited. I didn't want anyone left out, but I made an executive decision. Those others don't need the extra cash. These folks do."

I glanced around the room. Everyone had overheard the exchange. They had all turned from their various conversations and now stared at me. Waiting.

"You're doing this to help those who need help, right?" asked Mabel.

219

True.

"They already know not everything's going in the show," she continued, "but I told them everyone would have at least something. Excluding the ones that don't need the money means these folks get more pieces exhibited."

She gave me a pointed look that dared me to disagree with her. I didn't. The last thing I needed was someone else pissed at me.

Besides, Mabel was right. This show was about helping the cash-strapped residents of Sunnyside become a little less cash strapped. Hopefully, those not included would understand. I'd make an extra effort to include them in the magazine article and have our staff photographer shoot them and their work at Sunnyside. A few classroom shots would round out the article nicely.

My dilemma resolved, I spoke to the gathered residents. "All right. Let's get to work."

"Are you going to take our pictures, too?" asked Sally. "I need my roots touched up."

"I need a new perm," said Barbara.

"Don't worry," I told them, "I'm just photographing your work today for the gallery owner. She'll choose the pieces to feature based on the snapshots I email her. Our magazine photographer will take your pictures at the opening a week from Friday. You'll all have plenty of time to look your best."

I had prepared a simple questionnaire and printed out copies of Trimedia's standard release form, stapling the two together. I removed the stack of papers from my tote bag and placed them on one corner of a table filled with dozens of beaded necklaces, bracelets, and pins. I recognized the work as belonging to Sally Strathower. "While I'm taking the photos," I said, "I need you to fill out some paperwork. Then we'll set up an interview schedule."

"What kind of paperwork?" asked Murray.

"The first is a standard release form to use photos of you and your work in the magazine. The other asks a few biographical questions."

"Like what?" asked Dirk, eyeing me suspiciously.

"You better not need my social security number or date of birth," said Murray. "I don't give out personal information to anyone. Not with all those damn identity thieves lurking everywhere. My kid was hacked last year. They got hold of his credit card number and password. What a nightmare that was!"

The other crafters all nodded in agreement.

"Those hackers should be ashamed of themselves," said Berniece. She bobbed her head with such emphasis that her helmet hair actually moved slightly. "They stole money right out of my bank account a few years ago."

"How'd they do that?" asked Estelle.

"They rigged the swipe machines at Michael's to obtain customers' debit card information. You must have read about it at the time. It was in all the papers."

"I remember that," said Sally. "My bank cancelled my credit card and sent me a new one because I sometimes shop at Michael's. I was lucky, though. They didn't get any money from me."

"I don't tell nobody nothing," said Dirk. "Better safe than sorry."

"I don't blame you," I told them. "I certainly don't need your social security numbers or anything else that might jeopardize your finances. The questions are mostly in regards to your artwork and crafts. I'll use your answers to help me develop the article I'll be writing about all of you. I don't think you'll find any of the questions objectionable, but if you do, just leave them blank."

"Fine," said Dirk. He grabbed the pile and began passing the papers out to everyone.

"Need pens," said Murray. "Can't fill out forms without a pen, Chickie."

Chickie? Was that a compliment or an insult?

I hadn't thought to bring pens for everyone, but I did have a few in my tote and rooted around until I found them. "You'll have to share these," I said, placing the four pens on the table.

Murray picked up two Bics. "We get to keep these?"

"Sure, Murray. Knock yourself out. Just don't fight over them."

He pocketed one and began writing with the second. Several others made a grab for the two remaining pens.

"You should bring more next time you come," said Mabel. "It's not fair some got and some didn't."

"They're only Bics, Mabel, not Mont Blancs."

"Doesn't matter."

Murray and two others scribbled away at their questionnaires. The rest of the group waited somewhat impatiently for a turn with a pen.

"Everyone loves free stuff," said Mabel.

Apparently so.

Leaving them to their forms, I began shooting the various crafts and artwork spread out around the room. The task took longer than I'd anticipated, thanks in part to a dozen self-appointed photo stylists. One by one they joined me, either before filling out their forms or afterwards. Each offered all sorts of unsolicited advice on how best to capture their particular pieces of art.

"You need to photograph that vase from several different angles," said Murray. "Each side is different."

"Not a problem, Murray." I took a few more digital shots of the vase and each of his other ceramic pieces before moving on to the table of jewelry.

"Shouldn't I be wearing my jewelry so the gallery owner knows what it is?" asked Sally.

"She'll know."

"I don't see how."

"Trust me. She does this for a living."

"I still think I should be wearing them. Don't you think so, Mabel?"

"Let her wear them," said Mabel.

With the death of Lyndella, Mabel had morphed into the Napoleon of Sunnyside, a bossy, four-foot-ten-inch high and almost equally as wide, rhinestone-studded commander on jeweled wheels instead of a white steed. Challenged by no one, Mabel had taken over for the much-hated Lyndella Wegner. Only instead of grumbling about her, the others apparently had anointed her. Mabel Shapiro reveled in her newfound power, showing off by bossing me around in front of the rest of the crafters.

Not that it mattered. Clara would have the final say as to which items were selected and which weren't. I shrugged my acceptance of Mabel's edict and waited for Sally to adorn herself, deciding not to mention that the delicate pastel beadwork would get lost against the bold rainbow stripes of her size twenty-four boat neck T-shirt.

By the time we'd finished, the residents were talking dinner, speculating on that evening's offerings. They packed up their crafts and artwork and headed off to their rooms. I scooped up the completed forms and headed for the exit, hoping to sneak out without running into either Shirley or Lucille. Of course, that would require luck, something I'd lost this past winter when Karl permanently cashed in his chips and my life crapped out.

What were the odds I'd meet both Shirley *and* Lucille in the hallway, coming at me from opposite ends, one power walking in her power suit du jour, the other shuffling along with her walker?

"Why are you here?" asked Shirley.

"It's about time you got here," said Lucille. "I'm all packed."

"What?" Shirley whirled around to confront Lucille. "You're not leaving. You haven't completed your therapy."

"I'm fine," said Lucille. "I dressed myself this morning and fed myself both breakfast and lunch."

That explained the stained shirt held closed with only one button. "Have you looked in the mirror, Lucille?"

"I'm not vain like you, Anastasia. I don't need to look in mirrors. Now let's go. I've been ready for hours."

"I can't release her until her doctors sign off that she's completed her therapy," said Shirley, "and that's highly unlikely, given that she's supposed to be here four weeks, and it hasn't even been a full week yet."

"This is your fault, Anastasia. If you'd arrived earlier, I wouldn't have to stay here another night."

"I don't think you're ready to come home yet, Lucille." *I'm* not ready for her to come home yet. However, Lucille coming home would certainly put an end to Mama's afternoon delights.

I pondered which was the lesser of two evils.

"You don't get to make that decision," she said. "I know my body better than any of you, and I'm fine."

Lucille smacked her hand on the top bar of the walker and lost her balance. Shirley grabbed her from the left; I grabbed her from the right. "Take your hands off me!"

"You almost fell," I said.

"I did not!"

"You shouldn't even be walking the halls by yourself," said Shirley. "The last thing I need is a lawsuit. Stay with her," she said to me. "I'll call for an aide."

Shirley dashed into her office.

"I didn't come to pick you up, Lucille. You're not ready. What if you fall when no one is home to help you?" I said.

"That won't happen."

An aide rounded the corner and headed toward us. I handed Lucille over to him and dashed off, without responding to her and before Shirley returned from her office.

FOURTEEN

I arrived home to a quiet house. No blaring stereo. No senior citizens' sexual escapades. Ralph snored on Lucille's bed; Catherine the Great sprawled across the back of the living room sofa. A glance at the boys' work schedules for the week told me they were both on the late afternoon/early evening shifts today.

Zack's car was missing from the driveway, which meant he probably hadn't returned from D.C. yet, and Lord only knew where Mama was, what she was doing, or with whom.

"Looks like you're my dinner companion this evening," I said to Ralph as I released him from his cage.

"*What an equivocal companion is this!* Brrraaack!" he fluttered his wings and took off, squawking, "*All's Well That Ends Well. Act Five, Scene Three.*"

Ralph settled on his perch of choice, the

top of the refrigerator, and alternated between preening his feathers and intently studying me while I whipped up a zucchini and tomato omelet for dinner. Once done cooking, I plated my omelet and moved to the dining room table where I could spread out Lyndella's journals to read while I ate. Ralph followed, perching himself on the back of my chair and peering over my shoulder.

"Let me know if I miss anything important," I told him.

"*What here shall miss, our toil shall strive to mend. Romeo and Juliet.* Prologue."

"Then let us both toil away, Ralph, and maybe between us, we'll solve a murder."

"*Confer with me of murder and of death. Titus Andronicus.* Act Five, Scene Two."

"Exactly."

I read for hours, taking notes, cross referencing with Lyndella's accounts ledger, adhering sticky-note flags on pertinent pages. Alex and Nick came home shortly after eight-thirty, and I reluctantly took a break, although I feared if I stopped my momentum, I'd miss something.

"What are you looking for?" asked Alex, eyeing the clutter of loose-leaf notebooks on the dining room table. "Need some help?"

Three pairs of eyes could scour through Lyndella's journals in one third the time of one set, but I hesitated. Earlier today the thought of either of my kids having sex had twisted my innards into a knot the size of Cleveland. I wasn't naïve when it came to what teenagers viewed and read behind their parents' backs. Or even did for that matter. Hell, I'd sneaked *Peyton Place* off Mama's bookshelf when I was younger than Nick and watched *The Devil in Miss Jones* one night while babysitting for a neighbor who owned a well-stocked X-rated video-tape collection.

However, I can't imagine the *ick* factor had my mother handed me *Peyton Place* or suggested we view *The Devil in Miss Jones* together. I would have needed therapy for decades.

"Thanks for the offer," I said, "but you guys must be tired after working all day. Why don't you go veg out. I think the Mets are televised tonight."

"And you didn't work today, Mom? You're not tired?" Alex picked up a legal pad on which I'd jotted some notes and read aloud. "Marriage. Wedding. Husband. Birth. Baby. Child. Daughter. Divorce. Death. What is this?"

I held out my hand for the pad. "Words

I'm searching for in these journals."

"Why?"

"I'm hoping they'll offer up some clues to who killed the person who wrote them."

"The woman the cops think Grandmother Lucille killed?" asked Nick.

"That's the one."

"You think maybe her daughter or husband killed her?" asked Alex.

"I don't even know yet whether she had a husband or daughter. That's part of the mystery I'm trying to solve."

"How come you have all her journals?" asked Alex. "Why don't the cops have them? Aren't they evidence?"

"Apparently, the cops didn't think they were important. I rescued them from landing in a Dumpster."

"You think the cops are wrong?" asked Nick. "That you'll find something in them?"

"I think the cops didn't look closely enough and dismissed them as merely journals recording her various crafts projects. However, I suspect they might contain facts relevant to the case. I'll know for sure after I finish reading through all of them."

"So let us help you," said Alex.

"I don't think Mom wants us to see what's in these," said Nick. He'd picked up one of

the journals and held it up for his brother to see.

"Holy shit!" said Alex. "Is that what I think it is?"

Heat rose up my neck to my cheeks. "This is why I don't want you helping me." I reached across the table and grabbed the binder out of Nick's hands.

"I thought Grandmother Lucille's roommate was practically ancient," said Alex. "Like in her nineties."

"She was."

He screwed up his face. "Eeuuww! That is just too gross. Guys don't really do that to themselves, do they, Mom?"

It was nice to know that my nearly grown son was still naïve when it came to certain less-than-mainstream sexual practices. As much as I hated to enlighten him, I couldn't lie. "I think some do."

Alex turned green. He looked like he was about to hurl at just the thought. "That's totally sick."

"Are all these notebooks filled with stuff like that?" asked Nick.

"For the most part."

"How can you even look at them, Mom?"

I glanced down at the photo of the ceramic sculpture in question, a lifelike rendition of a tattooed and pierced piece of male

anatomy, and wondered if Lyndella had created it for shock value alone or if she'd actually used it, either on herself or someone else. "It isn't easy," I said.

"I may need to bleach my brains to get that image out of my head," said Alex.

"Ditto," said Nick.

That made three of us. The more I combed through Lyndella's journals, the dirtier I felt. If what I suspected about her past was true, I could understand how and why she felt forced to turn to prostitution. I sympathized with Lyndella, the girl; I disliked Lyndella, the woman. Immensely. From what I was learning, she took extreme pleasure in hurting everyone with whom she came in contact. And she certainly had a strange way of getting her kicks. No wonder the other residents of Sunnyside rejoiced in her death.

I continued reading, partly because no matter how bleary-eyed I grew, I couldn't stop myself. Lyndella's journals presented a fascinating puzzle. Every so often I'd discover a full name written somewhere within a craft journal page. Just a name. No other reference. Often the name was hidden within the text of the directions. When I cross referenced the start and completion dates of the craft project with the accounts journal, somewhere within the corresponding dates I'd find a client with the same first name.

And sometimes I'd recognize a name. A congressman. A senator. A former cabinet member. Even one sitting Supreme Court justice. I suspected if I were familiar with Georgia politics the last half of the twentieth century, I'd recognize far more names. With all these politicians as clients, was Lyndella's establishment in some way responsible for Savannah being known as the Hostess City? How ironic would that be?

I jotted down each man's name as I came across them. Once I read through all the journals, I'd Google each name.

Was it possible Lyndella had been blackmailing some of the former patrons of The Best Little Whorehouse in Savannah, as I'd come to think of The Savannah Club for Discerning Gentlemen? Did one of them hire a hit man to rid himself of a potentially damaging scandal? A plausible theory that contained one huge hole. If Lyndella had been receiving blackmail payments, why did she remain in a shared room at Sunnyside? With all her accumulated crafts and her active sex life, wouldn't she want a single if she could afford one? She certainly couldn't have been stashing the cash away for her old age. For that reason, I dismissed the blackmail theory.

Lyndella also made cryptic references to other people and events without actually naming names or places, but I began to see her writings as a breadcrumb trail that if I followed to its end, might reveal the truth of her murder.

I also continued to read because I wanted to wait up until Mama arrived home. She, too, was becoming something of a puzzle lately. Her deliberate sidestepping of all my questions concerning this new mystery man in her life was driving me crazy. Who was this guy? Why didn't she want me to know? Should I be worried for her?

Three hours later, Mama still hadn't appeared. Bleary-eyed and knowing I should stop for the night, I made myself a cup of coffee and kept reading.

At one in the morning, Mama waltzed through the front door, but I barely noticed. I had finally hit pay dirt, having discovered a huge clue in unlocking the mystery of Lyndella's past and quite possibly the name of her killer.

Now what should I do?

I needed to brainstorm with someone, but Zack must have decided to spend the night in D.C. Either that or he'd flown off on some clandestine mission, and his meeting in D.C. had been nothing but a bogus cover story. Photos of siren-sounding lemurs aside, I still didn't know what to believe and what not to believe when it came to Zachary Barnes, photojournalist/secret agent.

I grabbed the phone to call Cloris, but hung up at the sound of the dial tone. She'd kill me if I woke her up at this hour. Worse, she'd never feed me again. I couldn't risk starving to death. So I crawled into bed.

Between the late-night coffee and my racing brain, I spent the remainder of the night trying to figure out what to do with the information I'd uncovered.

Going to the police seemed useless. Detective Spader would listen to what I had to say and write me off as a raving lunatic grasping at straws to keep her mother-in-law out of prison. The police dealt with hard evidence, not conjecture and speculation, which was all I really had. But that conjecture and speculation made a hell of a lot of sense to me. Too bad I couldn't prove any of it.

Or could I?

I never fell asleep. At four in the morning I realized I'd forgotten to download the crafts photos to my computer and email them to

Clara. Since I couldn't sleep, anyway, I dragged myself out of bed and fired up my computer. Then I nuked a cup of milk in an unsuccessful attempt to catch at least a couple of hours of sleep.

The milk didn't work. At six I rose and padded into the kitchen to start a pot of coffee. While it brewed, I took a long, steamy shower, then dressed, walked Mephisto, and ate breakfast, all while Mama and the boys slept.

At seven twenty I was ready to leave the house. Having decided what I needed to do, I was antsy to get under way, but it was too early. The person I wanted to speak with wouldn't be available until eight thirty. So I caught up on a few chores — throwing in a load of wash, emptying the dishwasher, wiping down the stove and countertops — all of which only ticked off another fifteen minutes.

By that point, I thought I'd jump out of my skin if I didn't get going. I stared at the clock. Seven thirty-five. I should have scrubbed the bathroom or cleaned Ralph's cage before showering and dressing. That would have killed sufficient time. Too late now, though.

I grabbed my purse and keys and headed out the door. The muggy heat immediately smacked me in the face and sucked the oxygen from my lungs. Not even eight in the morning and already close to ninety degrees. When would this weather break?

I glanced around at the yard as I headed for my car. Only early July and already every plant and blade of grass had withered and died. By August my yard would look as bleak as a moonscape.

Up and down the street my neighbors' yards weren't faring much better, even the ones who had in-ground sprinkler systems and enough money not to worry about their water bills. That made me feel better. At least mine wasn't the only dead yard on the block.

I slid behind the steering wheel of my Hyundai, cranked down the window, and started the engine. I'd rather cool my heels at Sunnyside. Maybe one of my crafters was an early riser, and I could squeeze in an interview for my article while I waited for Shirley Hallstead.

"Girl, you're here early," said April when I entered the building. She'd traded her *Jerseylicious* T-shirt for one that stated *Jersey Girls Do It Down the Shore,* written in flowing hot pink glitter script on a black background. "You scheduled to work today?"

"No, I was hoping to catch Shirley before

she got busy with her day."

"She generally arrives around eight fifteen. Grab yourself a cup of coffee at the nurses' station. You can wait for her in her office."

I decided to forego tracking down one of my crafters for an unscheduled interview. Being allowed to wait in Shirley's office meant she'd have to make time to speak with me.

I grabbed some coffee and settled in behind Shirley's desk to wait for her. Part of me itched to nose through her files, but the sensible side of me figured she wouldn't dare keep any evidence at Sunnyside. She'd made too much of an effort to conceal the facts to be that careless. Instead, I settled back, sipped my coffee, and watched the second hand journey around the dial of her crystal desk clock.

At precisely eight twenty-one, with Birkin in hand and wearing her double-breasted cherry red power suit and matching stilettos, Shirley Hallstead entered her office. "What are you doing here?" she demanded.

"April suggested I wait in your office. We need to talk, Shirley."

"Your mother-in-law is not ready to leave, Mrs. Pollack. I spoke with her doctors yesterday, and they all agreed she needs more time until she's capable of getting around on her own. You saw that for yourself yesterday when she lost her balance. Now if you don't mind, I'd like my chair."

I stood but didn't move from behind the desk. "That's not what I came to discuss."

"Then what? I have a very busy schedule today, and I really wish you'd make an appointment ahead of time when you need to speak with me."

"Next time I will. For now, though, do the police know that Lyndella Wegner was your grandmother?"

FIFTEEN

Shirley froze; all the color drained from her face and neck. Without saying a word, her body language confirmed my hypothesis. She stared at me for several seconds before regaining a semblance of composure, then she closed the door behind her, but held fast to the doorknob. "I don't know how you found out," she said, "but if you're inferring I had something to do with her death, you're wrong."

"Why the secrecy?" I asked.

She released the knob and slowly walked across the room to her desk. When I stepped aside, she sat down, clutching her Birkin to her chest as if the pricey bag were a talisman that could ward off evil. I took the seat opposite her.

"Not that it's any of your business, but I suppose if I don't tell you, you'll go to the police."

"Which wouldn't look very good for you,

considering you told me that when murders occur in assisted living facilities and nursing homes, a staff member is usually charged and convicted. Even if you're innocent, the negative publicity would most likely ruin your career."

Shirley emitted a sigh of resignation. "How did you find out?"

"Lyndella wrote about you."

"Wrote about me?" The thought seemed inconceivable to her. "Where?"

"In her journals."

I wouldn't have thought it possible, but Shirley grew even whiter, and she began to tremble. Her voice came across as panicky. "Wh . . . what journals?"

"She kept binders of her various crafts projects."

"I know about those. I told Reggie to toss them with the rest of her crap." She paused and eyed me for a moment. "She didn't, did she?"

"No, she gave them to me, along with all of Lyndella's crafts. The ones you destroyed. Is that why you fired her and told the police you thought she killed Lyndella?"

"I fired Reggie for incompetence and disobedience. She never should have been hired in the first place, but my hands were tied."

"I heard."

Shirley raised an eyebrow. "For someone who's only been here a few days, you seem to know an awful lot about what goes on at Sunnyside."

"People talk."

"Don't believe everything you hear."

"Like the fact that you deliberately steered the police toward Reggie? You know she didn't kill Lyndella. That kid is scared of her own shadow."

"I know no such thing. Reggie fit the profile, an incompetent malcontent with self-esteem issues. The police agreed with me. That's why they picked her up for questioning. My call to them only sped things up a bit."

"Is she under arrest?"

"No, they let her go for lack of evidence, but that's beside the point. You haven't told me what those binders have to do with these journals you mentioned."

"They're one and the same. Lyndella wrote about what was going on in her life during the time she crafted each piece. Little notes scrawled in the margins of each page of directions. I read through them, hoping to find a clue to the identity of her killer."

"And did you?"

"You tell me."

"I already did. I didn't kill her. I tried to help her. If I'd wanted to kill her, why would I wait twenty years?"

"Maybe you finally snapped? She certainly took pleasure in yanking your chain."

Shirley's panicked expression grew more panicked. "She wrote that? What did she say?"

"She called you a tight-assed old prude." Actually, Lyndella had called Shirley far worse, but tears were beginning to well up in the eyes of the woman sitting across from me, and I saw no point in twisting the dagger I'd already plunged into her gut.

"What else?"

"She suspected you of destroying her business."

Shirley sniffed. "Is that what she called it? Her *business*? I was trying to protect her."

"She didn't see it that way."

"No." She took a shaky breath. "So what are you going to do with this newfound information, Mrs. Pollack? Go to the police? Blackmail me?"

"Blackmail?"

"I know you need the money. Why wouldn't you stoop to blackmail?"

"Because I'm not that kind of person. As for going to the police, they didn't bother taking the journals as evidence when they had the chance. I suppose they didn't look closely enough at them when they searched Lyndella's room. I have the big picture, but why don't you fill in the details for me? Then I'll decide what to do."

Shirley picked up her phone. "April, hold all my calls until further notice." After she hung up, she closed her eyes, and took several deep breaths, exhaling slowly between each before she finally spoke.

"I was adopted as an infant," she said, her eyes still closed. "My adoptive parents were wonderful people, but I was always curious about my birth parents. As I grew into adulthood and established my career, I became more and more obsessed with the blank spaces in my life. Gaps that could only be filled by learning more about who I really was, where I came from."

She opened her eyes and her voice grew strident as she said, "Working in healthcare, I came to realize that everyone should have the right to know about his or her background for medical reasons if nothing else."

"So you tracked your mother down?"

"No. I tried. Through various channels available to me, but I failed to find anything. The adoption was private, handled by a doctor and lawyer. Both had died, and my parents — my adoptive parents — never knew anything about my birth mother other than she was an unwed mother. They didn't even have a name."

Shirley let go of the death grip she'd maintained on her Birkin and placed it on her desk. She stood and began pacing back and forth across the small office as she continued speaking. "A little more than twenty years ago I had a health scare. Knowing my medical history would have helped tremendously at the time. After the crisis passed, I hired a private investigator. I didn't care how much it cost me; I needed to find my mother."

"Did you?"

She shook her head. "She died shortly after giving me up for adoption. Drug overdose, according to what the P.I. uncovered. But he did find an address for my maternal grandmother. For Lyndella."

"I can imagine that came as a bit of a shock."

Shirley laughed. "Did it ever! The investigator told me she ran a *dating service* in Savannah, Georgia."

"Which you took literally, not realizing he'd employed a euphemism?"

She nodded. "I was a lot younger and much more naïve back then. I decided to fly to Georgia to meet her." Shirley laughed an ironic laugh. "When I rang her doorbell, she thought I was applying for a job. She sized me up in a glance and dismissed me as lacking what she called the *je ne sais quoi* demanded by her upscale clientele. Can you believe that? The gall of the woman, telling me I wasn't good enough to be one of her hookers!"

That sounded like the Lyndella I'd come to know from our short acquaintance, her journals, and the other residents' stories about her. The woman never minced words, always spoke her mind, and didn't give a flying fig whom she hurt in the process.

"When I told her I was her granddaughter, she didn't believe me at first, but she finally came around and invited me in."

"Was this at The Savannah Club for Discerning Gentlemen?"

"You even know the name of the place?"

I nodded.

"No. She lived separate from her bordello. You have to understand, at that point I didn't know she ran a bordello. I still thought she operated a dating service. I was thinking in terms of a modern-day Dolly Levi."

"Who?"

"You know, like in *Hello, Dolly*?"

"Right."

"I had read some people still relied on matchmakers to find them the perfect marriage partner."

Living in New Jersey with its large Indian population, I knew about matchmakers and arranged marriages. However, I had no idea whether the custom extended to other immigrant groups, let alone non-immigrants.

"Anyway, once Lyndella accepted me as her granddaughter, we established a relationship. Every six to eight weeks I'd fly down to Georgia for a weekend. She told me about my mother, how she'd run off as a teenager, got mixed up with the wrong crowd, and gotten herself pregnant. According to Lyndella, my mother didn't even know who the father was. Lyndella convinced her to give me up for adoption."

"Because Lyndella knew how hard it was to raise a child as a single parent?"

Shirley shook her head. "She never mentioned that, but I came to suspect it because she never spoke about my mother's father. I don't even know if they ever married."

"I don't think so. Her journals suggest she became pregnant when she was only fifteen. She made plans for a wedding, but I came across no indication that a ceremony ever took place."

"I'm not surprised. Anyway, a few weeks after my mother gave me up for adoption, she OD'd. I guess I was lucky."

"How so?"

"I might otherwise have been raised by Lyndella."

A valid point. It couldn't have been easy for Shirley's mother, growing up in a whorehouse. Maybe Lyndella bore a good deal of the blame for her daughter running off and turning to drugs.

"Eventually, I learned the truth about Lyndella's business."

"You didn't suspect anything by the type of artwork in her home?"

"That trash decorated her business, not her home. I never saw any pornographic artwork or crafts until I moved her to Sunnyside."

"Then how did you find out about her business?"

"She wanted to groom me to take over for her when she retired."

"I'll bet that came as a shock."

"That's the understatement of the year. I was absolutely horrified when I found out."

"What did you do?"

"The only thing I could do. After all, she was my grandmother. I had to save her."

"Save her?"

"Her soul. She had to see the error of her ways and repent for her sins if there was any hope for her."

"Did you call the vice squad?"

Shirley shook her head. "Lyndella bragged that the police commissioner was one of her best clients. Along with the mayor and several other big city officials."

"I know."

"How could you know that?"

"She was in business for decades. Along with her craft journals I discovered an accounts ledger. Her clients wcre referred to by numbers and first names in the ledger, but she'd often embed the full name of someone within the directions for a craft. Her clientele went way beyond mere city officials."

"I suppose that shouldn't surprise me," said Shirley. "Not with all the political sex scandals of the last few years. Congressmen. Senators. Governors. It's disgusting."

"So what did you do?" I asked, steering the conversation back to Lyndella.

"I called an investigative reporter at the *Atlanta Journal-Constitution.*"

"Why an Atlanta paper?"

"I couldn't trust that a Savannah paper wouldn't bury the story. Or refuse even to investigate. Anyway, after the exposé the reporter wrote, the cops had no choice but to shut Lyndella down for good."

"And after that she chose to move to Sunnyside? I'm surprised she even spoke to you at that point."

"She didn't know at first that I was responsible for outing her. Besides, she had little choice. The D.A. froze her bank accounts and seized her assets. She was left with next to nothing."

"But she didn't go to jail." I knew this for a fact from Lyndella's journals. She cut a deal. In exchange for no jail time, she wouldn't name names. Given that many of her former clients now held positions at the state and federal levels — including one U.S. senator, four current and nine former congressmen, one current and one former cabinet member, and quite a few federal judges, not to mention one Supreme Court justice — the D.A. was pressured into making the offer.

"Lyndella was free but broke," I said, "so you offered her a place to live at Sunnyside."

"Where she proceeded to make everyone's life miserable for the next twenty years and probably would continue to do so for years to come had she not been murdered. I don't think that woman was ever sick a day in her life."

"Her way of getting back at you?"

"Yes, but I didn't kill her."

I believed her. Everything Shirley had said corresponded to the timeline of events I had pieced together from Lyndella's numerous journals and her accounts ledger. Shirley had dropped her defenses and bared her soul. I doubted the confession came easily.

In addition, I felt sorry for her. Although she hadn't said so, I imagine Shirley had hoped for a loving relationship with the grandmother she unexpectedly discovered two decades ago. Lyndella certainly hadn't lived up to anyone's idea of a grandmother.

And I thought my kids had it bad with Lucille. Lyndella Wegner made Lucille Pollack look like Cinderella's fairy godmother.

Someone knocked on the door. "Not now," yelled Shirley, her voice filled with annoyance.

The door opened and one of the nurse's aides poked her head in. "Sorry to interrupt but you're going to want to hear this, Ms. Hallstead."

Shirley morphed into her no-nonsense business persona. "What is it?"

"Mabel Shapiro has died."

"How?"

"Apparently, in her sleep, sometime last night."

Shirley opened the top drawer of her desk and pulled out a large magnifying glass. Then she accompanied the aide to Mabel's room. I followed.

Since Mabel lived in a single, no room-mate could supply any details of the previous night. Mabel reposed peacefully on her side under a quilt, her head facing away from us. Shirley rounded the bed and felt for a pulse.

"I already did that," said the aide. "Tried to wake her, too. She's definitely dead."

Shirley rolled Mabel over onto her back. "Bring that floor lamp closer," she told the aide, "and turn it on."

Mabel's face flooded with bright blue-white light. Shirley raised one of Mabel's eyelids, leaned over her, and stared into the magnifying glass.

"What are you looking for?" I asked.

"Petechial hemorrhaging." Under her breath she added, "Damn."

"What's wrong?" I asked.

She turned to the aide. "Call nine-one-one. We have another murder victim."

"How do you know?" I asked after the aide ran out of the room.

"The tiny red splotches on her eyes. They indicate Mabel was probably suffocated." She handed me the magnifying glass. "See for yourself."

I bent over Mabel and squinted through the glass. At first I didn't see anything, but with careful searching I finally noticed them. "They're barely the size of pin pricks."

"Which is why the nurse on duty last Saturday missed them on Lyndella."

"I thought Lyndella was strangled."

"She was, but petechiae can occur from strangulation as well."

"Is it normal to check deceased residents for telltale signs of foul play?"

"At this point do I need to remind you that mercy killings are not uncommon in assisted living facilities?"

"Or that someone on the staff usually turns out to be the killer," I added.

Shirley ignored my pointed comment. "I've taken seminars on signs to look for when a resident dies suddenly, especially residents in seemingly good health."

"So you think there's a serial killer running loose at Sunnyside?"

Shirley sighed. "It's beginning to look that way." She collapsed into one of Mabel's chairs and covered her face with her hands. Her shoulders shook as her tears flowed.

"How could this happen to me?" she choked out between huge sobs. "First Lyndella. Now Mabel. What did I do to deserve this? Why me? Why?"

Why *her*? Mabel Shapiro lay suffocated to death mere inches away from us, and all Shirley could do was feel sorry for herself? What about feeling sorry for poor Mabel? I shoved my hands deep into the side pockets of my skirt to keep from smacking Shirley. Not that I would have smacked her, but if anyone deserved a good smack at this moment, Shirley Hallstead was the prime candidate.

My sympathies belonged to Mabel. That feisty, bejeweled dynamo hadn't lived long enough to enjoy her new status as Queen of the Sunnyside Crafters, and that was a damn shame. Mabel had possessed serious spunk, and I liked that about her. Although she'd grown bossy — or bossier — since Lyndella's death, the other residents and the staff also seemed to like her well enough.

Who would want to kill her? One of the crafters she didn't tell about the gallery show? That hardly seemed motive for murder, especially if those residents didn't need the extra income, as Mabel had assured me.

Was her death related in some way to Lyndella's death? Or was the killer nondiscriminatory, simply taking advantage of opportunity, the identity of his victims not mattering because one dead old person was as good as another?

When the police arrived, they'd round up the staff and residents to start interviews. Under the circumstances, chances were slim that I'd be able to conduct any of my own interviews for my magazine article. I decided to leave for work before the police arrived, or I'd be forced to hang around for hours.

Feeling no obligation to hand-hold, I slipped out of Mabel's room while Shirley continued to wallow in her self-pity party.

SIXTEEN

When I arrived at work, I filled Cloris in on what I'd discovered about Shirley's relationship to Lyndella, and both deaths.

"Sounds awfully coincidental," she said. "Are you sure Sunnyside's director didn't kill them both?"

"I'm not sure of anything, but I saw a different side of Shirley Hallstead today. At first I found her controlling, arrogant, and dictatorial, a woman who'd stop at nothing to get her way. You should have seen the way she destroyed Lyndella's crafts because she'd wanted them thrown away, and I told the aide to bring them to me instead. Shirley could have just tossed them in the Dumpster when she learned they were in the arts and crafts room. Instead, she spent hours creating a pile of paper, wood, and fabric confetti."

"Maybe she's obsessive-compulsive. Or passive-aggressive."

"Probably both, but I think her behavior covers up a very sad and lonely woman who has little in life besides her job. She's defined by it; she'd be nothing without Sunnyside. You should have seen the way she twisted Mabel's death into her own personal crisis. For that reason, my gut tells me she didn't kill anyone. She'd have far too much to lose."

"Maybe your gut is just telling you you're hungry. You'll find raspberry apricot blondies in the break room, assuming the vultures left any. I'm off to a photo shoot."

I ducked into the break room and found one lone blondie sitting on a platter from the test kitchen. I grabbed it before anyone else came goody sniffing, poured myself a cup of coffee, and headed for my cubicle.

After checking my email and printing out a list of the crafts Clara had chosen, I phoned Kara. Maybe she had something more to offer about Lyndella and Mabel that might point me in the direction of their killer.

Kara answered on the second ring. "I was wondering when you'd get around to calling," she said.

"You didn't warn me I was walking into a geriatric soap opera, complete with a killer on the loose."

258

"A killer? What do you mean? Who's dead?"

"Haven't you heard from anyone at Sunnyside?"

"Not a word. What's going on?"

"How much time do you have?"

"From now until junior decides it's time to make his grand entrance. I'm on mandatory bed rest. Dish, girl!"

I quickly caught Kara up on everything that had happened at Sunnyside since she left last Friday.

"Unbelievable," she said. "And now Shirley thinks Mabel was murdered, too?"

"Mabel's death should at least cause the police to look elsewhere for their killer. As far as I know, my mother-in-law had no interaction with Mabel. Not that I believe she killed Lyndella."

"I agree with you about Reggie. That kid wouldn't have the strength to strangle or suffocate anyone, let alone the disposition. Shirley, on the other hand? I wouldn't put anything past her, but why now?"

"Exactly. Reading through Lyndella's journals, I came across no evidence that anything had changed in her relationship with Shirley. The two of them carried on a mutual animosity for twenty years. Lyndella wrote nothing about any recent escalation from either of them."

"I saw nothing different over the last few weeks. Shirley made a point of keeping her distance from Lyndella as much as possible. Then again, so did most of the staff and residents. Lyndella was Shirley's grandmother? I can't get over that." Kara chuckled.

"Can you think of anyone who'd want both Lyndella and Mabel dead?"

"Lyndella, yes. Mabel? Definitely not. People liked that feisty little broad, especially for the way she refused to take shit from Lyndella." Kara paused. "Really, I can't think of anyone. Sorry. But I'm sure the police will find whomever killed both of them."

"Hopefully, before he strikes again."

"Or she," added Kara.

Funny how I kept thinking of the killer in terms of a *he* when every suspect on either the police radar or mine was female. Why did I have difficulty thinking of women as killers when two of them had nearly killed me only weeks ago? Maybe because it seemed so wrong that the part of the population that brings new life into the world could be capable of taking away life. Something about that seemed so wrong.

When I thought about male suspects,

though, I drew a blank. Unless the killer was a staff member performing random mercy killings, no man stuck out as a possibility. Yet, if the murders were mercy killings, wouldn't the killer strike critically ill residents where he'd more likely be able to get away with his crimes?

Both Lyndella and Mabel were in excellent health for women their age. Lyndella's death was ruled a homicide as soon as the medical examiner looked at her body. According to Shirley, the same would happen when he examined Mabel's body.

Surely, a staff member on a killing spree would employ less detectable methods of murder. The nurses, nurses aides, and doctors all had access to a host of barbiturates and other medications that could be administered by syringe to an IV line or directly into the person's body without drawing suspicion to themselves.

If I ruled out staff members, that left male residents of Sunnyside, quite a narrow pool of candidates. The women residents outnumbered the men by at least four or five to one. None of the men ever did more than grumble about Lyndella, and I don't remember hearing a single unkind word said about Mabel from any of them.

Who did that leave? As far as I knew, no

one. Was it possible we were dealing with two separate killers?

I decided I needed to devote additional time to studying Lyndella's more recent journals. If we were dealing with one Sunnyside killer on the loose, it now seemed unlikely that the killer was someone from Lyndella's past.

I'd written off Shirley as Lyndella's killer. A killer with a long-standing grudge against Lyndella from her past seemed unlikely. Besides, such a person would have no reason to target Mabel. From everything I'd pieced together, Lyndella and Mabel first met when Lyndella moved to Sunnyside twenty years ago.

I had only one other theory involving someone from Lyndella's Savannah days. With a clientele list that had included many past and present politicians, what if the killer was a former client currently contemplating a run for national office? Someone like that would be intent on ridding himself of any unsavory connections to his past.

Perhaps he'd already dealt with all his previous dalliances, systematically working his way up to the former madam of The Savannah Club for Discerning Gentlemen. A little Googling around the Internet might turn up whether there had recently been a rash of ex-call girl murders in Savannah.

But would a man with such high aspirations hire out his dirty work, setting himself up for future blackmail, or would he carry out the murders himself?

And where did Mabel fit into such a scenario?

"Is it possible Mabel Shapiro was just the victim of being in the wrong place at the wrong time?" asked Zack. I needed a sounding board, and to my great fortune (the only type of fortune I was ever bound to experience the remainder of my days on earth), he'd returned from D.C. Or whichever nameless locale he'd really flown to in order to do whatever bidding he really does for the guys in the dark suits.

I played nice, though, and didn't ask. He wouldn't have told me the truth, anyway. Meanwhile, wherever he'd been and whatever he'd been doing, he must have received partial payment in cow and maize. Zack had arrived back in Westfield bearing a cooler of T-bones and freshly picked sweet corn, which he was currently grilling to perfection on my back patio. The aroma definitely made up for standing outside over a hot grill in yet another scorcher in our endless summer heat wave. Although Mama and the boys played it smarter by waiting inside the slightly cooler air-conditioned house.

"If so, why would he wait three nights after killing Lyndella to kill Mabel? If she saw something, he ran the risk of her talking to the police in the interim."

"What if at first he didn't know she saw or heard something?"

I mulled that over. "He still wouldn't have known whether or not she had spoken to the police."

"True. Unless she told him. These are ready to flip." He reached his hand out for the jar of garlic powder I held.

I unscrewed the lid and handed him the jar. "That would have been pretty stupid of her, and Mabel never struck me as stupid."

"It also eliminates anyone in the public eye," added Zack as he first sprinkled the garlic, then flipped the steaks. "I think people at Sunnyside would have noticed a political wannabe roaming the halls."

"Definitely. Besides, by definition those guys aren't capable of milling around senior citizens without glad-handing everyone in sight."

Zack turned to face me. "Which means it's more likely that the politico hired himself some muscle, and there's a professional killer on the loose at Sunnyside."

"If it is a politico. I want to comb through Lyndella's journals again tonight. Maybe I've overlooked something."

Zack's serious face grew more serious. "Maybe it's time to give that detective a call."

"Tomorrow. I need more credible evidence. Otherwise, Detective Spader will dismiss me as nothing more than a conspiracy theory crackpot."

Zack raised his eyebrows at that. He already thought I was a conspiracy theory crackpot where he was concerned. I guess he figured what's one more crackpot theory when you already wear the crackpot title.

Once the steaks and corn were cooked, the five of us gathered around the kitchen table to devour Zack's bounty. I'd managed one heavenly bite of T-bone when Mama said all too casually, "Oh, I forgot to mention, dear. Ira called before you and the boys arrived home."

I had hoped after Alex and Nick's disastrous Parents Day trip with Ira to his kids' camp that we might not hear from Karl's half-brother again. Apparently, the day in the Catskills didn't bother Ira as much as it bothered his kids and mine. "What did he want?"

"He's invited us over for a barbecue

265

Friday evening to meet his wife. I checked Alex's and Nick's work schedules for Friday. Neither of them is working that night, so I accepted for all of us."

"Mom!" Alex groaned.

"Do we have to go?" asked Nick.

Mama jumped in before I could respond. She patted Nick's hand and said, "Don't be silly. Of course you're going. Ira is family, and you have little enough family as it is."

"And what if I had plans for Friday evening, Mama?" Like a date with a bubble bath, followed by one with my pillow.

The added stress since settling Lucille in at Sunnyside last Friday — not to mention the unending heat wave — had totally zapped me. I'd give anything for just one lazy, stress-free day, but I'd settle for a few hours Friday evening. Which is what I had planned. Now I wouldn't even have that.

"Don't worry, dear. Ira invited Zack, too. He even suggested springing that batty Bolshevik for a few hours, but I talked him out of that. Why ruin what promises to be a delightful evening, right?"

My mouth dropped open. I literally did not know how to respond to this ambush from my mother. I turned to Zack for help and found his mouth hanging open, too.

■ ■ ■ ■

Whether Zack thought he was humoring me or protecting me, he stuck around after dinner and helped me pore through Lyndella's journals yet one more time. Alex and Nick were much smarter, accepting an invitation to swim at a neighbor's pool. Mama joined them. I thought about sneaking down the street and hiding in the bushes to see if she hooked up with a special someone while there, but my work ethic got the better of me. Besides, I could always cross-examine my sons about their grandmother later that night or tomorrow.

My eyes grew gritty from the strain of reading Lyndella's miniscule script, but I continued to read every word, this time concentrating on the last six weeks of her life. At one point I found a single tantalizing inscription — *found a golden ticket* — but no clue as to what the phrase meant. I doubted it referred to Willy Wonka.

I had previously created a list of all Lyndella's clients from her accounts ledger and matched them to names I found hidden in her crafting journals from corresponding time periods. Zack decided to go over the names from the last ten years that The Savannah Club for Discerning Gentlemen had been in business, hoping to spot someone currently making a name for himself in politics.

"If only we were more familiar with Georgian politics," he said. "None of these names is jumping out at me."

"Do you think it's worth searching further back, beyond ten years?"

"Pointless. What are the chances that someone old enough to frequent a gentleman's club over thirty years ago would just be getting into politics now?"

"Slim to none?" Neither of us had heard of any potential national candidates from Georgia or elsewhere older than their early sixties.

"If I never see another handcrafted sex toy in my life, I'll die happy," I said at one point after reading through directions for dildos made of every conceivable medium known to the arts.

"It's a shame Sunnyside's director destroyed all of Lyndella's artwork," said Zack.

"Oh?" I bemoaned the loss of such fine craftsmanship, even given the subject matter, but I questioned Zack's interest in the vandalized pieces.

"She was Lyndella's only living heir, right?"

"As far as either of us knows."

"I'll bet the Museum of Sex in Manhattan would have paid a fortune for that collection."

I'd braced for some prurient comment, and Zack handed me a goldmine of an economic one. I laughed in spite of myself. Or maybe I should be crying. If only I'd had room in my car for additional cartons Sunday afternoon, I might now find myself out of hock and firmly planted back in middle-classdom.

After hours of reading with not a hint of a suspect, I finally stumbled across something I'd missed earlier from one of Lyndella's last craft projects. "Look at this." I pointed to a cryptic line written within the directions for a pair of cloisonné nipple clips. The letters were so tiny that at first I'd mistaken the writing for a wavy underline. Had Lyndella written her comment with the aid of a magnifying glass? I certainly needed one to read what she'd written.

"Ouch!" said Zack. "I wonder who modeled those for her."

"I don't want to know." The body in the photo was way too young by half a century or more to be Lyndella. One of Sunnyside's staff perhaps? I slapped my hand over the photo so that Zack would instead concentrate on the writing on the page. "Take a look at what she wrote at the end of the list of supplies."

Zack squinted at the print and read aloud, *"Disturbing. I never used to forget a face."*

"Now look what's buried within the fourth step in the directions, between the second and fourth lines."

I pointed to another wavy line that was actually a sentence. Zack read, *"Why can't I place him?* Not much to go on," he said.

"But there's more." I showed him the last clue, the *coup de grace* sentence I'd found between the fifth and seventh lines of the ninth step in the directions. My cheeks infused with heat as Zack stared wide-eyed at Lyndella's words: *A good fuck should refresh my memory.*

SEVENTEEN

"Well," Zack finally said.

"Yeah."

"So you're thinking —"

"The killer had to be someone fairly new to Sunnyside. Someone Lyndella thought she recognized but couldn't place. He certainly wouldn't have used his real name if he came to kill her."

"And luring him into her bed would clear the cobwebs from her mind?" Zack laughed. "Sex usually acts as a soporific on the brain, not a stimulant."

"But maybe if you've had as much sex over a lifetime as Lyndella did, you come to realize that no two men make love the same way. If she'd previously slept with the guy, the way he performed might trigger a memory."

Zack saw where I was going. "You're thinking Lucille wasn't dreaming Friday night, that Lyndella did have sex with

271

someone, and that someone was her killer."

"Given what she wrote, it's a plausible theory. All I need to find out is which male residents and staff members were new to Sunnyside."

"No," said Zack.

"No?"

"What you need to do now is hand over those journals and your theory to the investigating detective. Let the professionals deal with this."

"Party pooper." Although I offered Zack my most petulant pout, I was relieved that I finally had enough credible evidence to take to the police. Maybe *credible evidence* was stretching it a bit. What I really had was a working theory and lots of circumstantial evidence, but it was credible circumstantial evidence that should cause Detective Spader to take me somewhat seriously.

At least, I hoped so. Having already suffered a close call with one quasi–hit man five months ago, I had no intention of deliberately putting myself in harm's way again. I had one major problem, though. I still had to spend time at a place where a hit man either lived or worked.

As soon as I arrived at work the next day, I phoned Detective Spader.

A woman answered. "Detective Spader's phone."

"Is he available?" I asked. "This is Anastasia Pollack calling. I'd like to speak with him about the Sunnyside investigation."

"Are you a reporter?"

"No, I work part-time at Sunnyside, and I have some information for him."

"One moment." Instead of placing me on hold, she covered the phone's mouthpiece, and I heard her shout a muffled, "Hey, Sam! Call for you."

Sam? The guy's name was *Sam* Spader? Once again the universe had punned me. Ever since Dead Louse of a Spouse died five months ago, I'd found myself dealing with a series of law enforcement types whose superiors had to have smoked wacky weed when they partnered up their cops. So far I'd come in contact with Officers Simmons and Garfinkle and Detectives Batswin and Robbins in Morris County and Detectives Phillips and Marlowe in Manhattan. Now Detective Sam Spader in Union County. I had to add his parents to my wacky weed theory. So far only Westfield patrolmen Harley and Fogarty seemed to have escaped pun-free, unless Harley's first name was Davidson.

"Spader here."

Luckily, he'd taken enough time getting to his phone that I'd overcome my urge to giggle. When I spoke, I sounded like an intelligent adult. After introducing myself, I asked if he'd made any headway in solving Lyndella's murder.

"I can't discuss an ongoing case, ma'am."

I knew he'd say that, but I figured it didn't hurt to ask. "I think I may have stumbled across something that might help you," I said. "Can we make an appointment to meet?"

"Are you at Sunnyside now?"

"No, I only work there on weekends. I'm at my full-time job up in Morris County."

"How about if you come over to headquarters on your way home from work this evening?"

"Would it be possible for you to meet me at my home instead?" The last thing I wanted to do was lug all those cartons of binders from my house to my car and then from my car into Union County police headquarters, all in blistering heat, especially when collecting evidence fell under Detective Spader's job description, not mine. I'd happily acquiesce the lugging to him.

After we agreed on a time, I hung up, ready to start my day. First up, I collated

274

the crafts Clara had chosen with the questionnaires the residents had filled out for me. To my great relief, Clara had decided to feature at least three items from each of the crafters in the group and as many as half a dozen from some.

To my great surprise, most of the questionnaires remained empty aside from the crafters' names. No one had even listed his or her age. Holy paranoia! It's not like I asked for their birth dates. Most hadn't even told me how long they'd been crafting. I suppose I'd have to wheedle the information out of them on a one-on-one basis. If they wanted to be part of the magazine article, they'd have to cough up at least some details of their lives.

By two-thirty I'd checked off the day's must-do items from our various in-production issues. With an hour to spare, I should have no trouble arriving back in Westfield in plenty of time for the first of the interviews I'd scheduled with the Sunnyside crafters.

Of course, I hadn't factored in the overturned semi and resulting five-car pileup that ground traffic on Route 287 to a standstill. After being diverted off the interstate and through towns with twenty-five-mile-an-hour speed limits, I finally arrived at Sunnyside forty-five minutes late.

I expected to find Mabel cooling her rhinestone bedazzled heels and walker in the lobby and braced myself for a lecture on punctuality until I remembered Mabel would never lecture me about anything ever again. Instead, April greeted me.

"Girl, you work as much as I do. What'cha doing here today?"

"Me? What about you? I've never seen another receptionist sitting at that desk."

April shrugged her shoulders, bouncing both her boobs and her mass of cornrows up and down. Today she wore a Kelly green T-shirt with a huge red *Jersey Tomato* stamped across the front.

"Shirley gives me all the hours I want. I'm saving to go to beauty school. Me and my cousin, we're gonna open our own day spa some day. Already have a name picked out for it. April May, and June. Her name's June. Cute, huh?"

"Definitely."

She beamed. "Oh, I almost forgot. Sally Strathower was looking for you. She said if you ever showed up to tell you she'd be in the computer room."

I didn't know Sunnyside had a dedicated computer room. "Where's that?" I asked.

"Four doors down from the arts and crafts room."

I thanked April and headed in search of Sally, my first interview for the day.

I found her sitting at one of six computer terminals that lined three walls of the small room. Five other residents worked at the other computers. The fourth wall held a printer, a shelf of computer manuals, and several reams of paper. "You're late," she said when I walked over to her.

"Sorry. I got caught behind a pile-up on 287. Can we go somewhere private to talk?"

"Soon as I finish updating my Facebook page."

Facebook? I glanced over Sally's shoulder to study her page. For someone concerned about identity theft, she certainly wasn't shy about posting all sorts of information about her private life for Mark Zuckerberg and the rest of the Facebook Nation to view.

While Sally typed away, I wandered around the confines of the tiny room, surreptitiously glancing at the other computer screens. Barbara was Tweeting, Estelle and Berniece were catching up on email correspondence, Jerome was surfing eligible women on eHarmony, and Murray was losing big at online poker. No wonder he needed extra cash.

"Okay," said Sally, coming up behind me and grabbing my arm. "I'm done. Let's go."

She led me to the library. Glancing inside, we found the room empty. "This work for you?" she asked.

"Sure."

After we settled in on one of the leather sofas, she asked, "How many of my pieces does the gallery want?"

I pulled out my paperwork on Sally and showed her copies of the photos Clara had chosen.

"Only six pieces? I was hoping she'd want them all since they don't take up much space." Sally had brought three dozen pieces of jewelry for me to photograph the other day.

"It's a small gallery," I reminded her. "You had more pieces chosen than many of the others, and no one had more than six items picked." This elicited a smile from her. "Plus, if the pieces sell, the gallery owner will want more from you."

Sally's eyes sparkled with glee. Or were those dollar signs I saw dancing in her eyes?

"I noticed you didn't fill out any information on your form," I said.

"Murray convinced us not to. He said you never know where personal information will wind up and how it will be used against you."

"When did he say this?"

"While you were taking the photographs."

"I didn't hear him."

"He whispered it to each of us."

I decided not to point out the hypocrisy of having a Facebook page. Becoming confrontational wouldn't get my article written. I took out my notebook and pen and said, "I see, but that causes me a bit of a dilemma. So how about if we compromise?"

"In what way?"

"For starters, instead of me mentioning everyone's age, what if you give me a range for the crafters? I don't even need names, just how young is the youngest and how old is the oldest."

Sally thought this over for a minute, a scowl on her face, her clear gray eyes focused on me throughout her thought process. "I suppose that wouldn't hurt," she finally said, "except I don't know everyone's exact age. Maybe late sixties through early nineties. Lyndella was the oldest, but she doesn't count anymore."

I made a note. "That works. And have you always done handcrafts?"

"I always knitted. My mother taught me

when I became pregnant with my first child, but I didn't take up any other crafts until I retired."

"What did you do before you retired?"

She scowled again.

I sighed. "I don't need a company name, Sally, just an occupation."

"Why?"

"Because this is a human interest story. Our readers want to be able to relate in some way to the people they read about in our magazine."

She nodded. "You can put down that I worked in the banking industry."

"Were you a teller?"

She squared her shoulders and puffed out her chest. "A branch manager, but don't say that."

If all my other interviewees were this close-mouthed, I'd wind up writing the most boring human interest story ever to grace the pages of *American Woman*. Naomi would pitch a fit, especially since the issue's slant had been my idea. I tried a different approach. "What got you interested in making beaded jewelry?"

"One of the other Sunnyside residents."

"Care to tell me which one?"

Sally shook her head. "Doesn't matter. She died a few years ago."

After pulling teeth with Sally for about fifteen minutes, I ended the interview, hoping I'd have better luck with some of the other crafters. Before I left, though, I changed the subject. "Sunnyside seems almost like a family to me. I imagine you all grow very close to the staff over the years."

Sally pulled a face and waved my words away with a flick of her hand.

"No?"

"This place is like a revolving door. No one hangs around all that long."

"Really? With jobs so hard to come by these days?"

"They don't leave until they've lined up something else, but would you work for Shirley Hallstead longer than you had to?"

"So in the last month or so would you estimate there have been many new employees?"

"At least a dozen. Nurses, aides, orderlies, cafeteria workers, housekeeping staff. You name it. Hard to keep them all straight half the time." She narrowed her eyes at me. "Why all the interest?"

I shrugged. "No reason other than curiosity." And the need to form a list of possible killers.

"Odd thing to be curious about. You sure there isn't something you're not telling me?"

"Me? Sally, what reason would I have for withholding information like that from you?" I stood, thanked her for her time, said good-bye, and went in search of my second interview subject.

Barbara proved no more forthcoming than Sally. Neither did Estelle, Berniece, or Dirk. I'd set aside two hours to interview four people. Even with arriving forty-five minutes late, I wound up finishing early. I expected just as little cooperation with the remaining crafters I still needed to interview.

I also realized that with Mabel dead, we were one crafter short. Did I choose someone else from the group of crafters not in need of extra cash, or should I ask Clara to pick some extra projects from those not chosen? I saw no point in asking my eleven surviving crafters for their input. I knew what they'd decide. So I made an executive decision to toss the problem off to Clara.

I ducked out of Sunnyside without encountering either Shirley or Lucille, and headed home. I still had one more interview to get through today, but I wouldn't be the one asking the questions.

EIGHTEEN

When I suggested Detective Spader come to my home, not only was I thinking about all those cartons of binders but Alex's and Nick's work schedules. Both boys would be working this evening.

As for Mama, given her mysterious and secretive ways of late, I didn't expect to find her home, either. If she was, I'd prep her ahead of time, warning her to keep her mouth firmly sealed regarding Lucille.

Mama would like nothing better than to see my mother-in-law locked up for the rest of her life, even if she had to spin a web of fiction to make it happen. Then again, if asked, Lucille would probably profess a similar desire regarding Mama.

I arrived home to find both the house and the driveway empty. I had no idea whether Zack was off running an errand or on assignment again in some faraway part of the globe. Our relationship hadn't progressed to the point where we shared our daily schedules. Something told me no matter how far the relationship progressed, I'd never really know where Zack was on any given day.

After walking Mephisto and letting Ralph out of his cage, I made myself a tuna sandwich, cut up some carrot sticks and cucumber slices to go with it, and ate dinner while watching the news. My doorbell rang as Diane Sawyer was signing off for the evening from *ABC World News.*

"Detective Spader," I greeted him. "Please come in." I led him into the dining room where I'd stacked the cartons of binders on the floor and left some pertinent ones spread out across the table.

"Have a seat. Would you like a cold drink?"

"A glass of ice water, if you don't mind, ma'am. This heat is something else."

Especially when you're lugging around an extra hundred pounds or so, I thought. Not to mention wearing a jacket and tie. I wondered if he also wore a bullet-proof vest under his shirt. I'd seen a piece on the news about a device that cops hooked up to the air-conditioning vent in their cars and slipped the other end between their vest and body. From the looks of him, I doubted

Detective Spader owned one.

I headed for the kitchen as Ralph zoomed into the dining room and perched on the back of the chair opposite the detective. "Don't mind Ralph," I called over my shoulder. "He's just curious."

When I returned with his water, Detective Spader already had his little spiral notebook out, a pencil stub poised in his hand, ready to take down any pertinent information I had to offer him. He took a long swig of water, then asked, "What was it you wanted to tell me, Mrs. Pollack?"

"I found some clues in Lyndella Wegner's journals. I thought you'd want to know about them."

"Journals? What journals? And how the hell did you get hold of them?"

I indicated the binders spread across the table and stacked in the cartons on the floor, explaining how I'd come into possession of them. "If I hadn't taken them, they'd be rotting in some landfill right now."

"We looked at those," he said, dismissing them with a wave of his hand. "They're not journals, just directions for craft projects."

"That's where you're wrong."

He glared at me. I suppose telling a detective he's wrong isn't such a smart move. I quickly pushed on. "One of them is an accounts ledger for the bordello she owned."

"How the hell do you —"

"And had you read through the others —"

"There was nothing to read through, just directions —"

"You would have found that Mrs. Wegner kept a diary of sorts hidden within the pages of those craft project directions."

The detective's angry glare morphed into a wide-eyed, jaw-dropping gape. "Seriously?"

"Seriously."

"Prove it."

Over the next hour I showed Detective Spader how I'd uncovered Lyndella's background and figured out her relationship to Shirley Hallstead. His jaw dropped farther. "I'm assuming Shirley didn't tell you she was Lyndella's granddaughter, did she?"

"I can't comment on an ongoing investigation."

He didn't have to. The anger in his narrowed eyes, the clench of his jaw, and the bulging veins in his neck told me everything I needed to know.

Or maybe he'd already figured out their blood relationship through other means not at my disposal. He may have been keeping the fact a closely guarded secret until he'd completed his investigation. Detective Spader's anger might be over the fact that I'd stumbled upon the same information.

I ignored his anger and pressed on. "I think that Lyndella wanted to keep detailed records of her clients but at the same time had to protect the privacy of those clients to sustain her business. She must have had a reputation for being very discreet for such an establishment to last as long as it had."

Detective Spader agreed. "If those records fell into the wrong hands, she'd wind up in all sorts of hot water."

"Both she and her clients, and not necessarily with law enforcement."

"Right. So you're saying she developed a sort of code for her record keeping?"

"Lyndella had a huge knowledge of art. Leonardo da Vinci kept notebooks filled with details that would have gotten him burned at the stake had anyone read them. However, because he wrote in code, no one could decipher those notes to determine what he had written."

"And you figured out Mrs. Wegner developed her own system of hiding information?"

"Hiding in plain sight. Just like da Vinci. I only figured all of this out because I was fascinated with her detailed documentation of her handiwork. No one else would have bothered to read through those directions line for line."

When I'd finished explaining how I'd cross-referenced the ledger with the journals, I showed him the list of past and present politicians and judges I'd compiled. "I know it's all circumstantial evidence, but I have what I think is a plausible theory as to who killed her."

He folded his arms across his chest and leaned back in his chair. "Okay, let's hear it."

I filled him in, ending with, "The killer has to be some guy fairly new to Sunnyside. Either a resident or one of the staff. And he was hired by one of Lyndella's former clients who couldn't afford to have his past membership in The Savannah Club for Discerning Gentlemen exposed. That most likely makes him from Georgia, in his fifties or early sixties, and on the political fast track for national office."

Detective Spader chewed on my words as he chewed on the inside of his cheek. "And you came up with all of this from bits and pieces she hid throughout those loose-leaf binders?"

I nodded.

"Very impressive, Mrs. Pollack."

I thought so, but opted not to agree with

him. No one likes a wise ass. Besides, he and his department had totally overlooked valuable evidence. No sense rubbing it in. After the turn my life had taken over the past five months, I'd learned it's best to have the cops on your side. Especially hometown cops.

"I'm going to need to take all of these," he said, making a sweeping wave of his arm to encompass all the binders.

"Of course. I don't suppose I could get them back at some point after they're no longer needed?"

He raised his eyebrows. "Got a thing for X-rated art?"

"No, detective, I've got a thing for expert craftsmanship. Lyndella was an artist. I might not care for her subject matter, but these are historical documents that would be prized by many museums. I only wish Shirley hadn't destroyed all of Lyndella's work."

"Destroyed? You didn't tell me that."

"I brought home the journals the day Reggie delivered them to the art room, but after hauling all these cartons out to my car, I didn't have room for the cartons of crafts. I left them in the art room, figuring I'd bring them home the next day. When I arrived at Sunnyside the next morning, I discovered someone had reduced all of Lyndella's artwork to dust, shards, and confetti."

"Ms. Hallstead admitted destroying them?"

"Not in so many words, but she didn't deny it."

He made a notation in his notebook. "Anything else you've forgotten to tell me, Mrs. Pollack?"

I thought for a moment. "No, I don't think so, but I have your card if I remember anything else."

He leveraged himself out of the dining room chair. "Then I'll take these cartons and be on my way. Thank you for your help."

"You didn't answer my question about the journals," I reminded him.

"If Ms. Hallstead is Mrs. Wegner's only living relative, the binders belong to her."

"She'll destroy them."

Detective Spader shrugged. "Her right."

I think he expected me to help haul the cartons out to his car. Instead I limited my assistance to opening and closing the front door to keep the cool air and the pets inside while he schlepped back and forth. If I couldn't keep the binders, I saw no reason to waste any further muscle power on them.

Once Detective Spader pulled away from

the curb, I considered the rest of my evening. Now that I no longer had Lyndella's journals to pore over, I should turn my attention to the job I got paid to do. Since I still had a carton full of Lyndella's fabric yo-yos, I could assemble the Christmas ornaments for the November issue in very little time. Or I could scrub the bathrooms and kitchen. I opted for the yo-yos.

Yo-yos can be used to make a variety of Christmas ornaments. Here are three quick and easy ones. For variety, make the basic tree, angel, and snowman ornaments, but use your imagination and various craft supplies you have on hand to decorate them as you desire.

Note: Fabric glue or a glue gun can be used for all gluing except when attaching plastic beads and gemstones. Use the glue gun or jewelry glue to adhere those items.

YO-YO TREE ORNAMENT
Materials
basic yo-yo supplies to sew 6 green print
   and 1 brown print yo-yo made from a 4″
   circle template and 1 gold print yo-yo
   made from a 3″ circle template
6 red 1/2″ buttons
25mm flat-back gold star acrylic gemstone

8" length of red 1/4" wide satin or grosgrain ribbon

glue gun or fabric glue and jewelry glue

Directions

Make the yo-yos following the Basic Yo-yo directions (pp. 32–34). Stitch a button over the center of each of the green print yo-yos.

Glue the star acrylic gemstone over the center hole of the gold yo-yo.

To assemble the tree, all yo-yos will slightly overlap each other in each step. Glue three green yo-yos in a horizontal row with middle yo-yo on top. This is the bottom of the tree. Glue two green yo-yos together for middle row. Glue bottom row centered over middle row. Glue middle row centered over remaining green yo-yo. Glue bottom row centered over brown yo-yo. Glue gold yo-yo centered over top green yo-yo.

Fold the ribbon in half. Glue cut ends to top back of tree for hanging loop.

YO-YO ANGEL ORNAMENT

Materials

basic yo-yo supplies to sew 1 print (color of choice) and 1 white yo-yo made from 6" circle template

1" two-hole wooden button, 2 black #8

glass beads

1″ flat-back heart acrylic gemstone in coordinating color

8″ length of 1/4″ wide satin or grosgrain ribbon in coordinating color

glue gun or fabric glue and jewelry glue

peach acrylic paint and brush (optional)

Directions

If desired, paint the wooden button. Allow to dry.

Make the yo-yos following the Basic Yo-yo directions. To form the wings, sew a running stitch from the top of the white yo-yo to the center hole. Pull to gather. Tie off thread.

Glue the heart acrylic gemstone over the center hole of the print yo-yo. This will be the body.

Glue the wings to the back of the body so that the gathered section extends above the top of the body. Keeping the button holes horizontal, glue the button to the top of the body. Apply a small amount of glue inside the buttonholes. Set a bead in each buttonhole for eyes.

Fold the ribbon in half. Glue cut ends to top back of angel for hanging loop.

Yo-yo Snowman Ornament

Materials

basic yo-yo supplies to sew 1 white yo-yo each made from 4″, 5″, and 6″ circle templates

2 black pebble beads

1 orange pony bead

1 brown chenille stem

3 15mm flat-back gold star acrylic gemstones

8″ length of 1/4″ wide satin or grosgrain ribbon

glue gun or fabric glue and jewelry glue

Directions

Make the yo-yos following the Basic Yo-yo directions.

Overlapping the yo-yos slightly, glue the 5″ yo-yo to the top of the 6″ yo-yo and the 4″ yo-yo to the top of the 5″ yo-yo.

Glue the orange pony bead over the center hole of the top yo-yo for a nose. Glue the two black pebble beads above the nose for the eyes. Glue a star over the center holes of the remaining yo-yos and another evenly spaced between the first two stars.

Cut a 5″ length of chenille stem. Glue to back of center yo-yo so ends extend out on either side for arms. Cut two 1″ pieces from remaining chenille stem section and twist onto each arm to form branches.

Fold the ribbon in half. Glue cut ends to top back of snowman for hanging loop.

By the time Mama and the boys arrived home, I'd completed the three Christmas yo-yo ornaments and typed up the directions. For once, I wouldn't be rushing at the last minute to finish up models in time for my scheduled photography session. Given the lack of cooperation I experienced earlier today, I had a feeling I'd need all the extra time I could snag to devote to my article on the Sunnyside crafters.

The next day I left work at noon to head to Sunnyside for the remainder of my scheduled interviews with the crafters. This time the traffic gods smiled down on me. If only the weather gods had been as accommodating, not to mention the interview gods.

The air-conditioning unit in my rust-bucket Hyundai finally died on me a few miles east of Trimedia. No longer did the vents whisper an occasional breath of cool air. Now they blasted me with nothing but engine heat. I turned off the useless contraption and continually sipped water as I traveled to Sunnyside.

The car had baked for hours sitting in Trimedia's shade-free parking lot. With an outdoor temperature of a hundred and two degrees, the interior temperature had to be a hundred and twenty. At least. Touching the steering wheel burned my hands. In order to drive, I had had to wad up tissues, using them as insulation between my palms and the steering wheel.

The blistering heat had one upside, though. Stepping on the scale this morning for the first time in two weeks, I discovered I'd shed five pounds, probably by sweating them off, but who's complaining? That's 10 percent of the fifty I'd tried to lose since forever. Only 90 percent to go. Maybe I should embrace the heat rather than complain about it.

By the time I arrived in Westfield, pools of perspiration had collected in every nook and cranny of my body. Whatever the cost of repairing the air conditioning, I knew I couldn't afford it. Until this heat wave ended (would it ever?), I'd have to travel with a spare set of clothes, washcloth, and towel in the car.

A sniff of my armpits told me I needed to stop at home to jump in the shower and change my outfit first. Better to be a few minutes late for my interviews than arrive dripping with sweat and smelling like a cave woman.

Luckily, Mama wasn't entertaining the mystery man she planned to make my next stepfather. I found her eating a ham sandwich at the kitchen table.

Without looking up from *Vogue,* she said, "How nice that you're home so early, dear! How would you like to take me shopping? We can both buy new outfits for the barbecue this evening. Look." She turned the magazine around to face me and pointed to the Lord & Taylor ad on the left-hand page. "Isn't that the most adorable sundress? I think it would look very flattering on you."

The barbecue! I'd totally forgotten. Just how I wanted to spend my Friday evening, sweltering outdoors with a total stranger and her nearly total stranger husband. "I'm only home to shower and change, Mama."

That's when she tore herself away from the pages of *Vogue* long enough to notice the limp rag that used to be her daughter. "Dear Lord, Anastasia! What on earth has happened to you?"

"What happened to me?" I slumped down into the chair opposite her. "I'll tell you what happened to me, Mama. Karl happened to me. And now I'm forced to drive a piece of shit with no air-conditioning, work

two jobs, care for his semi-invalid mother, and deal with my own mother who's so out of touch with reality that she thinks I can afford a four hundred and fifty dollar sundress to spend an evening with the half-brother of the man who screwed up my life!"

"Well, if you don't like the dress —"

"Mama, did you listen to anything I just said?"

"Of course I did, dear. And I totally agree with you. Karl screwed up your life, and it's a damn shame you're stuck with that commie curmudgeon. Which is why you need an evening out to forget about your troubles. Ira mentioned he has one of those fancy drink machines." She reached across the table and patted my hand. "A few frozen margaritas and you'll feel like a new woman."

A few frozen margaritas in this heat and I'd pass out. I stood up and headed for my bathroom without saying anything else. What was the use? Mama lived in her own world.

I suppose I could refuse to attend the barbecue this evening, but if I copped out, I'd have to let Alex and Nick do likewise. That would only postpone the get-together to another evening.

For some reason Mama had formed an

alliance with Ira and conspired to force a family relationship. For the life of me, I couldn't understand why. Ira came across as wishy-washy dull. According to Alex and Nick, his kids were total spoiled brats. Under the circumstances, the chance of Ira's wife and me becoming BFF's was non-existent. Why would my mother, who was normally so anti-Pollack, want us to have anything to do with these people?

Fifteen minutes later I headed out to Sunnyside, dressed in a clean pair of khakis and white scooped T-shirt, my wet hair pulled back into a ponytail.

April greeted me as soon as I stepped into the lobby. "Girl, you are not going to believe what went down here this morning!"

NINETEEN

Before I had a chance to ask her, April continued. "A couple of cops marched into Shirley's office around nine o'clock and marched out with her sandwiched between them."

I wondered if that was my doing. Detective Spader certainly didn't seem too happy last night when he learned Shirley had withheld information concerning her relationship with one of his murder victims. As a matter of fact, *pissed off* hardly began to describe his reaction. The guy looked like he was about to pull a Vesuvius. "Did they arrest her?"

"They didn't cuff her, so I guess not."

"Then the detective handling the case probably just had her picked up for questioning."

"She sure didn't look happy. Her face was the same shade as my shirt." April threw back her shoulders, better to show off a magenta T-shirt with white lettering that read *Jersey Girls Don't Pump Gas.*

I wondered if she owned any T-shirts without Jersey slogans. I'd yet to see her wear one. Given the size of April's chest and her obvious New Jersey pride, the state tourism council should pay her an advertising fee.

"Why would they question her for so long?" asked April. "You think Shirley killed Lyndella and Mabel?"

"No, I don't. Maybe she's helping the police piece together who did."

"I suppose."

The phone rang, and as April picked it up, I waved and headed off to find my first interview subject of the day.

I found Murray at one of the potter's wheels in the nearly empty arts and crafts room. At the other end of the room, three wheelchair-bound residents sat hunkered around a table. I recognized Lucille from the back of her buzz-cut head.

An aide and a woman I didn't recognize — most likely the art therapist — helped the other two residents, a man and another woman, string pony beads onto plastic lanyard. Although I couldn't see her, Lucille seemed to have no trouble stringing the beads herself. The aide and the art therapist paid no attention to her. Maybe she really was almost ready to come home after only a week of therapy.

Then again, maybe Lucille refused to play at stringing beads and sat with her arms crossed over her chest. From my vantage point, I couldn't tell. Since I had no desire to get sucked into any of her drama right now, I refrained from walking across the room to get a better take on the situation.

Instead, I walked over to where Murray worked, bent over the wheel. "Be right with you," he muttered.

I watched as he took a wire clay cutter and deftly sliced a thrown bowl free of the wheel. A shiver coursed up my spine. Ever since *The Godfather,* I've squirmed at the sight of wire clay cutters. They reminded me too much of how Luca Brasi was garroted and dispatched to sleep with the fishes. In the wrong hands a wire clay cutter was a deadly weapon. However, neither Lyndella nor Mabel had died by garrote.

Murray headed for the sink, leaving the bowl to dry a bit on the wheel before attempting to remove it. "Where you want to do this?" he asked, heading back after washing his hands.

I suggested the library. He removed his canvas pottery apron, hung it on a wall hook, and followed me out of the room and down the hall. Once again, no one else occupied the library. We settled onto leather chairs opposite one another.

I pulled his paperwork out of my tote, and after offering him a smile asked, "Murray, how come you're making my job so difficult?"

He raised his wiry unibrow. "How'm I doing that?"

"By convincing all the other crafters not to fill out the information forms I requested. No one wrote much beyond his or her name."

He shrugged. "Better safe than sorry."

"I need some personal information for the article. What can you tell me about yourself that won't concern you regarding possible identity theft?"

"I like to throw pots."

"I know that, Murray. And you're good at it. What else do you like to do?"

"Skydive."

Was he pulling my leg? I checked his facial features for any winks or smirks. He looked dead serious.

"Can't do it anymore, though," he added.

"Why's that?"

"Too damned expensive. Maybe if I sell

enough pots. How many'd that gallery take?"

"Four." I showed him the pictures of the two vases and two bowls Clara had chosen.

He frowned. "Not gonna get a jump out of four pots."

"I'm sorry, but if they sell well, the gallery owner may want to carry some on an ongoing basis. You might get that jump in eventually."

He shrugged again. "If I'm still around."

"You planning on leaving?"

"Who knows? I'm no young rooster, chickie."

There's that *chickie* again. I bit my tongue. No matter how condescending and sexist a term, I had an article to write, and handing Murray a lecture on gender bias would work against me. At least he didn't call me Sweet Cheeks the way Ricardo had. "You look like you've got plenty of good years ahead of you, Murray. How old are you?"

He answered with a blank stare.

"Come on, Murray. I'm not going to steal your social security checks."

"How old you think I am?"

"Seventy-two?"

Another blank stare.

"Am I close?"

"In the ballpark, give or take."

"Am I giving or taking?"

"Can't say, chickie."

"How long have you lived at Sunnyside?"

"Not long."

"Where did you live before moving here?"

"Here and there. Moved around a lot."

And so it went. With Murray and the rest of the crafters. Well before the end of the afternoon I'd finished all the remaining interviews but had little to show for my time. I wondered how much creative leeway I could get away with in my article.

April stopped me as I headed toward the exit. "Shirley never came back."

"Maybe she went home after leaving the police station."

"Without her car? It's still parked in the employee lot. I checked a few minutes ago."

Interesting. Maybe Detective Spader hadn't bought into my theory and had one of his own, one that had Shirley killing Lyndella. But what about Mabel? Shirley may have finally snapped and taken out her years of frustration and disappointment on Lyndella not measuring up to Shirley's grandmother standards, but what would be Shirley's motive in killing Mabel?

I'd seen how Shirley reacted to Mabel's death. Either she had nothing to do with it, or she should head to Hollywood because her performance was worthy of an Oscar.

I still believed my theory to be the more plausible one, even though mine, too, had no explanation for Mabel's murder. However, with Shirley away from Sunnyside, I might be able to prove mine with a little help from April. "Do you know how many new employees Shirley has hired over the past several weeks?" I asked.

"Sure. I process all the paperwork into the computer for her." She tapped a few keys. "How far back we talking?"

If someone hired a hit man to do away with Lyndella, how long would he hang around Sunnyside before striking? Long enough to establish himself and fit in without raising suspicion, I thought. He'd still be here, too. Otherwise, he would have leapt to the head of Detective Spader's suspects list.

"Since the beginning of June." That would have given the killer a month to blend in and become one of the countless nearly invisible employees who kept Sunnyside running on a daily basis.

"Only three, but that includes Reggie," said April.

Three? Sally had suggested at least a dozen. Three considerably narrowed the suspects pool.

"Why you want to know?" asked April.

"Humor me for a bit. I've got a theory about Lyndella's killer."

"Girl, you think one of the new hires offed her?"

"I think someone fairly new to Sunnyside may have been hired by someone else to come here to kill Lyndella. Tell me about the other two."

She chewed on her lower lip. "I don't know. I could be breaking some sort of confidentiality rules." Then she scowled at the computer screen. "It's an interesting theory, but I don't think it works."

"Why?"

"Well, I guess I can tell you this since the killer can't possibly be either of them. Besides Reggie, you've got Maria Gomez. She's fifty-three years old, about four-eleven and a hundred and thirty-five pounds, hired to work in housekeeping. No way she could have killed Lyndella. Besides, she barely speaks English."

I had to agree with her. Maria Gomez sounded like an unlikely suspect. "And the other new hire?"

"Franklin Applewood. He works the early morning shift in the dining room and kitchen. Busses tables. Sweeps up. Washes dishes. That sort of thing."

"What disqualifies him?"

"For one, he works from five-thirty in the morning to one-thirty in the afternoon. He'd stick out like a wide receiver at the opera if he wandered around the residents' rooms late at night. We've got security cameras at all the residential entrances. No way he'd get from the cafeteria to here without showing up on tape. On top of that, the dude's an ADA hire. Down Syndrome."

Mr. Applewood certainly didn't sound like prime hit man material. That left one other group as potential suspects. "What about new residents?"

"Older residents I'd believe," said April. "They all hated Lyndella. You thinking some new resident came here specifically to kill her?"

"I think it's a theory that's worth exploring."

April tapped a few more keys on the computer. "You got to promise me you won't tell anyone about this. I can't afford to lose my job."

"I won't breathe a word."

"Same time period? The past month?"

I nodded.

"Got plenty to choose from in this group. Four new couples in the independent living apartments, five new residents in this section, and seven rehab patients, including your mother-in-law and her new roomie."

"I think the chances of a husband/wife hit squad are slim, so let's rule out those new to the apartments. Same for the rehabs." I checked my watch. I needed to get home for Ira's barbecue. Too bad I couldn't use ferreting out a killer as an excuse for not attending. "Can you print out the paperwork for the remaining five for me?"

April hesitated. "I really shouldn't. I could get in a heap of shit if Shirley finds out."

"I won't tell her, and you won't tell her." I glanced around the lobby. April and I were alone. "And there's no one else skulking around to see what you're doing."

April drummed her nails on the desk as she weighed the possibility of getting caught, then came up with a way of easing her conscience. "You being staff and all, I suppose you'd be entitled to see this stuff, right?"

I grinned at her. "I don't see why not."

She returned my grin, and hit several keys. A few seconds later the printer began spitting out sheets of paper. April had just finished stuffing all the pages into a large envelope when I saw Shirley striding down the corridor, coming from the direction of the back entrance.

"Thanks, April! Gotta run." I grabbed the envelope, turned, and bolted out the main door. I didn't know if Shirley had seen me, but I had no intention of hanging around to find out.

I arrived home to find Mama, the boys, and Zack all waiting for me.

"Hurry and change, dear," said Mama.

I checked the clock on the microwave. "Isn't it too early to leave?" We weren't due at Ira's until seven, and it was only a little after six. Then again, I realized I had no idea where Ira lived.

"We have to drive all the way out to Lambertville," said Zack.

I stared at him. Dumbfounded, for a minute I couldn't even speak. When I finally found my voice, I said, "We're driving nearly to Pennsylvania on a Friday night?"

I don't suppose someone — namely Mama — could have clued me in to that minor fact at some point before this very minute. I turned to her. "You do realize my car has no air conditioning, we all can't fit in Zack's two-seater, and last I looked, the temperature outside still hovered around ninety-nine degrees in the shade?"

Mama crossed the kitchen and grabbed hold of Zack's arm. "I'll ride with Zack. You

310

really should get your car fixed, Anastasia. It's much too hot to drive around without air conditioning."

"Tell me something I don't already know," I muttered.

"What was that, dear? Speak up."

"The cost of fixing the air conditioning would probably run more than the car is worth, Mama."

She let loose a dramatic sigh. "I do wish you'd kept your Camry. That was such a comfortable automobile."

"And I wish Karl had hit the jackpot in Vegas instead of blowing our life's savings and leaving me up the wazoo in debt. Too bad neither of us is going to get her wish."

"Maybe we should call Ira and cancel," suggested Zack.

"Oh, no, we can't do that!" said Mama.

"Why not?" I asked. "I'm about to commit matricide. Surely that's a legitimate excuse for getting out of attending a barbecue."

"Really, Anastasia!"

I noticed the boys had ducked out of the kitchen. Of the five of us, only one of us wanted to show up at this shindig. I wondered if it had anything to do with her secretiveness over the last few days. "What aren't you telling me, Mama?"

"Nothing other than I brought you up to have better manners."

Zack extricated himself from Mama's grasp and placed both his hands on my upper arms. "Go get changed," he said. "I'll drive everyone in your car."

"That will only make for more body heat in a confined space."

"If three of you have to suffer through the heat, we'll all suffer."

The corners of Mama's mouth turned down. "Is that really necessary, Zachary, dear?"

He answered her without taking his eyes off me. "Yes, it is, Flora. Your daughter looks like she's had a rough day. I don't think she's up to driving this evening. So either I drive everyone, or we don't go."

My hero! If we'd been alone, I would have jumped his bones right there in the kitchen. To hell with my reservations and taking things slowly.

Mama sighed in resignation. She smoothed out a few imaginary wrinkles in her — *new sundress*?!?

My jaw dropped. "You went shopping this afternoon?"

"I was wondering when you'd notice." She held out both sides of the bold yellow, green, and black floral print skirt and

312

executed a pirouette. "Do you like it?"

I'm reduced to scavenging the street for dropped pennies while my mother blows four hundred and fifty dollars on a sundress? What is wrong with this picture? "Mama, you and I need to have a chat this weekend."

She smiled. "How nice! We should go out for brunch. Just us girls. There's that cute new place on Central Ave. They have a fabulous brunch menu. You'll love it, dear."

I fisted my hands in my pockets to keep from strangling her. "I'll be working tomorrow and Sunday morning."

"Dinner, then. But we'll have to go somewhere else. The place on Central is only open for breakfast and lunch."

I turned to Zack. "Do you believe this?"

He regarded Mama as he answered me. "Have the talk if it makes you feel better, but I doubt it will make any difference."

I didn't bother changing out of my khakis and white scooped-neck T-shirt, and I kept my hair pulled back in the ponytail I'd fashioned after stepping out of the shower earlier in the day. I didn't bother with makeup. What was the point? No matter how fresh I looked stepping into my car, I'd arrive sweltering, limp, and bedraggled. And the only person I cared to impress would be arriving equally sweltering, limp, and be-draggled.

All I really wanted to do was draw myself a cool bath and read through the paperwork April had printed out for me. I felt so close to finding the identity of Lyndella's killer that my nerve endings tingled in anticipation. Or maybe the tingling was from Zack running the tips of his fingers up and down my arms. Nothing would come of either right now.

Nearly two hours later we arrived at Ira's home — unfashionably late. Mama had called ahead to alert him while we sat in bumper-to-bumper traffic on Rt. 202. At least we wouldn't arrive to find the burgers burned to a crisp.

Ira lived in an over-the-top housing development that had cropped up on some old farmland on the outskirts of Lambertville during the housing boom before the subsequent bust. Making a conservative estimate, three of my ranchers would easily fit into his McMansion.

He greeted us at the front door, then led us through a marble foyer the size of my living room and into a gourmet kitchen as large as my entire downstairs. If I had any money, I'd bet the kitchen alone cost more than what Karl and I had paid for our house eighteen years ago. From the kitchen we passed through an enclosed sun porch that ran the width of the house, then exited onto a designer hardscaped patio.

"I'll make quick introductions, then get everyone drinks," said Ira. Pointing to us one at a time, he continued, "Flora O'Keefe; Anastasia, Alex, and Nick Pollack; and Zachary Barnes. This is my wife, Cynthia Pollack, and of course you already know her father Lawrence Tuttnauer."

I was about to say that no, we didn't all know Lawrence Tuttnauer. How would we? I didn't need to, though. Mama had sidled up next to him and looped her arm through his. Lawrence responded by patting her hand.

Mama barely came up to Lawrence's chest. I pegged him at six-six minimum and possibly several years younger than Mama. I could see why she'd fallen for him, given his athletic body and a face reminiscent of Cary Grant, right down to the shock of silver hair and black-rimmed glasses.

Mama craned her neck, smiled up at him, and batted her eyes in adoration. I bit firmly down on my tongue to keep my thoughts from spewing out of my mouth. Then I tossed my sons a *don't-say-a-word Mom Look.*

The stepfather-in-waiting cleared his throat. "Actually, we haven't met yet, Ira."

"Oh, sorry, Dad. I thought —"

Lawrence Tuttnauer didn't let his son-in-law finish. He stepped forward and extended his hand toward me. With a knowing twinkle in his eye, he said, "I've been looking forward to meeting you, Anastasia."

I'll just bet he had, now that the horn dog was fully clothed.

TWENTY

Cynthia Pollack offered us the kind of tight smile hostesses bestow upon unwelcome company. She didn't want us in her home — or more accurately, on her designer patio — any more than everyone except Mama wanted to be here. I caught an almost imperceptible scrunch of her nose as she sized up my wrinkled khakis, my sweat-drenched T-shirt, my wide butt, and my utilitarian ponytail.

In contrast, Cynthia gave off the aura of a woman who spent her days at the local spa, from her not-a-hair-out-of-place, expertly styled and highlighted blonde head down to French pedicured toes that peeked out of strappy white Manolos. Not a single wrinkle nor sweat stain marred her size zero designer outfit, a pair of perfectly pressed white linen slacks topped with a scooped-neck midnight-blue silk shell. Diamonds the size of Cleveland graced her left ring finger and dangled from her ear lobes. Another hung from her neck and nestled in the unnatural indentation made by boobs too perfect to have come from nature.

Was Cynthia Ira's trophy wife? Either she spent a fortune on Botox or a huge age gap separated her from her husband. The woman didn't look old enough to have given birth to eleven-year-old twins and their nine-year-old brother. If Cynthia was their stepmother, that would explain why she'd opted to visit her sister instead of attending parents' visitation at their camp.

Right then and there I realized two things: Ira was loaded, and it was going to be a very long evening.

"Drinks, everyone?" Clueless as ever, Ira excused himself and headed over to an outdoor kitchen that contained a built-in gas grill, stove, sink, refrigerator, and prep station. He whirred something pink and frothy in a hi-tech blender, then poured the contents into six chilled margarita glasses he removed from the refrigerator and placed on a tray next to the blender.

After adding two cans of Coke from the refrigerator, Ira slowly and gingerly carried the tray back toward where we remained standing. Too bad he hadn't thought to balance his load better. Throughout his unsteady progress, the tray wobbled precariously, and the drinks sloshed over the lips of the glasses.

I held my breath, expecting disaster to strike at any moment. Instead of offering her husband a hand, Cynthia stepped far enough to the side to avoid any fallout that might occur should Ira lose his battle with gravity.

"Let me help you with those, Ira." Zack stepped up and grabbed the Coke cans off the tray and passed them to Alex and Nick.

"Thanks." Ira set the tray on the table and began mopping up the mess. Then he passed around the sticky glasses to us. "To family," he said, raising his glass. "Old and new."

We dutifully raised our glasses to acknowledge Ira's toast, all except Cynthia. She placed her glass back on the tray without taking a sip, then strode over to the sink to wash her hands.

Mama and Lawrence settled themselves on lounge chairs as far away from the rest of us as possible. When Cynthia returned from cleaning her hands, she exerted no effort to make her guests feel comfortable, not even attempting any small talk about the weather. Apparently, she had no desire to learn anything about me or my children and deemed information about herself or her family none of our business.

However, I did notice that she couldn't tear her eyes away from Zack. He also noticed and in response, wrapped his arm possessively around my sweaty waist and drew me closer.

I opted for a less subtle approach. After downing my raspberry margarita in one long draught, I said, "Cynthia, I can't help but notice you keep staring at Zack. Any particular reason why?"

That rattled her cage. "I . . . uhm . . . er . . . you look very familiar," she said to Zack, totally ignoring me. "Have we met?"

"I'm sure I would have remembered," he said without a hint of a smile on his lips or in his voice.

"You probably recognize him from *People* magazine," I offered, giving her a huge smile.

Cynthia's eyes lit up. "You're a celebrity?"

"Only in my publicist's dreams," said Zack, continuing his deadpan demeanor.

Puzzlement clouded her eyes. I think she may have tried to pull a frown, but I wasn't sure. Too much Botox, I suppose. "Then why have you been in *People*?"

"Because he shoots people for a living," I said.

Cynthia's eyes grew wide.

"One of the best in the world," I added.

Zack tilted his head and whispered to me, "Better go easy on the margaritas, sweetheart. You're enjoying yourself way too much."

I smiled up at him and whispered back. "Tell me the bitch didn't have it coming?"

Before Zack could answer me, Ira gestured for all of us to gather around the large teak picnic table. Mama and Lawrence reluctantly gave up their seats to join us.

"Isn't this nice?" continued Ira, passing around a platter of crudités he had removed from the refrigerator. "I hope we'll be able to get together often, especially once the kids are home from camp."

Did the man not feel the tension emanating around him? Was he really that clueless? Alex and Nick rolled their eyes. I kicked them both lightly on their shins under the table, then shot them my *Mom Look.*

Cynthia obviously didn't share her husband's sentiments. I wondered what she thought about my mother getting cozy with her father. Although the two of them sat at the table with us, they were off in a world of their own, acting like hormone-possessed teenagers.

And speaking of teenagers, bored out of their minds, my poor sons slipped away from the table and began to wander aimlessly around the yard. They kept eyeing the Olympic-sized swimming pool at the far end of the property and edging closer and closer to it.

Too bad *Uncle* Ira hadn't mentioned having a pool or suggested the boys bring their suits. No matter how much Alex and Nick commented on the heat or dropped hints about how inviting the pool looked, Ira didn't offer to lend them swim trunks.

The boys had kicked off their sneakers and were skimming the water with their toes. Any moment now I expected them to take the plunge. Nick caught me watching them and pointed to the water.

Hell, why not? I thought. Did I care if the back seat of the Hyundai got wet? In this heat they'd dry off before we drove home, anyway. I gave a slight shrug.

A huge splash caught everyone but me by surprise.

"Ira!" Cynthia's voice sounded too controlled for her blood pressure. In the dimming twilight I noticed a vein pulsing along her neck. "I told you I didn't want any strangers in my pool. Tell them to get out."

Ira shrugged. "They're not strangers, honey; they're my nephews. Besides, what's the harm?"

"The harm is I don't want them in my pool."

Her pool? Not *our* pool? Did she think my sons would pollute her pristine chlorinated water with their sub-standard genetic material?

Ira waved to the boys, then headed over to the grill and slapped on hamburgers. As Cynthia fumed in silence, Ira attempted to engage us in conversation. He flitted from one subject to the next, but none took off beyond a sentence or two before quickly petering out.

Had Cynthia acted less icy, the evening might have been only marginally better. Truthfully, it was too damn hot to make any effort at conversation. Moving required too much work, even just moving my mouth.

I found it even too hot to eat. As I half-heartedly nibbled the edges of my over-cooked hamburger, my gaze drifted longingly toward the air-conditioned McMansion behind me, then to our hostess. Apparently, Cynthia didn't possess any sweat glands because she seemed unbothered by the oppressive heat and extreme mugginess. The rest of us dripped sweat, but the Ice Queen's face remained moisture free, and her silk shell amazingly void of any dark underarm stains. I'd love to know what brand of antiperspirant she used. Mine had conked out within minutes of leaving Westfield.

We remained outside well after the sun set and the mosquitoes had taken wing in search of their evening meal. Neither the electric bug zapper nor the citronella torches Ira lit around the perimeter of the patio stemmed the vampiric onslaught.

Itching from head to toe, I finally stood and announced, "Ira, Cynthia, thank you for the dinner, but I'm afraid we're going to have to call it a night." (The universe will note I did not thank them for a *lovely* evening. I hate telling lies.)

Mama objected to our departure. "Don't be such a party pooper, dear. The night is young."

"Your pumpkin is about to leave, Cinderella. The boys and I have to work in the morning."

With a disgruntled sigh, Mama tore herself from Lawrence's arms. "Before we leave," she said, "Lawrence and I have an announcement to make."

I'd braced myself all evening for what Yogi Berra used to call *déjà vu all over again*. After all, I knew my mother. Instead of looking at her and Lawrence, I kept my gaze focused on the Ice Queen. Did Cynthia have any idea what was about to transpire?

Lawrence cleared his throat. Without any pomp or preamble, he blurted out, "Flora and I are getting married."

Cynthia's jaw dropped. "Daddy! How could you?"

Ira strode over to his father-in-law and slapped him on the back. "Congratulations, Dad! The moment I met Flora, I knew the two of you were perfect for each other."

Cynthia turned on her husband. "Ira, this is *your* doing? Are you out of your fucking mind?"

Off to my left I heard Alex and Nick choking back laughter. I guess they hadn't thought the situation through. A marriage between Ira's father-in-law and their grandmother meant we'd be seeing a lot more of Ira and his family. The thought nearly brought me to tears.

Or maybe that was the salty sweat dripping into my eyes and the dive-bombing mosquitoes feasting on my limbs.

"Never again," grumbled Alex as we piled into the car.

"Ditto," said Nick.

"You both deserve medals," I told them.

"You owe us, Mom," said Alex.

"Me? I think that's your grandmother's department. I had nothing to do with accepting Ira's invitation." I settled into the passenger seat and turned to Mama as Zack started the car. "And as for you, don't you think you're jumping into this relationship with Lawrence a bit too quickly?"

"I'm not getting any younger, dear, and neither is Lawrence. We need to grab happiness wherever we can and hold tight."

"Yes, that worked so well for you with Lou Beaumont." I faced forward and clicked my seat belt into place as we pulled away from the curb. "Exactly how many *hours* have you known Lawrence, Mama?" Ten o'clock at night, hot and muggy with no breeze, and a car loaded with itchy, sweaty passengers had a way of ramping up my crankiness a few hundred notches.

"Time is irrelevant, dear. I only hope that someday you and Zack will understand that."

Zack reached over and squeezed my hand. Through the light of oncoming traffic, I caught his slight head shake. I think he was suggesting I ignore Mama.

I decided I didn't have the energy for a battle, anyway. Mama would do what Mama did best: marry. Ira, Cynthia, and his three little monsters would become permanent fixtures in our lives, whether I liked it or not, for as long as the marriage lasted.

On the upside, given Mama's track record with husbands, neither the marriage nor Lawrence had much chance of longevity. I wondered if Lawrence had any idea about the nature of the select club he'd soon be joining. Should I warn him? I tossed my head back against the seat, closed my eyes, and sighed.

The next thing I knew, we were back in Westfield. "Did I miss anything?" I asked Zack.

He laughed as he motioned toward the back seat. Mama and the boys had all conked out. "Should we leave them there?" he asked.

"We'd never hear the end of it." Alex leaned against one door, Nick against the other, so instead of opening the back doors, I twisted around and shook their knees to wake them. "Arise, my sleeping princes."

That did the trick. Alex undid his seat belt and climbed out of the car. Nick first had to remove his draped grandmother from the right side of his body. Mama didn't stir as he pushed her away from him. Shaking her knee accomplished nothing. Neither did gently calling her name.

"We could carry her," offered Nick.

"She'd have a cow if she woke up," said Alex.

I climbed into the back seat and vigorously shook her shoulder. "Wake up, Mama! We're home."

Her eyes popped open. "Honestly, Anastasia, you don't have to shout! I was only dozing."

Right.

She scooted out of the car, smoothed the wrinkles from her four hundred fifty dollar wilted sundress, and flipped her hair like a consummate beauty queen. "Thank you for providing transportation this evening, Zachary. Now, if you'll all excuse me, I have a date with a cool bath."

She'd have to wait her turn. The boys had already dashed into the house.

"If I don't hurry, she'll commandeer my bathroom for the next several hours," I told Zack as I scratched at the bites on my arms. I needed my own date with a cool bath. And then a bottle of calamine lotion. I hope I had some in the medicine cabinet.

"Go," he said, giving me a quick kiss.

Unfortunately, I was already too late. I doubted the other Pollack household ever played musical bathrooms. With the size of that McMansion, Cynthia and Ira most likely had his-and-her ensuites, complete with every high-end amenity ever shown on HGTV. All three kids probably had their own bathrooms, as well. Must be nice.

I wondered if Mama and Lawrence planned to live in their own wing of the Mc-Mansion when they married. No one mentioned whether Lawrence lived there now. Too bad Lucille wasn't Ira's long-lost mother. I'd be able to palm them both off on Mr. Moneybags and his Trophy Wife. Of course Trophy Wife would probably jump ship, but that wasn't necessarily a bad thing, was it?

While I waited for a bathroom to free up, I pulled out the paperwork April had printed for me. Five people had moved into Sunnyside within the last month, two men and three women. I immediately zeroed in on the two men. I knew them both. Dirk Silver and Murray Seibert.

TWENTY-ONE

Neither Dirk nor Murray fit my precon-
ceived notion of a hit man, but maybe that's
what the killer had going for him. Who'd
suspect a little old man, especially in an
environment such as Sunnyside, of being an
assassin? He'd blend in without raising any
suspicions. For that matter, so would a little
old lady. Even more, given the ratio of men
to women at Sunnyside.

I began reading through all five sets of applications, hoping to find a link between any
of the men or women and Lyndella's previous life. I began with the women.

I hadn't crossed paths with either Lorraine
Melrose, Charlene D'Amato, or Rosemary
Ledbetter. Although all three lived in the
same wing of Sunnyside as Lyndella had,
none of them lived on the same floor.
Lorraine suffered from rheumatoid arthritis,
Charlene recently underwent hip replace-
ment surgery, and Rosemary was eighty-

eight years old. Hardly typical assassin material.

Lorraine had lived the last forty years in Westfield, having moved here from Staten Island. Charlene had spent most of her adult life in Scotch Plains and taught first grade in North Plainfield until retiring five years ago. As for Rosemary, her paperwork stated she'd worked as a claims processor for the Social Security Administration in Elizabeth her entire adult life. Unless these women had blatantly lied on their admissions applications, they had no connection to Lyndella, Savannah, or The Best Little Whorehouse in the Hostess City.

I set aside the paperwork for the women and turned my attention to Dirk and Murray. Dirk pretty much kept to himself, rarely saying more than a few words to me or anyone else in the arts and crafts room. He spent most of his time at an easel, painting exceptional still lifes, mostly florals and bowls of fruit, from arrangements set up on a display stand within the center of the circle of easels. No matter the schedule, whether the room was filled with scrapbookers, quilters, or potters, I'd usually find Dirk at his easel.

Either he possessed innate talent, or he'd had some training. However, although

Savannah was home to the renowned Savannah College of Art and Design, how many hit men have attended art school? Dirk seemed an unlikely assassin.

Murray, on the other hand, was a royal pain in the ass. He, too, camped out in the arts and crafts room most of the day but confined himself to the pottery area. A real skinflint and conniver, he absconded with anything not chained down. On more than one occasion, I'd seen him pocket items others accidently dropped or inadvertently left behind — mostly magazines, packs of cigarettes, or candy bars. I was lucky I carried around cheap Bics in my tote and not more expensive pens. He also refused to divulge any information about himself and had encouraged the others not to, either.

Murray's paperwork listed him as having last lived in Bridgewater. Who moves from out in Somerset County into a retirement home in Westfield? Especially someone who complains so vocally about his lack of money? Surely, he could have found an equally nice and less expensive retirement community near Bridgewater.

Then again, I could imagine someone with a penchant for skydiving being a killer. Both activities involved adrenalin junkie behavior and both risked life and limb.

A lot of circumstantial evidence seemed to point to Murray being the hit man.

I saw one major flaw in my reasoning, though. If Murray was the killer, wouldn't he be getting paid well for the hit? Murray, more than anyone else I'd come across at Sunnyside, openly complained about his lack of money. Then again, Murray might have a huge stash somewhere and his grumblings were just another part of his charade. For all I knew, Murray had never lived in Bridgewater, and Murray Seibert wasn't even his real name.

So how did I out him?

The answer to that question kept me tossing and turning most of the night. As Mephisto and I headed over to Sunnyside Saturday morning, I still had no idea how to prove a connection between Murray and Lyndella.

As soon as I arrived, April greeted me with a warning. "That woman is definitely off her meds. Stay as far away from her as you can today."

"Shirley?"

"The Queen of Bipolar herself."

"Did something happen?"

"She's had one serious stick up her ass ever since she returned yesterday afternoon.

Chewing everyone out nonstop. Notice anything different?"

I did. For the first time since I'd met her, April wasn't wearing a New Jersey billboard plastered across her chest. Instead, she wore what I suspected might be her grandmother's Sunday go-to-church dress, a modest pastel blue and lavender calico print shirtwaist with a white Peter Pan collar and elbow-length sleeves. Instead of her usual dangling chandelier earrings and nose stud, she wore one small white pearl in each ear and nothing piercing her nose. "New look?"

She grimaced. "I was told my wardrobe didn't meet Sunnyside standards. No more T-shirts. I've worked here two years, and she never once said a word. Then yesterday afternoon, she's all over me like she got picked up by the fashion cops for the way I dress."

"Sorry to hear that. I'll heed your warning and stay hidden in the arts and crafts room all day."

April called after me as I headed down the hall to deposit Mephisto in Lucille's room. "Won't help. She knows where to find you."

And she did. Shirley Hallstead was waiting for me when I entered the classroom. She wore her navy power suit, a Hermes scarf tied around her neck, and a huge scowl. Several of my students were already at work on their pottery and sculpture projects. Dirk had taken up his usual station at his easel.

I sensed a tension in the room that explained the lack of socialization which normally accompanied everyone's crafting.

Deciding to play dumb, I graced Shirley with a huge smile and said, "Good morning, Shirley. Is there something I can help you with?"

She raked her gaze from my pale blue and white striped T-shirt to my chambray skirt, to my bare legs and sandals. "From now on, Mrs. Pollack, you will dress in suitable business attire while working here. That means a dress or business suit, stockings at all times, and absolutely no T-shirts or sandals under any circumstances. Do I make myself clear?"

I know my mouth opened to speak, but no words came out. Was she out of her freaking mind? Stockings in this heat wave? Stockings when she kept the Sunnyside thermostat set at eighty-two degrees? And a dress or suit in an art room? I wondered if she made the same demands of her nurses and nursing aides.

Say good-bye to your scrubs, ladies and

gentlemen. From here on the women will change catheters and take blood dressed in Pierre Cardin suits and Nine West pumps. The men will wear three-piece Hugo Boss suits and Cole Haan oxfords.

Was this Shirley's way of punishing everyone for her deceit over her relationship with Lyndella? I'd love to know exactly what happened yesterday down at the police station. Too bad I had no way of finding out.

I don't know how long I stood there with my mouth gaping, but it was definitely well after Shirley had departed. I snapped out of my stupor only when Murray asked, "Want us to take out a contract on her?"

My head whipped around to where he stood at the glazing table. Had he just let an important piece of evidence slip? "You have connections, Murray? Are you a made man?"

"Me? Hell, no."

"Then how would you go about orchestrating a hit on Shirley? Or anyone?"

He laughed.

"What's so funny?"

"This is New Jersey, chickie. There's bound to be someone at Sunnyside with connections."

"He's right," said Estelle. "My old next door neighbor was a DiNapoli, and her

336

daughter married a Gambino."

"My George worked for a Bonanno until we retired," said Sally.

I raised my eyebrows but decided to keep my mouth firmly shut. I'd ask April what George Strathower did for a living before moving to Sunnyside.

"I went to school with a Colombo son and two Genovese cousins," said Jerome. "You can't spit in New Jersey without hitting someone connected to one of the five families."

So I'd heard, but rumor was one thing. I certainly didn't have any such connections, and I'd lived in New Jersey all my life. Then again, Erica Milano, *American Woman's* former assistant fashion editor, now in Witness Protection, was Joey Milano's daughter. And Ricardo, the loan shark who'd tried to kill me, had worked for Joey. So in a way, I, too, had loose ties to organized crime. Not connections I could call upon, though.

Having all these people mention their ties to the Mafia turned rumor into reality. It also considerably widened the pool of suspects. Anyone with a grudge against Lyndella may have paid to have her snuffed out.

Maybe that's why so many of my crafters were in dire financial straits. What if they'd all pooled their money to have someone knock off Lyndella Wegner? It might sound like something out of an Agatha Christie novel, but hey, this was New Jersey, and not far removed from the realm of possibilities in a state that had an intertwined history with organized crime. Had Mabel been killed because she suffered from buyer's remorse and threatened to spill the beans?

However, before I started generating additional murder scenarios, I had to eliminate the ones I already had. Once everyone went back to his and her projects and chatter filled the room, I sidled over to Murray.

After watching him dip the top half of a vase in glaze, I asked. "Hey, Murray, what's it like in Savannah this time of year? Hotter than here?"

I had hoped to startle him, but Murray didn't startle, didn't skip a beat. He set his vase down to dry and turned to me, a puzzled expression on his face. "Why ask me about Savannah? Never been there."

"Really? I could have sworn I heard someone mention you once lived in Savannah."

"Wasn't me." He picked up a bowl, poured some glaze into it, and swished the glaze around to create an abstract pattern. "Never been south of D.C. Can't stand those

Southern rednecks. Lincoln should've let them all quit the Union when he had the chance."

That was certainly more information than I'd pried out of Murray since meeting him. Too bad it didn't help me. Was Murray Seibert that good a liar, or were my Sherlocking skills that bad?

Since I didn't know how else to keep the Savannah conversation going without raising Murray's suspicions, I decided to ponder my next move as I began collecting the remainder of the pieces for the Creative Hearts & Hands exhibit. Given Shirley's mood and her wholesale destruction of Lyndella's crafts, I had decided against a staging area in the arts and crafts room. Each day I'd been to Sunnyside since Clara picked the items she wanted, I'd brought some of them home with me. Clara and Ronnie would pick them all up at my house later this afternoon.

During lunch, before walking Mephisto, I carted the remaining artwork out to my car, keeping my fingers crossed I wouldn't bump into Shirley. When April had suggested Shirley was off her meds today, perhaps she wasn't being sarcastic. A bipolar Shirley would certainly explain her roller-coaster personality.

I contemplated the possibility as I tried to coax Mephisto out into the blistering midday heat. "Don't make me lift you up and haul you out," I told him as he dug in his paws at the entrance. "Shirley's already on the warpath. If you pee on her floor, we're both toast, and I need the extra income to keep you in Kibble."

He lifted his head and presented me with the most pathetic doggie-eyed expression I'd ever seen. "Save it. I'm not that much of a pushover. Now, march!"

Mephisto let out a long-suffering doggie sigh, but he exited the building, found a small spot of shade under a tree, and did his business in record time. I had to run behind him as he made a beeline back to the entrance and the relative comfort of eighty-two degree air conditioning.

We found Lucille waiting at the reception area. "Why are you making my darling run in this heat?" she demanded, yanking the leash from my hand. "Have you no common sense, Anastasia?" With Mephisto dragging behind her, she shuffled her walker back to her room.

"Looked to me like you were running to keep up with the mutt," said April. "You should stick up for yourself, girl. That mother-in-law of yours needs a good talking to. She's as bad as Lyndella was, just in a different way."

"Have at her, April. I've given up trying." Thanks to Dead Louse of a Spouse, I was stuck with Lucille until death do us part. At this point in my life, I only hoped the Grim Reaper came for her first. Until then, I'd continue to try not to let her get to me. *Try* being the operative word. I didn't need an ulcer on top of all my other problems.

My painting and drawing class started filing into the room as I finished my last spoonful of yogurt. The seniors had previously made it abundantly clear to me that they neither needed nor wanted instruction. However, I felt I should be doing something beyond proctoring to earn my thirty-five dollars an hour.

Over the course of the week, I'd accumulated a box of interesting objects, everything from a chipped conch shell to a broken locket to a bent wire whisk and more. I added a few balls of yarn, lengths of ribbon, and buttons from the arts and crafts room supply closet and placed the box in the middle of one of the tables.

"For those of you looking for new subject matter to draw or paint, help yourselves to some of the items in the box and arrange them to form a still life."

A few of the men and women wandered over to the box and pawed through it, helping themselves to some of the items. I felt useful for the first time. The others headed for the circle of easels to work on their current still lifes.

"Any chance you could talk Shirley into coughing up money for a live model?" asked Estelle. "I'm getting sick of still lifes."

"Me, too," said Berniece. "Kara used to take some of us over to Mindowaskin Park to work on landscapes, but it's too hot to paint outside."

"Preferably nude models," said Murray from the pottery table where he'd begun to knead a lump of fresh clay.

I raised my eyebrows at that. "Are you planning to move from pottery to painting, Murray?"

"Hell, no, chickie. I just like to look."

This produced a titter from some of the women and chuckles from the other men.

"Don't hold your breath," I told him. "Shirley doesn't strike me as being in the giving mood lately."

"Unless she's giving grief and aggravation," said Sally, apparently referring to my dressing down this morning over the new staff dress code edict.

I gathered up the box of found objects to

make room for those who might want to use the table and placed it on one of the shelves under the windows. "Help yourselves to any of the remaining items at any point," I told them. "I'll leave the box here."

"I'd rather help myself to a nude model," said Murray.

"Enough with the nudes, Murray. Not going to happen. Not now. Not ever. Shirley would have a cow at the mere suggestion, and I'm already *persona non grata* with her."

Before anyone else responded, we heard a rap at the door. Detective Spader, accompanied by Officers Harley and Fogarty, stepped into the room and headed straight for Dirk. Harley nodded to me as he and Fogarty took up positions slightly behind and to either side of Dirk.

"Mr. Silver," said the detective, "we'd like to ask you a few more questions."

" 'Bout what?" asked Dirk, continuing to focus his attention on his acrylic painting. "Already told you everything I know."

"That may be true, sir, but based on some new evidence we've uncovered, we need to re-interview the entire staff and all the residents."

"I'm busy. Start with someone else."

"I'd prefer to start with you, sir."

Dirk scowled. "You'll have to wait while I

clean my brushes. Can't leave paint drying on 'em."

I stepped in between Dirk and Spader and held out my hand. "I'll clean your brushes for you, Dirk."

He moved to hand me his brush, but instead, he grabbed my arm and twisted me into a chokehold. I have no idea where it came from, but the very sharp point of a knife pressed up against my jugular.

"Go for your guns, and the bitch dies," he said.

TWENTY-TWO

This was no palette knife Dirk held against my neck. Not even an X-Acto knife. This was an I-can-slit-your-throat-with-the-flick-of-my-wrist sort of knife. Big. Pointy. And exceedingly sharp. To prove his intent, Dirk pressed the tip a fraction of an inch, pricking my skin. A trickle of blood flowed down my neck. Someone gasped, but I wasn't sure if the sound came from me or one of my students.

My life should be flashing before my eyes, but all I could think of was where the hell did that knife come from, and how had Dirk managed to pull it out from its hiding place and press it up against my throat before Harley, Fogarty, or Spader reacted the way cops do on TV? Shouldn't one of them have pulled a gun and shot Dirk the moment he flashed that whopper of a knife?

I also wondered how I could have been so wrong as to suspect Murray instead of Dirk.

This is why I shouldn't be stumbling across dead bodies. I'm a lousy amateur sleuth.

Not that I had to worry about that for much longer. Given the current situation, I might not live to trip over another dead body. Worse, if I died, I'd saddle Alex, Nick, and Mama with all the debt Karl had racked up *plus* his mother. I couldn't let that happen. Somehow I had to get out of this situation alive.

An eerie silence settled over the arts and crafts room. My students had frozen in place, looking like they were about to turn blue from holding their collective breaths. That or drop dead from fear. I knew the feeling.

I stared at Harley, Fogarty, and Spader, silently pleading with them for help, but they, too, stood like statues. Hopefully not from fear but because they were weighing their options and formulating a game plan that would result in keeping me alive while taking down the bad guy with the knife to my throat.

"This is how it's gonna work," said Dirk. "You three dicks line up facing the wall, about two feet away, legs spread. Place your arms behind your heads and bend forward until your heads touch the wall." He waved the knife at everyone else. "The rest of you, face down on the floor."

The seniors dropped to the linoleum, grabbing onto tables and chairs to aid in lowering themselves as their joints creaked and popped. The cops stood firm. Dirk poked the knife into a fresh spot on my neck, this time deeper and producing far more than a few trickling drops of blood. "Now!" he yelled at Harley, Fogarty, and Spader. "Or I slit her throat."

"Please," I whimpered through the pulsing pain in my neck. "He means it."

The cops complied. Once they lined the wall in the awkward position Dirk demanded, he dragged me across the room toward them. He lowered his one arm from a choke hold to grasp me across my shoulders, trapping my back against his torso, then transferred the knife to that hand. The point now poked me under my chin in such a way that if I moved my head in any direction, I was a goner.

With his free hand Dirk removed the cops' guns, shoving all but one into the pocket of his painting smock where they pressed painfully up against my lower back. He placed the barrel of the last gun against the side of my head.

"Murray!" he yelled. "Get your ass over here!"

Murray dragged himself off the floor. With a shaky gait he made his way across the room.

"Grab their handcuffs and cuff 'em together. Real tight." Murray did as Dirk directed. "Now take the last pair of cuffs. Place one on Spader's free wrist. Hold on to the other end."

Murray stared at the three cops. "Which one is Spader again?"

"Fucking amateur," muttered Dirk. He smacked Murray between the shoulder blades with the broadside of the gun but not hard enough to knock him off balance. "The one in the suit."

When Murray had snapped the cuff on Detective Spader's left wrist, Dirk took over. He slammed the gun into Spader's gut. "Slowly walk over to the corner." After he got the cops in position, he said to Murray, "Now loop that last cuff around the steam pipe and snap it onto the other cop."

Once the cops were secure to the pipe in an outward circle, Dirk gave Murray one more order. "Take their cell phones and keys and toss them out the window. Then get back on the floor."

We waited while Murray fumbled around

in the cops' pockets, then struggled to open the window, Dirk growing more and more impatient. "Don't toss them on top of the bushes. Pitch them hard onto the sidewalk."

When Murray had finished his task and was once again on the floor with the others, Dirk said, "No one move. Stay put, and you all live. Try being fucking heroes, and I'll make sure none of you sees your next birthday."

"What are you going to do with me?" I asked as he dragged me from the room.

"You're my insurance policy," he said as he flipped the knife closed and added it to his apron pocket while still keeping the gun trained on me. "We're going for a ride. Where's your car parked?"

"Out front."

Dirk dragged me down the corridor. "Don't do anything stupid," he warned.

With a gun shoved in my ribs? Hardly. My only concern at the moment was staying alive, and that meant total compliance to keep this hit man from making me his next hit.

However, I couldn't control the stupidity of others, especially my mother-in-law, who at that moment shuffled toward us with Mephisto at her side, his leash looped around her walker. "Anastasia, I refuse to spend

349

another night in this hell hole. Whatever you're doing, stop it right now and get me signed out of here."

Lucille planted herself directly in our path and took on her I-budge-for-no-one stance. Mephisto zeroed in on Dirk and emitted a deep, prolonged growl.

Dirk forced the gun barrel deeper into my flesh. "Get rid of her."

Easy for him to say. He didn't know Lucille. I gave it my best shot. No pun intended. "Fine, Lucille. I'll take care of it."

"Now," she demanded, "and I'm coming with you to make sure you do."

This time Dirk shoved the gun so deep I felt my flesh splitting. Tears flooded my eyes, and a wince erupted from my throat. How self-absorbed could my mother-in-law be? How clueless? Didn't she notice the gun? "Dirk is helping get something out of my car. I'll be right back. Why don't you wait for me outside Shirley Hallstead's office? I'll be there momentarily."

"I'll come to the car with you. Manifesto needs his exercise."

Couldn't she hear the fear in my voice? See it written across my face? "It's too hot for you outside, Lucille. I'll take him for a long walk in a few minutes."

Dirk grew impatient. "Enough of this.

Let's go." He yanked at my arm and started to drag me around Lucille's walker.

That's when Mephisto pounced, hurling himself against Dirk's chest. As Dirk fell backward, his legs twisted up in mine and brought me down with him. The gun discharged before it flew from his hands, the bullet missing both of us by mere inches.

I yanked from Dirk's grasp and scampered on all fours out of his reach, but I needn't have worried. The walker, still attached to Mephisto's leash, had followed behind the dog, dragging along Lucille, who toppled over the walker, pinning Dirk to the floor, her knee jabbed into his groin.

"Son of a bitch!" yelled Dirk.

With that, Mephisto clasped Dirk's neck in his jaws and continued his menacing growl. Between Lucille's bulk, her optimally placed knee, and the canine's canines — not to mention the gun I grabbed off the floor and aimed at his head — Dirk Silver wasn't going anywhere. At least not until the cavalry arrived.

"April!" I yelled down the hall. "Call nine-one-one!"

Instead of April, I heard the unmistakable clickity-click of Shirley Hallstead's stilettos headed our way. "What the hell is going on here?" she demanded. Then she noticed the gun in my hands. "Mrs. Pollack! Have you lost your mind? How dare you bring a gun into my facility and threaten one of Sunnyside's residents!" She stooped to grab the gun out of my hand. "Hand that over at once!"

I shifted my body, still keeping the gun pointed at Dirk. "And let your killer go free? I don't think so."

"Killer? Dirk? Don't be ridiculous."

"Why don't you go down to the arts and crafts room and ask the cops handcuffed to the steam pipe?"

"You handcuffed the police?"

"Not me, you imbecile, Dirk."

"You're the one with the gun."

The adrenaline that had sustained me to this point was dissipating from my body. My neck throbbed, and my arms and hands trembled and ached from grasping an extremely heavy gun. Who knew Glocks or Berettas, or whatever make this gun was, weighed so much? I had no strength to argue with Shirley. Instead, I heaved a sigh, executed a lame eye roll, and yelled again for April.

This time I heard her racing down the hall. "On their way," she said. "And an ambulance. I didn't know if that bullet I heard hit anyone." Then she saw my neck.

"Sweet Jesus, girl! You're bleeding."

"I'll be okay." However, I was beginning to feel a bit dizzy and hoped I held out until the cavalry arrived. No telling what would happen if I lost consciousness and dropped the gun. I certainly didn't trust Shirley to do the right thing.

Other staff members and residents began to congregate. In the commotion that ensued, Dirk started to squirm, trying to shift Lucille off him. That's when I remembered the other guns and knife in his apron pocket.

"No you don't," I said, inching closer and placing the gun against his temple, then directed two of the orderlies to help Lucille up and another to disarm Dirk.

Shirley stood off to the side, her expression both grim and petulant, her eyes narrowed, her lips pursed into a thin line. I couldn't decide if she was more upset by the capture of an assassin at Sunnyside or angry at the fact that the others were lauding me as the heroine of the moment. Either way, from the looks of it, I'd earned a few more black marks on her mental score sheet. Not that I cared.

What I did care about were answers. Before the cops arrived and while I still had a gun trained on Dirk, I asked, "Why Mabel?"

"I never kiss and tell," he said.

"Not good enough, Dirk." I slammed the barrel of the gun into the fleshy part of his cheek and repeated the question. Mephisto seemed to understand my intent and clamped down a little harder, threatening to break Dirk's windpipe. Still, the hit man kept to the hit man's code, if there is such a thing. He neither flinched nor uttered another word.

An hour later, dressed in a blue hospital gown, I lay supine on a gurney in the emergency room at Overlook Hospital. A doctor had stitched up the knife slits in my neck and given me a tetanus shot and a prescription for painkillers, even though I told him I didn't want any.

I'd seen and read too many stories in the news about people getting hooked on pain-killers after accidents. I'm no martyr, but I figured I'd rather soldier through the pain with over-the-counter ibuprofen than risk addiction. He told me I'd probably change my mind once the local wore off and placed the prescription on the chair with my clothes.

"Do you know anything about my mother-in-law's condition?" I asked before the ER doctor left the room.

"The woman brought in with you? They took her for X-rays. I'll have one of the nurses update you."

Lucille had complained vociferously throughout the short ambulance ride to Overlook because she hadn't wanted to leave Mephisto behind at Sunnyside. She didn't appear hurt, Dirk having cushioned her fall, but Shirley insisted. I'm sure her concern centered more around a lawsuit than Lucille's physical well-being.

As for me, right now all I wanted to do was go home and hug my kids and Mama. Then I wanted to crawl into bed and sleep for a week. I wondered if Shirley expected me to show up at Sunnyside tomorrow. I fully expected her to dock my pay for not putting in a full day today, even though I deserved hazard pay in addition to my hourly rate.

The door opened a couple of inches and Detective Spader called in, "Are you decent, Mrs. Pollack?"

"Depends on the context but you can come in."

He entered the room, pulled up a chair, and sat down next to me. "Up to talking?"

I swung my legs over the side of the gurney and leveraged myself into a sitting position. "Are you?"

355

"I'm trained for situations like that. You're not."

Hmm . . . seemed to me he and his colleagues could use a bit more training. Granted Dirk was a hit man, but the odds had been stacked in the cops' favor three-to-one, and still Dirk got the drop on them.

"How are you holding up?" he asked.

"I survived. In the greater scheme of things, I'm fine, considering what might have happened."

"I like your attitude. Harley and Fogarty are right about you."

"Talking behind my back?"

He chuckled. "Seems they're charter members of your fan club. Anyway, I just stopped by to thank you. I'm not sure we would have broken this case without your help. Our CSI guys totally overlooked the importance of those journals."

"Not to mention Lyndella's accounting ledger."

"Yeah, I gave them hell over that one. From now on they've got orders to go through every page of every book at a crime scene."

So many questions still remained unanswered, though. At least for me. I doubted Detective Spader would satisfy my curiosity, but I had to ask. "How did you figure out Dirk was the hit man? I never suspected him. I was positive the killer was Murray Seibert."

He gave me his *ongoing investigation* look but then said, "Hell. The story's going to break on the evening news, anyway. His prints popped in the system under a different name. Dirk Silver is really Dante Silvestri, and he's got a rap sheet going back decades."

"Was he hired by one of Lyndella's former clients?"

"That's where the case gets really interesting. Silvestri worked security for Adeline Hunter."

"The congresswoman?" Adeline Hunter was a newly rising star in national politics, riding the conservative coattails of Sarah Palin, Michele Bachmann, and Nikki Haley. She'd recently started showing up with increasing regularity on the Sunday morning talk show circuit. "How is she connected to Lyndella?"

"Turns out Congresswoman Hunter put herself through college and law school working as one of Lyndella's girls."

"And she feared that information getting out?"

"Exactly. She had no idea the vic was even still alive until she received a blackmail

357

threat from her. Instead of paying off Mrs. Wegner, Hunter dispatched Silvestri to deal with the problem."

"How'd I miss that in Lyndella's journals?"

"I don't think you did."

I thought back to Lyndella's entry about finding a golden ticket. "Lyndella must have caught Hunter on television and recognized her."

"Yeah. It's doubtful Hunter turned tricks under her real name when she worked for the vic. Until she saw a picture, Lyndella wouldn't have known the congresswoman and her former employee were one and the same."

"Which must have happened the day she wrote the entry about finding a golden ticket. And days later, Dirk moved into Sunnyside. But how'd you find out all of this?"

"Once we made the connection to the congresswoman, she realized her only recourse was to cooperate. I'm guessing it has to do with Georgia being a death penalty state."

"But what about Mabel? Why did Dirk kill her?"

"So far, Silvestri's not talking. If I had to guess, I'd say Mrs. Shapiro just got on his nerves for one reason or another."

Mabel had grown rather bossy in the days after Lyndella's murder. I suppose it doesn't take much sometimes to give a killer incentive to kill. Poor Mabel. "He seemed like such a bland, mild-mannered guy. Half the time I didn't even notice him around."

"Those are the most dangerous killers. They're great actors. They blend into their surroundings, and you never see them coming until it's too late."

"Dirk is an excellent artist. It's hard for me to reconcile someone who can create such beauty on one hand while taking lives on the other."

"He'll have plenty of time to paint where he's going, and he won't be taking any more lives."

He also wouldn't be taking part in the gallery show. I'd have to call Clara to tell her we'd lost another exhibitor. Whether I wanted to or not, I'd also have to go to Sunnyside tomorrow. With the opening less than a week away, we'd need to fill some large holes.

The door swung open, and Lucille shuffled her walker into the room. A nurse followed behind her. "Your mother-in-law checked out okay," she said. "A few minor bruises but nothing broken. She's free to leave."

"We're picking up Manifesto, and you're taking me home," said Lucille. "I'm not spending another minute in that hell hole full of lunatics running around with guns. That man nearly killed me!"

Actually, he nearly killed me, but why argue? "All right, Lucille, but I don't have a car here."

"I can give you a ride back to Sunnyside," said Detective Spader.

"Fine," said Lucille. "Let's go."

"Do you mind if I get dressed first?" I asked her.

That's when my self-absorbed mother-in-law noticed the hospital gown. "What happened to you?"

"Someone tried to kill me."

Lucille scrunched up her nose and skewered her mouth in disbelief. "Exaggerating as usual, I see, Anastasia. Well, you'll get no sympathy from me. If you hadn't forced me into that place, none of this would have happened. This is your own fault."

So what else is new?

TWENTY-THREE

When we arrived back at Sunnyside, pulling in the back entrance to avoid the news vans parked at the front entrance, Detective Spader decided I shouldn't drive the short distance home. He placed a call to Harley and Fogarty while I retrieved Mephisto. With any luck, I'd avoid Shirley and the bureaucratic paperwork involved in Lucille's release until tomorrow.

Once inside, I tiptoed down the hall past Shirley's closed door and made my way to the lobby, keeping off to the side to avoid the gaze of the reporters gathered like a flock of vultures at the front entrance.

"Girl, you okay?" asked April when she saw me.

I glanced up and down both halls before answering her. No Shirley in sight. "Sure. Just a few scratches."

"Shut up! Looked like a lot more than scratches from where I stood."

"I'm fine," I assured her. "Can you bring Mephisto to me? I don't want any of the reporters to know I'm here."

"Sure thing." She unhooked Mephisto's leash from the back of her chair and walked down the hall with him. Anyone peering inside would think she was taking him for a walk.

When April had traveled beyond the view of anyone on the outside, she handed the leash off to me. "I'm bringing my mother-in-law home," I said. "She's refusing to come back to Sunnyside."

"Can't say as I blame her. Not with what's been going down here lately."

"If Shirley says anything, let her think Lucille's spending the night in the hospital. I'll deal with her and all the red tape tomorrow."

"Don't worry. Shirley left for the day. That woman was one out-of-control, power-suited basket case in stilettos, especially once the news crews started showing up."

I can imagine. Talk about a PR nightmare. I wondered how Shirley would spin the events to her Board of Directors, not to mention the press.

"You got any inside info to spill?" asked April.

"Watch the news tonight." Then I added,

"National."

April's eyes bugged out. "You shitting me, girl?"

"Would I do that?" I tugged on Mephisto's leash and headed toward the employees' entrance.

Lucille, Mephisto, and I rode in Detective Spader's mercifully air-conditioned unmarked sedan. Fogarty drew the short straw and drove my stifling rust-bucket with Harley following in the police cruiser. When we arrived, I offered the three officers cold drinks, but they all declined.

Once inside the house, Mephisto scurried to his air vent of choice, and Lucille shuffled off to the bedroom she shared with Mama. I released Ralph from his cage. As I refilled his water bottle, I heard Mama scream.

Shouting ensued. Mama, Lucille, and one very decidedly male voice rose in discordant cacophony. I raced down the hall, Ralph flapping along ahead of me.

Lucille stood in the entrance to the bedroom. I poked my head into the room and found Mama and Lawrence Tuttnauer huddled together in Mama's bed, the sheet drawn up to their chins. "Mother!"

"Mother, mother, mother!" squawked Ralph flying into the room. He landed on the headboard and stared down at Mama and

Lawrence. "*Hamlet.* Act Three, Scene Four."

"Get out!" shouted Mama. She pulled her arms out from under the sheet and flapped them at Ralph. "Shoo, filthy bird!" Then she turned to me and Lucille. "Both of you, get out, and take that flying rodent with you!"

"I will not," said Lucille. "This is my room."

"What's she doing back here?" asked Mama, directing her question to me. "She wasn't supposed to come back until the end of the month."

"Well, she's back early," I said. "You and Lawrence will have to move your afternoon delights to his home."

"We can't do that," said Mama.

I raised my eyebrows.

Mama scrunched up her nose. "Cynthia. She doesn't approve of our engagement."

Which was the one thing Cynthia Pollack and I had in common. "Then I guess the two of you will have to get a room." And because I'd reached my limit (can you blame me with the day I'd had?), I added, "There are several motels out on Route 9 that rent by the hour."

"Anastasia! How can you say such a thing to your mother and future stepfather?"

Easy when my mother and Future Stepfather Number Six acted like rutting sheep. I sighed. My neck hurt like hell, and my head was following suit. I needed a quiet soak in a cool tub and a very strong margarita. It didn't look like I'd get either any time soon. "Mama, I've had a rough day. Get dressed. You're welcome to entertain Lawrence in my home, but from now on you'll both remain clothed with at least three feet on the floor at all times."

That said, I marched back down the hall, into the kitchen, and out the back door to the one place where I could find escape from perpetual family drama. The darkroom sign had better not be hanging on the door.

It wasn't. I knocked. A moment later Zack opened the door. He took one look at my bandaged neck and I thought he'd throttle me. "How the hell —"

I placed my hand across his mouth. "Don't. I'll tell you all about it. After I calm down. Or better yet, we'll watch the news together, and I'll let Diane Sawyer fill you in. Just please tell me you have the makings for a supersized, industrial-strength margarita. With lots of salt. If not, I might cry."

He pulled me across the threshold and into his arms. Before he could tell me whether he had the makings for a supersized, industrial-strength margarita with lots of salt, I began crying anyway.

Actually, I blubbered. I'd reached that point where the remainder of adrenaline that had carried me to this point finally deserted me. I was now officially running on empty. After a few minutes, I didn't even have enough strength to continue crying.

Zack led me to the sofa and sat me down. Then he pointed to my neck. "Are you sure alcohol is a good idea?"

"Right now I don't care if it's the worst idea in the world. I want one."

"Okay, one very supersized, industrial-strength margarita coming up."

"With salt."

"With salt. Will you be okay while I make it?"

I nodded. "Just don't take too long. I'm on the verge of implosion."

Three minutes later he placed a highball glass in my hand. I licked the salt from one side of the glass, then gulped down half the drink without coming up for air. The salt and fruit juice replenished my electrolytes, bringing life back to my nerves and muscles, while the alcohol helped numb the pain in my neck, although it would probably eventually contribute to the pain in my head. At the moment I didn't care.

I placed the glass against my forehead, leaned back, and closed my eyes.

Two hours later, Zack nudged me awake. "I would have let you sleep, but I figured you'd want to see this." He pressed the remote to unfreeze the ABC *Breaking News* logo on the television screen. We watched in silence. At the end of the report, Zack turned off the TV. "So you almost got yourself killed again." He pointed to my neck. "How bad is it?"

"Hardly more than a couple of scratches."

"Scratches don't require stitches."

"Deep scratches do."

"How deep?"

"You don't want to know."

"I want to know everything. But not now." He drew me into his arms and kissed me in that way he has that feels like no other kisses I've ever experienced.

"I'm ready for more," I said.

"More margarita?"

"More you."

Zack made sure the door was locked before leading me into the bedroom.

Twenty-Four

Thanks to all the local and national press coverage surrounding the arrest of Dirk Silver, aka Dante Silvestri, and Georgia Congresswoman Adeline Hunter, we had an extraordinary turnout for the opening at Creative Hearts & Hands the following Friday evening. Besides friends and family of my crafters and most of the Sunnyside staff, total strangers crammed into the small Hoboken gallery. The overflow poured out onto the still steamy sidewalk and into the street.

But the best news? People came to do more than gawk. They bought. And bought. And bought. Two hours into the opening every single item contained a sold sticker, and Clara was busy taking orders for more of my students' artwork and craft pieces.

With Mabel's artwork removed from the show at the request of her family and Dirk's removed at the request of the police, the gallery had room to include at least one piece each from all the crafters Mabel had originally excluded. They might not have needed the money, but they did need the affirmation and boost to their egos. Every one of my students strutted around the gallery with heaping plates of hors d'oeuvres in their hands, wide grins spread across their faces, and their chests puffed out with pride.

The one person who didn't show up was Sunnyside's director, not that I expected her, but according to my crafters and some of the staff, no one had seen or heard from Shirley Hallstead since shortly after Dirk's arrest.

"Sorry I'm late," said April after inching her way through the crowd toward me. She was back to wearing her Jersey pride T-shirts. Today's chest billboard, a scooped-neck hot pink number with puffy paint black lettering, read, *Jersey Babe and Proud of It!* "I've finally got the 411 on Shirley, and girl, you are not gonna believe it."

"Spill, April."

"She's gone."

"As in quit?"

"As in fired. The board axed her ass. Turns out Shirley never paid for Lyndella to live at Sunnyside. She cheated the place out of

369

twenty years' worth of fees and covered it up with money she skimmed from the Mildred Burnbaum arts and crafts grant funds. Not only did the Board of Directors fire Shirley, but she's got to pay back the money she embezzled, plus interest, PDQ. Otherwise they're filing charges against her."

April swiped a mini quiche off my plate and popped it in her mouth. "Can't say as anyone will miss her. That woman had serious issues."

I agreed. With the killer caught, Shirley gone, and my crafters flush with newfound discretionary funds, the remainder of my time at Sunnyside should prove blissfully uneventful. Too bad I couldn't say the same for my personal life.

Being with Zack had surpassed my wildest imaginings. Granted, my pool of personal comparisons was limited, but I'd read my share of romance novels, and last Saturday night surpassed even the steamiest of them.

However, sex is a temporary panacea. After the rush of endorphins wore off, I still had to contend with Mama and Lucille.

Mama was barely speaking to me, especially after I'd walked back into the house last Saturday night, and she immediately guessed from the expression on my face that

I'd gotten some. This only hours after I'd told her she could no longer have any — at least not under my roof.

The only impediment keeping her and Lawrence from running off and eloping was the not-so-minor problem of where they'd live. Like most of Mama's previous husbands, Lawrence had little savings. Between the two of them, they couldn't afford an apartment of their own, not with the prices of real estate in New Jersey.

Cynthia had made it clear Mama wasn't welcome at the McMansion, and I certainly didn't have room for the geriatric lovebirds at *Casa Pollack.* Over the last few days they'd begun working on Ira to foot the bill for an apartment. Personally, I hoped he'd agree. I love Mama, but she needs a man in her life, and for my own sanity, not to mention my budget, I need one less relative under my roof.

Of course, I'd rather have Mama than Lucille, but I had no way of palming Lucille off on some man. Or anyone else for that matter. Lucille was Karl's albatross of a parting gift that would keep on giving. And giving. And giving.

And just because my home life wasn't stressful enough, my mother-in-law now claimed I'd corrupted her dog. After considerable mutual animosity from the time he'd moved into my home, Mephisto and I had now bonded. Unfortunately, he'd made it clear that he preferred my company to Lucille's.

I also had to brace myself for the inevitable meeting between Ira and Lucille and the fallout of such a meeting. Were Lucille and Isidore ever married? If so, had they divorced? As much as I hated to admit it, I leaned more and more toward Mama's theory that neither had occurred and Lucille had legally changed her name to his. I awaited confirmation from Patricia's intern's records search, but my gut told me no such records existed.

One way or another, eventually, I'd have to decide whether or not to confront Lucille. I'd already kept several devastating secrets about Karl from her, believing she was better off not knowing her son's true nature. Should I keep yet another secret from her, knowing any number of people might spill the Isidore beans?

But with all the current family drama and the drama yet to come, at least I was finally getting some. I scanned the crowd until I found the giver of what I was getting. Zack inclined his head toward the exit and raised his eyebrows in question. I pushed through the crowd to where that sexy silver sports car of his waited at the curb and asked myself, how lucky could one pear-shaped, cellulite-riddled, slightly overweight, more than slightly in debt, middle-aged widow get?

ABOUT THE AUTHOR

Lois Winston straddles two worlds. She's a critically acclaimed, award-winning author of mystery, romance, romantic suspense, women's fiction, and nonfiction under both her own name and as Emma Carlyle, and she's also an award-winning designer of needlework and craft projects for magazines, craft book publishers, and kit manufacturers. Like Anastasia, she worked for several years as a crafts editor. A graduate of the prestigious Tyler School of Art, Lois often draws on her art and design background for much of the source material in her fiction.

Lois loves to hear from readers. Visit her at: http://www.loiswinston.com and http://www.emmacarlyle.com.

Visit Anastasia at the Killer Crafts & Crafty Killers blog: http://www.anastasia pollack.blogspot.com.